The Health of Strangers series

'An intriguing tale of crime in a post viral Edinburgh, told with panache.' LIN ANDERSON

'Lesley Kelly has a knack of leaving you wanting more...' *Love Books Group*

'A crime thriller in a dystopian and ravaged Edinburgh with a great cast and the pages which virtually turned themselves. I bloody loved it.' *Grab This Book*

'*The Health of Strangers* moves along at a cracking pace and the unsettling sense you get of an all-too-believable future, helps draw you into what, at its heart, is a really well constructed and extremely entertaining thriller.' *Undiscovered Scotland*

'Laced with dark humour and a sense that the unfolding fiction could become a reality at any moment, there's a mesmeric quality to Kelly's writing that ensures [*Songs by Dead Girls*], like its predecessor, is a real page turner.' LIAM RUDDEN, *Edinburgh Evening News*

'A dark, witty mystery with a unique take on Edinburgh - great stuff!' MASON CROSS

'*Death at the Plague Museum* demonstrates skilful storytelling and it grips from the first page.' *NB Magazine*

'Can't wait to read more about Mona and Bernard and the rest of the Health Enforcement Team.' *Portobello Book Blog*

A Fine House in Trinity

'Written with brio, A Fine House in Trinity is fast, edgy and funny, a sure-fire hit with the tartan noir set. A standout debut.' MICHAEL J. MALONE

'The storyline is strong, the characters believable and the tempo fast-moving.' *Scots Magazine*

'This is a romp of a novel which is both entertaining and amusing... the funniest crime novel I've read since Fidelis Morgan's The Murder Quadrille and a first class debut.'
Crime Fiction Lover

'Razor sharp Scottish wit... makes *A Fine House in Trinity* a very sweet shot of noir crime fiction. This cleverly constructed romp around Leith will have readers grinning from ear to ear.' *The Reading Corner*

'A welcome addition to the Tartan Noir scene, Lesley Kelly is a fine writer, entertaining us throughout. This is a book perfect for romping through in one sitting.'
Crime Worm

Lesley Kelly has worked in the public and voluntary sectors for the past twenty-five years, dabbling in poetry and stand-up comedy along the way. She has won a number of writing competitions, including The Scotsman's Short Story award in 2008, and was long-listed for the McIlvanney Prize in 2016.

She lives in Edinburgh with her husband and two sons.

The Health of Strangers Thrillers

The Health of Strangers
The Art of Not Being Dead
Songs by Dead Girls
Death at the Plague Museum

Also by Lesley Kelly

A Fine House in Trinity

MURDER
AT THE
MUSIC FACTORY

A HEALTH OF STRANGERS THRILLER

LESLEY KELLY

SANDSTONE PRESS

First published in Great Britain by
Sandstone Press Ltd
Willow House
Stoneyfield Business Park
Inverness
IV2 7PA
Scotland

www.sandstonepress.com

Copyright © Lesley Kelly 2020
Editor: Moira Forsyth

Sandstone Press is committed to a sustainable future. This book
is made from Forest Stewardship Council® certified paper.

ISBN: 978-1-912240-93-7
ISBNe: 978-1-912240-94-4

Cover design by David Wardle
Typeset by Iolaire, Newtonmore
Printed and bound by Totem, Poland

To Barbara, Carol, Deirdre, Eddie, Iain,
Ian, Joe, Linda, Mick and Tricia

CONTENTS

MONDAY

ARTHUSIAN FALL

I

It was the kind of gun to give you nightmares: black, shiny, approximately three foot long, and far, far, too close for comfort.

The months that he'd spent working for the North Edinburgh Health Enforcement Team should really have prepared Bernard for moments like this, should have given him the negotiation skills required to face down a hostile armed man, and the confidence to stand his ground. There had been an afternoon on guns and other weapons as part of his induction, delivered by an enthusiastic demobilised soldier fresh from a tour of Afghanistan. At the end of three hours Bernard could just about recognise the difference between a rifle and a carbine, but had learned precious little about what to do if you found yourself on the business end of either of them. More time on the subject might have helped, but he was pretty sure that even if he lived to be a hundred he would never, ever, feel at ease dealing with an authorised firearms officer.

The firearms officer who was currently alarming him was stationed in front of the public entrance to the Scottish Parliament, and seemed to be ignoring Bernard's attempts to politely signal that he needed to enter the building. He continued staring straight over his head, his eyes scanning the activity taking place on the street behind him. It was busy, Parliament staff hurrying along in between the tourists stopping to get their pictures taken next to the ornamental pond, and dodging the parkour enthusiasts, who used the steps and landscaping around the Parliament as their own personal gym.

'Ehm, excuse me, I need to get into the building.'

The police officer shook his head. 'No can do. No-one is allowed in.'

'But I'm here for the Virus Parliamentary Committee.' He attempted to get his ID into the officer's line of sight.

'Sorry, sir, even so. Nobody's coming in here.'

'Why not?'

The question was ignored. 'If you can just step back from the building please, sir.'

He took a few paces backwards, then stood watching as a number of other people received the same treatment.

'Bernard.'

He turned to see a tall, well-built man with a crew cut striding toward him. *His boss.*

'What's going on here?'

'I don't know, Mr Paterson. They're not letting anyone into the building.'

Something bumped into his lower leg, and he moved hurriedly out of the way of a large Alsatian dragging a man in black along in his wake. They watched in silence as the armed officer stood to one side to let dog and handler into the building.

'Sniffer dogs?' said Paterson. 'That can't be good.'

'You don't think they're looking for—'

The expression on Paterson's face silenced him before he could say the word 'bombs' out loud. He lowered his voice before continuing. 'Do you think this is anything to do with Bryce?'

'Why on earth would you think it was anything to do with our former colleague?'

'Well...'

'I mean, just because he proved himself pretty damn handy with an incendiary device when he blew up the HET's offices, are you going to blame him for every unexplained outbreak of chaos?'

This was probably sarcasm, but sometimes it was hard to tell with Paterson. He was staring in a manner that suggested he was waiting for a response.

'Well...'

'Of course it will be Bryce's work! He's not done with us, is he? Do you think he left a 'Watch this Space' sign on our website just for the fun of it? He's probably already updated it with his plans to blow the MSPs to kingdom come.'

'That's a good point.' Bernard pulled out his phone. 'I'll check if it *has* changed.'

'Let's get a bit further away from the building while you do that—'

'John, Bernard!'

One of the glass doors of the Parliament had opened, and the familiar figure of Cameron Stuttle gestured to them to come towards the building.

'Must be a fuss about nothing.' Paterson headed swiftly towards his boss. Bernard hurried after him, hoping he was right. Both Paterson and Stuttle had a considerably higher threshold for danger than he did. Their 'nothing' was quite often a substantial 'something' in his opinion.

'Right.' Stuttle stepped out of the building, and an armed police officer immediately positioned himself in front of the door. 'The Virus Committee has been postponed and we have to get this area cleared.'

'Why?' said Bernard and Paterson in unison.

'You take the park side, Bernard, I'll take the area round the pond thingy, and John, you take from here to the Queen's Gallery.'

'And we're telling people . . .?'

Stuttle strode off.

'What are we supposed to say to them?'

'As little as possible. Which shouldn't be too difficult seeing as we know bugger all.'

Bernard sighed. Ordering people around really wasn't one of his talents. Paterson and Stuttle had had decades of practice at it in their previous lives as police officers. As a Health Promotion Officer, he had extensive experience of supporting people in a non-judgemental manner to realise for themselves that smoking and over-eating were bad for them. Not the ideal skill set for today's task. He approached a couple of young women in business suits, both heading towards the Parliament entrance. 'Are you members of the Committee? I'm terribly sorry but we've had to cancel today's meeting.'

They stopped, frowning at him.

'Oh. Why?'

It wasn't an unreasonable question. Unfortunately, he didn't have an answer. 'Political reasons . . . Unavailability?'

'Yeah, right.' One of the women laughed. 'I heard a rumour there was going to be an illegal demo here today. Is that it?'

He shrugged in a way that he hoped was neither confirming nor denying her accusation, while wondering if she was correct.

'So,' began her friend, 'do we just go back to the office then, or what?'

'Yes,' he said, confidently. 'Back to the office.'

The two of them drifted off, occasionally looking over their shoulders at the confusion.

Buoyed by this success he moved on to a group of men. One of them raised his phone as he approached and took a picture of him. Bernard got a flash of a press pass and a strong impression of testosterone. His heart sank. Journalists. *Political* journalists. They weren't about to turn tail and head home without having their questions answered.

'What's the deal here? Why's Cameron Stuttle running round shouting at people?'

Bernard looked over in Stuttle's direction. He did appear to be taking a rather more assertive approach in clearing the area.

'The Parliamentary Committee is cancelled today.'

'Why?'

'Political unavailability.'

There was a round of catcalls at this.

'Who's unavailable? Carlotta? Is she in Africa?'

Bernard attempted some Stuttle-type assertion. 'I can't answer your questions, and I have to insist that you vacate the area.'

Nobody moved their feet, although several mobiles were produced.

'You're clearing the area? Can you confirm that there's been another bomb threat?'

'I . . .ehm, look, you just need to get out of here!'

Stuttle appeared at his side, as if he had some sixth sense for a cover story going south. 'Sorry, gentlemen, but I really need to insist you move.'

'Another bomb threat, Cameron?'

'Sorry, gents, time is of the essence. Press conference this afternoon.'

A couple of Police Scotland vans pulled up on the road, to Stuttle's obvious relief. Uniformed officers materialised, and started moving people away from the building.

Stuttle grabbed Bernard's arm. 'About bloody time this lot got here. I've been calling for immediate backup for about half an hour now. They've all been at some unscheduled demo over at the university.'

Bernard's source had been half right. He couldn't help but notice Stuttle was shepherding him back in the direction of the Parliament building, and this time he was absolutely sure it wasn't a fuss about nothing. He wondered about making a break for it, but Stuttle was still holding tight to his arm.

'What's going on, Cam?' Paterson asked as he rejoined them.

Stuttle stopped, looking round to make sure he couldn't be overheard. 'We had a phone call forty-five minutes ago telling us to get everyone out of the building or we'd regret it.'

'Bryce?'

'We're certainly entertaining that possibility.'

'Is it another bomb, Mr Stuttle?'

'The caller didn't specify. And as we know from your spate of calls to the HET they are as likely to be hoaxes as real.'

'Well, at least you've got everyone out of the way.' Bernard and Paterson looked round at the dispersing crowds.

'We haven't. The MSPs are still in there.'

'What?' There was a collective dropping of jaws. 'Why?'

'Because if it is Bryce's work, we can't be sure this

isn't all part of his plan. Get all the MSPs out in the open so he can take a pop at them. We can't use any of the usual emergency plans, because Bryce is a former—' He stopped, suddenly mindful of the level of security clearance of his audience. 'Because Bryce has prior knowledge of them. He knows all the ways we're likely to respond to this kind of threat, and could use that to his advantage.'

'But if he has actually planted a bomb in there . . .'

'They get blown sky-high. Whatever we do has the potential to go very wrong.'

'So what are you doing?'

'We're moving them out four at a time, straight into armoured vehicles. The army's overseeing that bit.'

'Sir.' A police officer bounded up to Stuttle. 'Message for you.' He handed over a folded sheet of paper.

'What now?' Stuttle read the note, and his face contorted. 'Carlotta Carmichael, our beloved Cabinet Secretary for Virus Policy, is demanding a meeting with me immediately, on the walkway leading to Dynamic Earth. Is she insane? Does she not realise we are under threat at the moment? She's going to get herself shot.'

'She is insane,' said Paterson, starting to run. 'We all know that. Come on.'

Bernard ran after his colleagues, happy at least that they were moving away from the building. Although he couldn't help feeling this was not an ideal place to request a meeting. The concrete pathway ran along the side of the Parliament building and, apart from a low wall, was otherwise open on its other side to the park land that led up to Arthur's Seat, Edinburgh's famous extinct volcano. If Bernard wanted to isolate someone and take a potshot at them, this was more or less exactly what he'd look for.

Carlotta appeared, the domed roof of the Dynamic Earth museum looming on her left. She was accompanied by the very tall figure of her secretary, Paul Shore. Bernard had met him a couple of times, and had found him to be one of the more pleasant people working in the world of politics. Or maybe that was just the way he seemed relative to his boss. Both of them were looking around at their surroundings as they hurried along, Paul with a protective hand on his boss's back.

She stopped directly in front of them.

'Minister—' began Stuttle.

'I can't believe this is your idea of a safe area, Cameron.' She pulled her coat collar up to her face, as if it could provide her with some protection.

'Safe area?' Stuttle frowned. 'I never said that.'

'Yes, you did,' said Paul. He waved a sheet of paper. 'We got your note, telling us that this was the designated safe area. You said to get here as quickly as possible.'

'Shit.' Stuttle looked round. 'We need to get you out of here.'

'I don't understand what's happening?' said Carlotta.

'Cameron!' Paterson shouted as a police marksman appeared at the top of the steps leading to Dynamic Earth. 'Over there!'

Both Stuttle and Paterson threw themselves in the direction of Carlotta Carmichael. Bernard looked at Paul, who appeared as confused as he did. A thought went through his head that they should probably get down behind the wall, but he couldn't get his legs to move. His eyes swivelled back to the marksman: his gun was raised and pointing in their direction. A shot rang out, and he heard Carlotta scream out Paul's name.

Bernard found himself sprawling on the ground, as the body of Paul Shore toppled onto him, a stream of blood pooling around them on the concrete.

He lay back and waited to see if he too was going to die.

2

Mona squinted into the light, a fuzzy ball of luminescence that was sending shooting pains through her eyeballs and straight into her frontal lobe. On the other side of the brightness she could just make out the outline of Dr Sangha, consultant neurologist. She narrowed her eyes to try to get a better look at him.

'Please don't do that. Just try and relax.'

'Sorry.'

Was he frowning? The lower half of his face definitely looked unhappy, his bottom lip puckered downward. Maybe it was just a look of concentration, his expression indicating nothing more than intense consideration of the matter in hand. Maybe this was the expression he always had as he stared deep into patients' eyes and tried to work out if their pupils were reacting in a way that indicated they had continuing brain trauma.

Some days she felt she didn't really need a brain to work at the North Edinburgh Health Enforcement Team. She and Bernard seemed to do nothing but knock on the doors of drug addicts and alcoholics who had missed their mandatory monthly Health Check and drag them kicking and screaming into the nearest doctor's surgery. Some of these people were so cavalier about their own health that she wondered if they had actually noticed that a million people had died in Britain from the Virus. Either way, dealing with them was strictly grunt work.

Other days, the days when she was negotiating the politics of the Virus, she needed all her wits about her to keep on top of the likes of Cameron Stuttle, who treated the North Edinburgh HET largely as his own personal task force, there to do his bidding on matters he would rather not have in the public domain. In July, she'd found herself dispatched to London to retrieve Scotland's leading virologist, Professor Alexander Bircham-Fowler, who had gone missing dangerously close to his scheduled Health Check. This 'routine' mission had resulted in having to take refuge with the Professor in the woods at the back of a motorway services station, while a lone gunman fired at them. It turned out the Professor was very good at accumulating enemies.

Despite this near-death experience, Stuttle had not held back from using her talents on difficult cases. A few weeks ago he had partnered her with Ian Jacobsen from Police Scotland, a man to whom Mona had taken an immediate dislike. A top civil servant working on Virus policy, Helen Sopel, had gone missing after a meeting with Carlotta Carmichael held in the picturesque surroundings of the Edinburgh Museum of Plagues and Pandemics. Ms Sopel was of interest to both Police Scotland and the HET; the HET's interest was, as usual, getting Ms Sopel to her Health Check, while Ian Jacobsen was intent on keeping her from revealing her knowledge of Carlotta Carmichael's involvement in some rather dodgy drug trials taking place in Africa. This divergence of mission had resulted in Jacobsen threatening to shoot both Mona and Bernard. Bernard had responded with an uncharacteristic outburst of violence, resulting in a broken arm and black eye for

13

their Police Scotland colleague. Ian had taken revenge by pushing Mona down a flight of stairs. The resulting collision between her head and a stone wall was what had led to her current period of care under Dr Sangha.

It would be unfair, however, to blame all their troubles on Stuttle's puppet-master tendencies. The HET team were perfectly capable of getting themselves into the deepest of trouble. Like the time they took on an Edinburgh drug dealer in order to—

Dr Sangha snapped the torch off, dragging her back to the here and now. He made an irritatingly noncommittal sound as he did so. 'Any headaches? Blurred vision?'

This was a difficult one to answer. Not because she didn't know, obviously; she was well aware of the happenings in her head. Her reluctance to reply was due to the consequences of giving either a positive or negative response. *Yes* meant continuing her period of sick leave, and missing out on any of the action resulting from the hunt for Bryce. *Yes* meant delaying her attempt to bring Ian Jacobsen to justice. *Yes* meant giving Cameron Stuttle time to renege on his promise to give her full authorisation on Milwood Orders, the highest level of security clearance available to a public servant in the UK. Under no circumstances did she want to be putting a hand up to any continuing brain dysfunction.

But saying *no* left her with a different set of problems. *No* potentially meant being signed fit for work, without further medical intervention. *No* meant that the brain-exploding pain she had continued to experience since the incident might never actually go away. Worst-case scenario, *no* meant ignoring a situation in her grey matter that might actually be deteriorating. *No* could mean her mother walking in to her room one day with an early morning cup of tea to find her staring glassy-eyed at the ceiling.

Yes no yes no yes no ...

'Actually, Doctor, I've been feeling fine. Just keen to get back to normal.' She held his gaze, and hoped that her left eye didn't start twitching, as it had been doing unbidden over the past few days.

'Huh.' That infuriating sound again. He typed something in his on-screen notes, his computer screen irritatingly not at an angle where she could read it.

'So, am I fit for work?'

'I would prefer it if you took another week off, just to be absolutely sure that there was no remaining damage.' He finished typing and turned to face her. 'But, I'm aware that your bit of the health service, like ours, is desperately short of staff. So, if you're absolutely sure that you're not still suffering any ongoing problems, I'll sign you back.'

'Absolutely, Doctor. I'm fine.' She nodded vigorously and recoiled in pain as the movement sent a shooting pain across the back of her head. Fortunately Dr Sangha was looking at the printer, which was clattering away as it produced her fit note. She dug her nails into the palms of her hands, and told her brain to get a grip.

'Here you go.' She took it gratefully, before he could change his mind.

She'd googled head trauma numerous times over the past few days, starting with the NHS website, working her way through a whole bunch of American web MDs, and ending up on a few of the more alternative discussion boards. They were largely in agreement about the trajectory of recovery. The headaches usually subsided of their own accord. Usually, everything returned to normal in its own good time.

She'd take her chances with *usually*. There was work to be done.

Mona walked up the solid stone steps of the Cathcart Building, the second floor of which housed the offices of the North Edinburgh Health Enforcement Team. She pressed her Green Card against the box at the front door, and was relieved when it gave a satisfied beep and allowed her entry. The Green Card system was meant to keep track of who had, and hadn't, attended their monthly Health Check. Failure to appear at a Health Check would result in a citizen's access to any public building being revoked and, of course, a visit from the Health Enforcement Team. The existence of a Virus that had already caused a million deaths in the UK had rewritten the book on civil liberties.

Mona should not have had any reason to doubt that her Green Card would let her into the building. Like all her colleagues, she was immune to the Virus, having already contracted a mild form of it less than two years previously. She'd spent a week in bed with it, feeling like death, but had come out unscathed. Lightning doesn't strike twice, criminals don't return to the scene of the crime, and influenza viruses don't infect the same person twice. At least not without serious mutation. The immune HET staff were ideally placed to track down health defaulters who may be out there infecting others, and their Green Cards were like American Express Gold Cards – welcome everywhere. Still, Mona couldn't quite shake the feeling that the Green Card might be used by her superiors for more than their stated purpose. Say, for example, keeping tracks on a member of staff who might have a grudge against a colleague . . .

16

The door to the Admin room was slightly ajar, causing her momentary alarm. This would be a bad time to bump into Marguerite, Admin assistant to the team and self-appointed gossip-in-chief of the administrative professionals. The sound of laughter echoed out into the hall; good to see they were hard at work as usual. She hurried past before she was spotted and interrogated with half an hour of questions about what treatment the hospital had subjected her to. Although – she paused for a second – Marguerite would be ideally placed to update her on what was happening with Ian Jacobsen. Stuttle had been extremely tight-lipped about how the police were dealing with his attack on her.

A quick glance at her watch persuaded her to keep going. The bus had taken forever to get here, frustrating her with its slow progress through Edinburgh's near permanent roadworks, and the necessity of stopping to pick up passengers, most of whom had appeared to be tourists without the correct change. She could have used her car, but maybe driving post-trauma wasn't a good idea yet. Damaging her own head was one thing, but she didn't want a sudden burst of crippling pain resulting in her taking out a bus queue.

The door to the HET office was firmly shut, no sounds of laughter, or even life, seeping round the door frame. She should probably have phoned ahead. It had definitely been her intention to call as soon as she was on the bus. Yet every time she looked at her mobile, she couldn't summon up the correct words to reassure her colleagues that she was fit and well. In all probability her colleagues would be harder to convince than Dr Sangha that she should be back at work.

If she were to make a prediction about how everyone would react, she'd say that Bernard and Carole would use their health backgrounds to browbeat her about the importance of rest after such a trauma. Maitland and Paterson might be a bit gung-ho about the HET getting revenge for an attack on one of their own. This was all supposition and speculation on her part though. She'd no real idea of what her colleagues thought because Stuttle had banned them from visiting her, insisting that her time in the hospital was spent entirely on recuperation.

The door handle was stiff, so after a moment's struggle she accidentally flung the door open wide, making far more of an entrance than she'd intended. Embarrassment was immediately replaced by a sense of anti-climax on discovering that the room was completely empty. *Oh well.* At least she could get back into the swing of things without anyone watching her. She switched on her computer, and several hundred e-mails slowly downloaded. If she'd been signed off for another week she might never have got to the end of her inbox.

'Oh, you're back.' Marcus walked into the office. In common with IT folk everywhere, he seemed to be carrying one more laptop than was ever necessary in civilian life. 'Feeling better?'

'Yes, I—'

'You'll have heard about all the excitement then?'

She was torn between irritation that he hadn't seemed more interested in her well-being, and curiosity about what the 'excitement' might be. 'No. What's happened?'

Marcus put one of his laptops down on a desk, placed the other one on top of it and flipped it open. 'There's been a shooting up at the Parliament.'

'A shooting?' Multiple scenarios raced through Mona's mind, from lone gunman to full-scale coup attempt. 'Who was shot?'

'Carlotta Carmichael's Parliamentary Assistant.'

'Not Paul Shore?'

'I think that's his name. The tall, pale one.'

'I met him a couple of times. Seemed a nice guy.' She frowned. 'Why would anyone want to shoot him?'

'I guess they were aiming for Ms Carmichael and the poor bloke got in the way.'

'That's awful. Is he badly hurt?'

'The website said he's in a critical condition.' He shook his head, as if he was still struggling to comprehend the situation. 'I suppose it's too soon to know much more.'

They stared at each other, until another thought occurred to her. 'Did they get the gunman? At least I assume it was a man?'

'Don't know. Everyone's on their way over for a briefing so we'll be updated with whatever management can tell us. In return, I'm going to update them on this.' He swivelled the laptop to face her. The screen appeared to be blank.

She blinked a couple of times, and hoped to God it wasn't her brain playing tricks. 'What exactly am I looking at?'

'Remember how Bryce left a parting shot on the HET website, a blank page with "Watch this Space"?'

'Yes.' She nodded, taking care not to move her head too quickly this time.

'Well, I have to hand it to my former colleague. He may be a mad psychopath, but he really knows his IT because we have been completely unable to remove it. The IT repercussions have been enormous; Lord help anyone who required tech support over the past few days. You picked a great week to be ill ...'

'I'm not sure ill is quite the right word ...'

'Anyhoo, the site has been updated to this...' He tapped the top of the laptop, and one by one words started to appear.

'*Your Health Is A Public Matter*? What does that mean? Whose health?'

He shrugged. 'I assume, and it is just an assumption, that he's referring to the wellbeing of Carlotta Carmichael. He did, after all, just attempt to ...' He made his fingers into a gun shape, and emitted click/boom sounds. 'Although beyond that I've got no idea what it means.'

'Does Stuttle know the message has changed?'

'Yes, sort of.' He grimaced. 'I had a bit of difficulty getting through to him. I phoned him three times, and the first two times he said, ehm, "F off, I'm busy dealing with murderously urgent stuff. I can't deal with this nonsense".'

In spite of the situation, Mona smiled. It was a typical Stuttle response. 'What did he say the third time you phoned?'

Marcus shuddered. 'That if I didn't F the F off he'd swing for me. Eventually I had to phone Bernard and get him to brave the monster and deliver the message in person.'

'Bernard was at the Parliament? How is he?'

'Not good. He was standing next to Paul Shore when he was shot.'

'Oh dear.' She winced. For a former Health Promotion Officer, Bernard really wasn't great with the sight of blood. Particularly blood that had been spilt in a violent manner. In his immediately vicinity.

'Mona!'

They'd been so engrossed in the laptop they hadn't heard Carole come in. Mona stood up to allow herself to be enveloped in a warm hug.

20

'Feeling better?' Carole held her at arm's length, scrutinising her.

'Yes, but . . .'

'So.' Carole was already turning away from her. 'I heard about the shooting. How awful.'

'Yeah.' Her colleagues weren't showing much interest in her injury. She could believe that Marcus's social skills were such that he'd forget to enquire after her health, but Carole was usually very supportive. She was a qualified nurse, and Mona had anticipated a full-on interrogation about her wellbeing and proposed treatment. Something was up; it was almost like they'd been told not to discuss it. Would Stuttle have done that? She'd get the full story out of Bernard later.

'Mr Stuttle and Mr Paterson are . . .'

The need for Carole to finish that sentence was relieved by the sound of the heavy footsteps and loud voices that generally announced the arrival of their senior management team. They walked into the room, and flung their bags in the general direction of a desk. Several paces behind them trailed Bernard, looking extremely wan.

Stuttle and Paterson seemed to be halfway through an argument.

'So you remember nothing about him, John, not one single thing?'

'No! I keep telling you that. Some bloke in a police uniform, who I obviously assumed was actually a policeman, handed you a bit of paper and ran off. It was chaos, and all I was bothered about was how we were going to get people away from the building.'

Paterson turned in Bernard's direction; Mona wouldn't have thought it possible but her colleague appeared to turn even paler.

'What about you, then? Anything at all? Hair colour? Height?'

Bernard shook his head, and slunk toward his desk.

'Oh, for God's sake! Call yourself policemen? You're like a couple of teenage girls trying to give a witness statement.'

'I'm not a policeman,' said Bernard weakly, from behind the safety of his computer monitor.

'Well, I *am* a proud former member of the constabulary, as are you, Cameron, although you seem to keep forgetting that.' Paterson was not taking the slurs on his work experience lying down. 'You were actually there too when he handed the piece of paper to you, and *you* seem to remember nothing about him.'

'I was facing in the opposite direction! Trying to get through to you two the importance of the situation.' He threw himself, rather heavily, onto a seat. 'Oh well, there's nothing we can do about it now. We'll just have to hope the CCTV has picked him up. Though it doesn't make us look good that we can't remember a thing about him.' He caught sight of her. 'Mona! I wasn't expecting you back just yet.' His expression was thoughtful. 'No bad thing to have you around.'

It wasn't quite the welcome she'd hoped for; she obviously wasn't going to need her prepared defence of her fitness to be at work. It wasn't that she wanted everyone fussing over her, God knows, she wasn't the attention-grabbing type, but the occasional 'Are you sure you're OK?' wouldn't have gone amiss.

'Yes, yes, everyone's glad Mona's back, but we need to get on,' said Paterson.

'Thanks for keeping me right, John. What would I do without you?'

'Sort out your own messes, I expect . . .'

Marcus moved hastily in between them, holding the laptop aloft. 'This is the new wording on the website, Mr Stuttle.'

Stuttle moved his glasses to the top of his head and stared at it. 'What's that supposed to mean? It would have been helpful if it was a little bit more specific. Do you think it's a threat?'

Marcus looked at Mona, then at Paterson, and reluctantly decided that no-one else was about to venture an opinion. 'I don't know. It could be, I suppose?'

'Is he likely to post again?'

'I don't know. It's pretty much impossible to say.'

Stuttle's mood wasn't improving. 'Well, you're not much use, are you?'

Marcus looked hurt. 'With all due respect, Mr Stuttle, I'm an IT officer, not a psychologist. I don't know what Bryce means, or intends to do. I'll keep monitoring it, of course, and will let you know as soon as anything changes.' He snapped the laptop shut, huffily. 'Assuming you take my calls.'

The argument was brought to a conclusion by the door flying open and Maitland staggering in, weighed down under a large number of box files.

'Got the lot, Mr Stuttle. At least, I hope that's all of them.' He dropped them gratefully onto Mona's desk and wiped his dusty hands vigorously on his trousers. She immediately opened one and started leafing through the papers it contained. The top one declared it to be a report by Bryce Henderson.

Shuttle opened the office door and poked his head out into the corridor. Satisfied that there were no stray members of the Admin team eavesdropping out there, he closed the door firmly. 'What I need to say stays in this room.' His eyes flicked over to Carole. 'Can I rely on everyone's commitment to confidentiality?'

They all muttered yes, Carole rather more huffily than the rest of them. Mona caught her eye, and she shook her head slightly, registering her annoyance. Mona smiled back, but privately she thought Stuttle had a point. Carole was currently attempting to sue the Scottish Health Enforcement Partnership, who had recently enforced a clause in the HET officers' contracts which prevented them from resigning. Invoking the clause was interfering with Carole's plans to move to England with her family and find a much less stressful job. Stuttle might be giving her some good ammunition for her court case. He seemed reassured by her commitment, however, and began to talk.

'So, Bryce, Marcus's fellow IT officer, appears to have been some kind of, well, undercover agent.'

Mona could see Bernard's face scrunching in a manner that suggested a question was on its way. She would have strongly advised against it, given Stuttle's current mood.

'Didn't you know that already, Mr Stuttle? I thought you would have to approve ...'

'It would appear,' he glared at Bernard, 'that he's gone rogue. Started working in someone's interest other than the HET's.'

Now Marcus was looking curious. 'But if he was an undercover officer rather than a HET officer by definition he would be working for ...'

Stuttle's voice was getting louder. 'What I need from you guys is to track down whether his head has been turned by one of the groups he was previously embedded with.'

'But wouldn't this be better—'

'NO MORE QUESTIONS! I don't have time for this. That's the information on the last two groups that Bryce was tracking before his HET involvement. John, get this shower organised, and track down these lunatics.' He patted the files. 'Mona, you're with me.'

Paterson glared at his boss. 'I could do with Mona here.'

'You'll just have to cope.' He nodded to her. 'Jump to it.'

Stuttle steered her down the stairs, past the curious eyes of the Admin team and into his car. Mona took a minute to admire the quality of the upholstery and dashboard: cream leather and mahogany. She had a feeling she should have wiped her feet before getting in.

'I'm not sure I'm ever going to get used to working with civilians, Mona.' Stuttle put the car into gear. 'All they do is ask questions. What ever happened to just obeying orders?'

If this was an attempt to dissuade her from any further probing, it failed. 'I'm not sure why you've got the HET working on this, sir. Isn't it a job for other spooks?'

He snorted. 'Given what happened with Bryce, I'm not entirely sure which of them I can trust. As your colleagues rather gauchely pointed out, I wasn't aware that we had an undercover officer anywhere in my team.'

'Why do you think he was there, sir?'

'Guesswork on my part, but I'll share my theory. You know that Carlotta asked me to identify which of the Edinburgh HET's were best placed to deal with any particularly difficult cases?'

She nodded. Paterson had enlightened her about the North Edinburgh HET's special remit. 'You suggested us. We get anything to do with sex, religion or politics, according to my boss.'

'He does have a knack of simplifying the complex, doesn't he? Anyway, I thought at the time it was one of Carlotta's better ideas. Keep all the difficult, messy stuff with the most competent – or least incompetent – of the HETs. And whatever your boss's many faults, I do trust him. My judgement was completely off on this idea, though. Carlotta's interest in having one elite team was less about operational efficiency, and more about her being able to spy on all the sensitive cases by simply embedding one operative in the technical support team.'

'He bugged our phones, and he'd have had access to all our e-mails in his IT role.'

'With the end result that Carlotta Carmichael probably had a better idea what was happening in the HETs than I did.'

'Possibly, sir, but only if Bryce was passing all the information on to her.'

'Good point.' He laughed. 'Judging by the fact he's just tried to shoot her, I think we can assume there's been some kind of falling-out. I'm surprised he missed, though. How do you think your colleagues are coping with events?'

'I think they're OK. None of them seems very interested or surprised to see me back at work.' She couldn't quite keep a tone of bitterness out of her voice. 'I thought they would be more concerned about my injuries.'

'Ah, yes,' he glanced over at her, 'I can explain that. I decided it might be for the best if we stuck with the story that you tripped going down the stairs and bumped your head. I told everyone you were a bit embarrassed about it all and it would be better if they didn't raise the subject.'

'Tripped?' The cadence of her voice changed immediately from hurt to fury. 'I did not trip! Ian Jacobsen pushed me headlong down the stairs with the deliberate intention of harming me. He was bloody lucky he didn't kill me.' A thought occurred to her. 'Have you even told the police what happened?'

There was a silence, which answered her question.

'OK, Mr Stuttle, can you drop me off at the next set of traffic lights because I want to report my assault to the police even if you don't.'

'That would be foolish, Mona.' He sighed. 'It's your word against his. Why would he want to hurt you anyway? All that stuff at the museum was just a communication breakdown. Ian knows it comes with the territory. People occasionally get hurt.'

'People like Helen Sopel? Because I got the distinct impression that Ian was planning to kill her.'

'You're being ridiculous now. Ian wasn't—' He stopped himself. 'You know that I can't discuss that particular operation with you.'

She nodded. 'Because I don't have Milwood Orders clearance.'

'At least, not yet.'

Not yet? She sat up a little bit straighter. *Milwood Orders.* Access to information about the most secret of government operations. Involvement in the inner workings of the Establishment. Colleagues like Ian – it wasn't all roses, obviously. She'd kill, though, to be part of that tiny elite who actually made a difference to the security of the country.

'Mona, Ian denies ever touching you.'

She whipped round to face him, and was rewarded

27

with another searing pain in her head. She gritted her teeth. 'Does he deny taking my mobile phone? Because when I came to that was gone.'

'Why would he want to hurt you? We're all on the same side.'

'Are we? I can think of plenty of reasons why he'd want to hurt me. We humiliated him. The crappy little HET team wasn't supposed to track down Helen Sopel and we certainly weren't supposed to fight back. Bernard left him with a broken arm, for Christ's sake. Isn't that reason enough to hate us?'

Stuttle had the particular look of annoyance he always had when faced with questions he didn't want to answer. 'I don't have time for this, Mona. We can sort out the nonsense between you and Ian once we've dealt with our immediate crisis. Right now my main concern is getting to Carlotta Carmichael and seeing if she can shed any light on who it was that gave her the note saying to head for the safe area. Here's hoping she was a bit more observant than your colleagues.'

And more observant than you, thought Mona.

'If it is Bryce, why do you think he was targeting Ms Carmichael?' she asked.

'That's what I'm hoping your colleagues can turn up. He could be annoyed with her about the African thing or any one of the other less than ethical things that she's been up to. Although that presupposes he's now some crusading angel. He spent years doing the bidding of politicians without these kinds of second thoughts. Something must have happened to make him have this sudden fit of conscience.'

'You really think he's been turned?'

'He wouldn't be the first one to go native, would he?

If you spend enough time embedded with these crackpots maybe some of their madness rubs off.'

She thought things over. 'Don't bite my head off, sir, but where is Ian Jacobsen?'

'Getting some rest and recuperation.' Stuttle's voice was back to smooth and reassuring. He'd obviously anticipated her question. 'You've no worries on that score. Bob Ellis is taking over all Ian's duties; he'll be your police liaison for any HET work.'

'He's not much of an improvement, sir.'

'Bob is a very competent operative. I've worked with him for many years, on some very sensitive projects, and found him to be highly professional. Although I do appreciate that he's not ideal from your point of view.'

Not ideal? He was Ian Jacobsen's closest colleague, and she was pretty sure he'd be gunning for her.

'I promise you when all this Bryce stuff is over, Mona, I will investigate it fully. If there is any evidence of wrong-doing by Ian I will ensure that he is prosecuted.'

'With all due respect, sir, there won't be any evidence. Bob Ellis will have seen to that.' If there had been any CCTV of her being pushed it would have disappeared. Any unfortunate witnesses who'd seen anything they shouldn't have would have been well and truly warned off.

Stuttle sighed, and she braced herself for a telling-off. Instead, he spoke softly. 'You may be right. We all tend to look after our own. But I want you in the fold, Mona. I haven't forgotten my promise about getting you security for Milwood Orders. You're just too good to be kept in the HET long term, despite our staffing issues. However, right now, I need to know, are you onside?'

She nodded, as vigorously as she dared. 'Yes, sir.'

3

'How did you think Mona was looking?' asked Carole, absent-mindedly curling a strand of hair round her finger.

Maitland shrugged. 'Same as always. Inexplicably pissed off at the world.'

'I thought she looked pale,' said Bernard. 'What did you think, Marcus?' If anyone was going to have an opinion on Mona's appearance it was going to be Marcus. He'd been carrying a misguided torch for her ever since he'd met her. Bernard had always thought that there was very little chance of Marcus's crush every being reciprocated, and he'd reassessed his friend's chances to zero after Mona had told him that she was gay. He still hadn't found the right time to update Marcus about Mona's sexuality; he was secretly hoping that someone else would let the cat out of the bag.

'What? Yes, very pale,' said Marcus, without taking his eyes from the laptop.

'Maybe she's come back too soon,' said Carole. 'Do you think we should have a word with her?'

'She's a big girl. She fell over, she bumped her head, and she's been signed fit for work. End of story.' Maitland passed them each a file. 'Can we focus on these?'

'What are they?' asked Carole.

'Case files. "Bryce Henderson", or whatever his name really is, was embedded with a couple of groups immediately prior to joining the HET. From the quick glance I've had at them, one seems to be student activists, and the other is some musician bloke and his mates. Both sets could be bloodthirsty anarchists set on destroying the state, or they could all be harmless nutters. Bryce's opinions on the risk they present is in the files, although given what we now know about Bryce I think we can take his findings with a pinch of salt.'

Bernard leafed through one of the files, accidentally spraying dust across his desk. It obviously hadn't been opened in a while. 'They seem very thorough.'

'Thorough doesn't begin to describe it. There's every single conversation Bryce ever had with anybody, times, dates, places that they were hanging out. Everything. He's obviously been embedded with them each for months.'

'Did he draw any conclusions about their activity?' asked Bernard.

'Well, here's the strange part. He spent months monitoring them, right, but the final report that he's produced, it's just like a paragraph long for each of them. There's nothing in the report that says why he was monitoring them in the first place, and nothing that spells out what the illegal activity is that he's been looking out for. Both reports conclude that these people are fantasists, no further action required. I wouldn't get away with producing something of that length for Paterson. I need more justification than that just to get him to sign my timesheets every month.'

'That's because he knows they're a work of fiction.'

'Shut up, Bernard.'

Bernard leaned back just in time to avoid being hit by a report that Maitland turned into a weapon.

'So, what do we do?' asked Carole.

31

'Well, obviously we don't take this as gospel. I think the only thing that we can do is go and speak to these people for ourselves, and make our own judgement.'

Bernard thought about this. 'It would help if we knew what Bryce was actually upset about.'

'Marcus knows him better than anyone,' said Maitland. 'Have you any thoughts?'

Everyone stared at Marcus, who kept his eyes fixed on his laptop. Bernard gave him a gentle tap on the shoulder, and he jumped in surprise. 'Sorry, what? I'm scared to take my eyes of this site in case it changes.'

'Any thoughts on what Bryce was upset about?'

'No. I've been through all this with the police and Mr Stuttle, and various other rather aggressive men whose job titles no-one took the time to explain to me. In the months that I worked with him, I never heard him express a negative comment about anyone. Well, apart from occasionally expressing the opinion that certain HET officers were arseholes for the way they spoke to him on the phone.' He looked pointedly at Maitland.

'Me? He's pissed off at me because I was a little bit short with him on the phone?' Maitland frowned. 'You don't think he'd shoot me just because of that?'

Bernard grinned. 'No, but we can live in hope.'

'Anyway,' said Carole, ever the peacemaker, 'maybe when he updates the website it will give us some clue to his motivation.'

Bernard returned to the files. There really was quite a mound of them. 'Which case files are we going to look at first?'

'I suggest we start with this one, mainly because they're about five minutes away.' Maitland waved one of the files about. 'This pair are students at Edinburgh University.

32

At least they were when Bryce was investigating them; I suppose they could have graduated by now.'

'OK, that makes sense.' Bernard nodded. 'Who's going to pay them a visit?'

'Tell you what, Bernie, why don't you come with me? I'll show you how an investigation is really done.'

'I suppose it will help your case to have somebody on your team who can actually read.'

He was slower this time, and Maitland managed to hit him with the file he was holding. It was surprisingly sore.

'Come on. Let's go.'

4

Carlotta Carmichael had been put in an empty waiting room. An armed guard stood in the doorway, his eyes constantly flicking up and down the corridor. He nodded to Stuttle as they approached. 'Sir.'

'Where's Bob Ellis?'

'Mr Shore is in theatre. Mr Ellis went with him to oversee security arrangements, sir.'

'How is Paul?' asked Mona.

'Don't know.' The guard appraised her for a moment before adding, 'Ma'am.'

Carlotta was on her phone, her coat neatly folded across her lap. She looked remarkably calm for someone who'd recently survived an assassination attempt. In Mona's police days she'd been used to dealing with civilian hysterics in the aftermath of shootings or stabbings, or supporting witnesses who had been shocked into silence by their experience. The MSP for Upper Nithsdale and Chair of the Parliamentary Virus Committee appeared to be made of sterner stuff, and not in any immediate need of trauma counselling.

Carlotta ended the call as soon as they walked in, without much in the way of leave-taking. Mona wondered which particular civil servant was bearing the brunt of her fury in the absence of Paul Shore.

Stuttle made his move. 'Minister—'

'I'm not leaving, Cameron, not until Paul's out of theatre and we know he's OK.'

She looked genuinely upset now. It was a side that Mona hadn't seen before, and she began to entertain the possibility that Carlotta Carmichael might actually care about something beyond herself, her husband, and their shared ambitions.

'We're all concerned about Paul, Minister, but we really need to get you to somewhere more secure.' He gestured toward the door, a mute suggestion that she might want to get weaving.

The suggestion was noted and ignored. 'The last safe area you suggested turned out to be anything but.'

'I didn't suggest that, Minister. You received a note telling you to head there, and we received a note purporting to be from you asking me to meet you there.'

Carlotta's face went through a number of different expressions as she took this in. 'We were set up?'

'It appears that way.'

'Is this the work of Bryce Henderson?'

There was a brief pause before Stuttle conceded, 'Possibly.'

'How was this allowed to happen?' Carlotta's voice was so loud the armed guard turned round in alarm, his gun poised.

Stuttle didn't say anything, his eyes firmly fixed on a point just beyond Carlotta's left shoulder.

She turned and stared at Mona for a second, as if estimating whether she had anything to offer to this conversation. Apparently she didn't, because Carlotta swivelled back to Stuttle. 'If you come out of this mess with your job, Cameron, I'll be very surprised.'

Not a single muscle on his face responded. 'I'll go and

find Bob Ellis, and then I'm afraid you will have to leave. We really can't guarantee your safety here.'

Mona wondered exactly how upset he would be if someone were to shoot Carlotta before she left the hospital.

Stuttle turned his expressionless face in her direction. 'Please discuss with Ms Carmichael any memory she might have of receiving the note.'

He exited without a backward glance, leaving her alone in the lion's den.

Carlotta frowned. 'I remember you.' The look on her face suggested she wasn't overjoyed to be renewing the acquaintance. Mona didn't blame her. The last time they'd been in a room together there had been a discussion about some impropriety on the part of her husband. She could probably have lived quite happily with never bumping into Mona again.

'Yeah.' Mona sat down on one of the plastic chairs and pulled out a notebook. 'Can you recall anything about the man who gave you the note?'

She shook her head, the irritation she'd shown to Stuttle earlier now being redirected at Mona. 'No, I didn't see him. Someone passed the note to Paul, and he updated me.'

'A policeman?'

She thought for a minute. 'I think that's what Paul said. Mainly we were concerned about what a ridiculous place Cameron Stuttle was suggesting for a safe area. Although nothing surprises me any more with the Head of the Scottish Health Enforcement Partnership. Enforcement! Ha! He can't even keep key members of our staff safe.'

Mona was pretty sure that the security of civil servants wasn't actually Stuttle's job, but she decided against raising the issue. 'So, you didn't personally see the man with the note?'

Carlotta shook her head, staring at her immaculately manicured hands. Her dejection reactivated Mona's earlier sympathy.

'Paul's getting really good care here, Minister. They'll be doing all they can.'

Carlotta's head snapped up. 'I want to be there when he gets back from theatre.'

'I'm really not sure that will be possible. Mr Stuttle ...'

'I don't care about what Cameron Stuttle says! Make it possible! When Paul comes round he's going to be spouting all kinds of nonsense, and possibly things which are classified. I don't want anyone without security clearance in his room.'

'But the nurses ...'

'We'll need to get them to sign something. Bob Ellis should be able to sort that.' Carlotta was staring at her as if she expected some response. As the only retort she could think of was 'You're being ridiculous, Minister,' she was delighted to be spared the need to reply, as the door opened and Stuttle reappeared.

Her relief was short-lived, as Bob Ellis trooped in right behind him. Mona felt an overwhelming desire to punch him, although given his size and solidity it would have had all the impact of a fly landing on a bull. Stuttle and Carlotta might be right to have faith in Bob's ability to resolve difficult issues; although no-one was rushing to explain to her what his actual job was, it was definitely one that involved sorting out messes for people in power.

'Bob!' Carlotta got to her feet. 'Thank God. These people are being very awkward.'

'Everyone is just concerned about your safety, Minister.'

'I'm concerned about national security.' She grabbed Bob's arm, her long pink nails digging into his bicep. 'Paul might reveal confidential information as he comes round. Can we get some nurses with security clearance over here?'

'Assuming he lives through the operation, Minister,' said Stuttle quietly.

'He's not going to die! Don't be ridiculous.'

There was a silence that stretched on too long. Eventually, Bob broke it. 'He is very ill, Minister.'

Carlotta redirected her fury at her favourite target. 'I'm holding you responsible for this, Cameron.' Keeping tight hold of Bob's arm, she reached for her coat and bag with her free hand. 'Come on, Bob. I'm sure *you* can find me somewhere properly secure. We can discuss Paul's nursing cover while we drive.'

The door slammed behind them.

'The hard-faced bitch didn't once ask how Paul was actually doing.' Stuttle said. 'Not once.'

'What do you think she's worried about Paul saying? Is it just a general concern about security or something in particular?'

'Knowing Ms Carmichael I would imagine it's something very specific, and probably much more closely related to her own personal future than to a matter of national security. And seeing as she herself has pointed out that I may not have a job after this, I see it as strongly in my own interest to find out what she's worrying about.'

5

'That's got to be unusual, hasn't it?' Bernard was mulling over the contents of the file on the students, Blair Taylor and Aaron Mitchell, as they walked across the Meadows, a large park in the centre of Edinburgh which was widely used by pedestrians and cyclists as a short cut across the heart of the city. It was a journey into the centre of student-land, in pursuit of Blair, identified in the files as a second-year Engineering student. 'It must be a bit strange that neither of them has ever had a Health Check. How could anyone avoid having a Health Check?'

The Health Check regime had been instituted when it became clear that the Virus wasn't going to die down of its own accord. Everyone was legally required to turn up for a blood test each month to confirm that they weren't carrying the Virus. Only those who had already had the Virus, and were consequently immune, were not required to do this. The HET team were the frontline of the Health Check regime, as their *raison d'être* was to track down people who had missed a Health Check. At least, that was what they were meant to be doing, when they weren't being given tasks directly by the Head of the Scottish Health Enforcement Partnership.

'It's not that odd. You could avoid an HC pretty easily, under the right circumstances. We only investigate people who haven't been reported as missing, so if this guy's mum or dad noticed that they hadn't heard from their loving son for a while, and drew that to the attention of the police then – bingo! Missing persons' enquiry, dealt with by our colleagues at Police Scotland. Would never have crossed our desk.'

'And *are* they both missing people?'

'That's the interesting part.' Maitland grinned. 'One of them is, one of them isn't. Blair Taylor, whose residence we're about to visit, was reported missing by his parents six months ago.'

Bernard moved out of the way of a rapidly approaching cyclist. 'Did the police investigate at the time?'

'Yes, in theory. With the resources available to them, I'm going to guess it was not a very in-depth undertaking. His parents didn't say he was vulnerable, so from the police's point of view he's just another student who's fed up with his course but doesn't know how to tell his mum and dad, or worst-case scenario had a few too many beers and his body is going to wash up in the canal at some point.'

'His poor parents.'

Maitland shrugged. 'For all we know he's turned up safe and well and is now working in McDonald's. Also, let's not forget we're looking for him for a reason. We don't know exactly what he's been up to, but obviously he's been up to something or else Bryce wouldn't have been sent to spy on him. He might have a very good reason for staying lost.'

Bernard wasn't quite ready to let this go. 'But if he is alive and well, he's still not part of the Health Check regime. Surely there is some method in place of monitoring people who should be having Health Checks?'

'There *should* be, but you know how it is. Back in the deepest, darkest days of the Virus the government threw loads of money at getting everybody on the electoral register signed up for a Health Check. But if they missed you on that first trawl, I don't think anybody is reviewing it to pick up people who were overlooked. Who'd have the time? Anyway, save these thoughts for later, because I think this is us.' He pointed at a door sandwiched between two shops on Bruntsfield Place.

Bernard peered at the list of doorbells, all of which had a handwritten name next to them. 'I don't see a Taylor listed.'

'His address is 3f3. Start with the top button. That's probably the third floor.' Maitland pointed at the bells, and Bernard realised he was going to be the one doing the talking. He gave an inward sigh. Talking to people he'd never met before was not one of his favourite things, especially when it wasn't face-to-face. He pressed the first bell and waited for a minute.

'Nobody home.' He tried again. After a second delay a woman's voice was heard.

'Hello?'

'We're looking for Blair Taylor. Is he still living here?'

'There was a silence. 'Are you from the police?'

'No. We're from the Health Enforcement Team.'

Maitland pushed him out of the way, and crouched down to speak into the door system. 'Which is a branch of the police.'

They could hear the sound of breathing as she pondered this. 'Is there any chance you could come back later?'

'No. Let us in right this minute, otherwise we will have to kick the front door in.'

After a second the door buzzed open.

'Why did you tell her that?' hissed Bernard. 'It's a complete lie.'

Maitland waved his concerns away. 'Because like everyone else she's never going to have heard of the Health Enforcement Team, but she knows who the police are, and I'm curious why she was so quick to think they would be interested in her flatmate.'

Bernard began mentally noting down what he would say if the woman made a formal complaint once she worked out that they weren't in fact serving police officers. Most of the report he was planning to write would be along the lines of *It was all Maitland's fault.*

The door to Flat 3 was firmly shut. The occupant may have been regretting giving them access to the building; maybe she was busy flushing drugs that the HET had no interest in down the toilet. Maitland knocked loudly in a manner that suggested he had a battering ram he would be perfectly willing to use if required.

'Just a minute.'

There was another brief delay before the door finally opened to reveal a young woman with glasses, and brown hair pulled up in a ponytail. She was an unlikely-looking drugs dealer.

'Hi.' Bernard decided to take the lead so he could put the record straight about who they were. 'I'm Bernard from the North Edinburgh Health Enforcement Team, and this is Maitland. We need to talk to you about Blair Taylor. Can we come in?'

She didn't move, obviously searching her mind for a legitimate reason to say no. Maitland took matters into his own hands, and pushed past her into the hallway. 'What is your name?'

'Kirsten Barnett. Although I don't know why you're asking me that.'

Her eyes followed him as he disappeared into her

home, and Bernard seized the opportunity to also squeeze into the hall.

She turned back. 'I don't actually live here. I'm just visiting my friend who does.'

'OK, but can we go inside and talk?'

Maitland had wandered around the flat until he found the living room, and installed himself on the sofa. They followed his lead, Bernard sitting down next to him, and Kirsten perching on the side of a large, sturdy armchair.

'What's the name of the friend you're visiting?' Maitland made a hand gesture in Bernard's direction that suggested he start writing this down. He pulled out a pad, and resolved to remind Maitland that he was a HET officer, not a secretary.

'Veronica Mathieson. She's at work at the moment.'

'Where does she work?'

'In the accounts department at City of Edinburgh Council.' Her eyes widened. 'She really wouldn't like you visiting her there though.'

Maitland leaned forward. 'Well, let's hope it doesn't come to that.' He spat the words out, softly but with unmistakable aggression.

Bernard resisted the temptation to roll his eyes. Maitland seemed to treat every interview as if he was a character from *The Sweeney* interrogating the lynchpin of a drugs cartel. He decided to jump in, with a tone he thought was more appropriate for the nervous twenty-something sitting opposite them. 'How well do you know Blair Taylor?'

'Not well.' She slid off the arm of the chair, and sat on it properly. 'I met him a few times, but I have to say I really didn't like him. Neither did Roni.'

'Why not?'

She wrinkled her nose. 'You know...' She paused while she thought how to explain her distaste. 'His attitude towards women was, you know, really appalling. In fact, he had lots of very strange views about life.'

Maitland was on the edge of his chair. 'Like what?'

There was a long pause as she stared at the ceiling and thought about things. 'He kind of believed that he was a lot smarter than us, you know? He reckoned he understood how the world worked and we were just stupid and young, even though we were exactly the same age as him.' She shrugged. 'It's quite hard to explain really.'

Bernard gave up and moved on. 'So, when did you last see him?'

'He stopped living here, I don't know, maybe about six months ago? A while ago, anyway. I think his parents reported him missing.' A look of concern crossed her face. 'Oh God, you haven't found a body or anything, have you?'

'No, no, nothing like that. Do you still have any of his stuff? Did he leave anything behind?'

She shook her head. 'His parents came and took most of his things. Well, the stuff that was left anyway. Roni had already thrown out quite a lot of his papers before his parents got here.'

Maitland raised an eyebrow at this. 'Not really her place to do that, was it?'

Kirsten shot a panicked look at Bernard, the obviously more sympathetic of her two interrogators. 'But some of the stuff in the leaflets was totally gross and his parents really didn't need to see them. They had enough on their plate worrying about where he was. You'd really be better speaking to Roni about all this.'

'We intend to,' said Maitland, sternly. 'In fact, I'm

expecting to see her here at nine o'clock sharp tomorrow morning. Tell her from us, if she's not here, we'll be looking for her at City of Edinburgh Council and making it very clear how unhelpful she's been.'

She nodded vigorously to show that she understood, and Bernard was sure he could see tears forming in her eyes. 'She'll be here.'

Maitland waited until the door slammed behind them and they were halfway down the stairs before he started to speak. 'That was odd, wasn't it?'

'I think everything that has happened today could be described as odd. Was there something specific you had in mind?'

'Well, she thinks we're the police . . .'

'Wrongly.'

' . . . so the obvious thing that the police would be contacting them about after all this time is that we've found her missing flatmate's body. Is that the first question out of her mouth?'

'No.' Bernard stopped on the landing as he thought about it. 'I don't think that occurred to her until near the end of the conversation with us. It's like it never crossed her mind. So why did she think the police were calling?'

'I don't know,' said Maitland. 'What I do know is that she wasn't telling us the full story.'

'Let's go back to the office and run a check on her, and Veronica Mathieson. I'd like a read of the file about the other student as well. Was he reported missing?'

'There's certainly no record of it in the file.'

'That's really sad. A lad that young should be missed by someone.'

Maitland laughed. 'Think anyone would miss you if

you vanished, Bernie? Who would report your disappearance to the authorities?'

'One of my colleagues I would hope!'

'Not that Lucy from the museum, then?'

Bernard said nothing, but inevitably the red rising in
his cheeks gave it all away.

'I knew it! You're seeing her, aren't you?'

He shrugged.

'You dog! Have you shagged her yet?'

'That's a hugely disrespectful way to talk about a
woman.' He hurried out of the front door. 'And mind
your own business.'

Behind him Maitland's laughter echoed off the stone
walls. 'Thought not. Still, I'm sure you're working on it.
I'll check back for an update in six to eight months' time.'

6

'Oh, look who's graced us with her presence.'

Everyone turned to look at Mona.

She sighed. Paterson obviously had the hump about her leaving with Stuttle, but as far as she was concerned he could save the attitude for the man himself.

'Hardly my fault I had to rush off, Guv,' she said.

'What did our Lord and Master want with you anyway?'

She looked around at her colleagues, all of whom were listening to the conversation with interest. 'Ehm, can we go into your office?'

'Oh yeah?' said Maitland. 'Top-secret stuff, was it? You and Mr Stuttle planning world domination?'

'No.' She tutted. 'I just thought that everyone, you know, looked busy, and I didn't want to disturb you'.

Paterson snorted. 'Half an hour in Stuttle's company and you've already mastered the art of an unconvincing lie. Come on then.' He gestured her in.

She sat on the uncomfortable plastic chair that was provided for visitors, then immediately stood up again to double-check whether any of her colleagues were hanging around outside. Paterson's office had been hastily created when they moved in to the building by cordoning off a corner of the room with MDF, and inserting a door with a small window in it into one of the makeshift walls. It had all the comfort and sound-proofing of a garden shed.

'Can you check your paranoia and get on with telling me what happened?'

'Sorry. OK, we went to see Carlotta Carmichael, who was at the hospital and refusing to leave. Stuttle tried to visit Paul Shore, and left me to interview her about whether she remembered anything about the person who gave her the letter, but she says she never met him.'

'That's good. If she'd given a full-on perfect witness statement it would have made us look even worse. How is Paul?'

'Still in surgery when I left.'

'Poor bastard.' Paterson shook his head. 'So, that's all Stuttle wanted you for? A woman-to-woman chat with Carlotta Carmichael?'

'Maybe, but I'm pretty sure that was just an excuse. I'm not sure that's why Stuttle really wanted me there.'

'Oh yes?' He was immediately suspicious. 'What's going on?'

Mona got up and peered through the window out into the main office. Everyone had their heads down over their files, even Maitland.

'Oh, for God's sake, Mona.' Paterson sighed. 'What's with the cloak-and-dagger stuff?'

'I'm sorry if I'm a little paranoid, but I think I've got reason to be. Stuttle told you I tripped and fell down a flight of stairs at the City Chambers, didn't he?'

He nodded.

'Well, I didn't. I was pushed.'

Paterson eyebrows shot up in the direction of his hairline. 'Who by?'

'Ian Jacobsen.'

'No.' Paterson frowned. 'No, no, no. That can't be right. Are you sure?'

Intense irritation flared up within her, and she struggled to keep an even tone to her voice. 'How long have you known Ian Jacobsen, Guv?'

'For years. He's been on the scene for ages.'

'Do you remember him as a beat officer?'

Paterson forehead creased as he cast his mind back. 'I don't think so. When I've come across him it's always been some kind of special project he's been working on.'

'Have you ever seen him in a police uniform?'

There was a pause. 'Well, no. I always just assumed he was a high-flyer, you know, the type that makes detective within a couple of years. Bit like yourself.'

'He pushed me, Guv. I'm 100 per cent sure.'

'OK.' Paterson closed his eyes as he tried to work things out. 'If he did push you, *why* did he do it? Was it some kind of accident?'

'It definitely wasn't an accident. I think he's having some kind of nervous breakdown. Obviously he's unhappy with me about the things that happened at the museum . . .'

'Not as unhappy as he is with Bernard. The man broke his arm after all.' Paterson looked thoughtful. 'You think this is personal?'

'I know it sounds paranoid but he *did* push me down the stairs. Bob Ellis is still around and from the look on his face when I saw him at the hospital I think he might be planning to finish off what Ian started.'

'Not on my bloody watch he isn't!'

'You believe me then, Guv?'

'I suppose so.' He sat back in his chair, arms folded. 'Why is Stuttle trying to keep this under wraps?'

She shrugged. 'I don't know, but he's sticking to the line that Jacobsen was under a lot of stress and just needs some rest and recuperation.'

'OK. Why are *you* keeping it under wraps?'

'Because I don't think anyone will believe me.'

Paterson raised an eyebrow.

'OK, yeah, and I'd also like a promotion.' She skipped over the whole Milwood Orders bribe. 'The problem with angling for a promoted post is that after everything that's happened today, it looks like Stuttle's job is in question. I'm not sure if that makes my position better or worse.'

'What happened today wasn't Stuttle's fault.'

'Yeah,' she nodded, 'no argument there, but Carlotta is gunning for him.'

'That's not good.' He tutted. 'I mean, somebody's head's going to roll for this, obviously. You could say it was the fault of the Parliament security. You could make the case that the army were there on the ground and somebody still got shot. However, when you've got a Minister offering up a sacrifice, everyone else is going to be very glad to take Stuttle's head on a plate instead of theirs.'

'So, what do we do?'

'We help him.' He thumped the desk, to emphasis his point.

'We do?' asked Mona, a little startled by his enthusiasm.

'Yeah, despite our disagreements, Cam and I go back a long way. He might be a devil but he's our devil.'

'I'm not sure what exactly we can do to help him.'

'Well, if it's a choice between him getting the sack or Carlotta resigning I know what I'm in favour of.' He pointed a finger at her. 'So get thinking.'

'Carlotta was really worried that Paul Shore was going to wake up and give away matters of state security.'

'Interesting. Do you think she had a particular matter in mind?'

'I got that impression. Maybe she's done something she doesn't want leaked into the public domain. If it was something illegal or unethical it might be enough to force her resignation.'

'Although she has proved remarkably adept at blaming her staff in these situations, and denying she knew anything about it. Worked for her with that whole Africa fiasco.'

There was a gentle and apologetic tap on the door which could only be the calling card of Bernard. Sure enough, he poked his head round the door. 'I wondered if you might have time for a bit of a briefing update?'

'For you, Bernard, anything. Mona, we'll continue this later.' He walked out into the main office. 'All right, what have you got for me?'

Now that Bernard had done the difficult work of getting Paterson out of his office, Maitland was happy to take the reins. 'We checked out Blair Taylor's last known address. Something a bit odd going on there, Guv.'

'Oh yeah? What kind of odd?'

'Well, the girl living there claimed only to be visiting, which we didn't really buy. She assumed we were the police ...'

Paterson raised an eyebrow. 'You set her straight that we weren't from Police Scotland, Maitland?'

'Of course, Guv,' he said and winked. 'Anyway, despite our best intentions, she thought we were the police, but didn't assume that we were there because her flatmate was missing, which makes me wonder what they *are* up to given she wasn't surprised to have the boys in blue knock on their door.'

'Did you run their names?'

'Yep, both registered at that address for the Green Card. No history at all of ever having missed a Health Check. Got the police to run a check, and neither of them has ever been stopped for any criminal activity, not so much as a speeding ticket.'

'OK, so they might be up to something, but we're probably not going to find they're making crystal meth in the bathroom. What's your next step?'

'We're calling back at nine tomorrow morning to talk to the one who actually lives there.'

'Sounds good, but, Bernard, just in case Maitland forgets, be sure to remind them that you are not from the police, you are from the Health Enforcement Team, OK?'

Bernard nodded enthusiastically.

Paterson turned his attention to Carole. 'And, Carole, what do you have for us?'

'I've been looking at the other case file we were given. I don't know what you guys thought, but I couldn't find anything to explain *why* this man was being investigated ...'

'Same with us,' said Maitland. 'Either that's filed somewhere else, or all this bumpf is just noise creation to look as if he's done a thorough job while actually covering up what was really going on.'

'That fits with Stuttle's "gone native" theory,' said Paterson. 'Anyway, carry on, Carole.'

'There was a lot of detail about meetings and things but from what I can make out it wasn't a terrorist group or anything like that that he was looking into. It appears he was tracking an individual who seems to have some pretty wacky views.'

'A musician, right?' asked Paterson.

She nodded.

'Anyone famous?' asked Maitland, sitting up.

'Sort of. I'd never heard of him, but according to Wikipedia, he was quite well known back in the 1980s.'

'Really? Will I have heard of him?' Paterson looked intrigued.

Mona had her doubts that Paterson had heard of anyone less famous than the Beatles. Although she did remember him once complaining that his wife was dragging him to a Take That reunion concert. He'd not been very complimentary about it.

'I don't know, Mr Paterson. Does the name Colin Karma mean anything to you?' asked Carole.

There was the sound of a coffee cup being brought heavily to rest on a desk top. 'Colin Karma?' Bernard eyes were huge. 'From the band Arthusian Fall?'

Mona exchanged a glance with Paterson. 'You know them?'

'They sold a lot of records in the 1980s. Not singles, they weren't on *Top of the Pops* every week, but their albums were massive.'

Maitland grinned. 'Didn't know you were a fan of 1980s pop, Bernard? Isn't it a bit before your time?'

'I'm not a fan. And I'm not sure you would describe them as pop. Or in fact as music of any kind.'

'That good, huh?' said Paterson. 'How do you know so much about them then?'

'Marcus is a fan. He said they were the perfect soundtrack for reading Tolkein.'

'Marcus is never going to get a girlfriend, is he?' said Mona.

'Not as long as he's still carrying a torch for you.' Maitland grinned. 'Barking up the wrong tree there, isn't he? You ever going to get round to telling him that you're gay?'

'Anyway,' said Paterson, with the haste of a manager spotting a conversation likely to end up at HR. 'So, what's the next step with this one, Carole?'

'I tried phoning his last known address and the person that answered said she was his wife, but they're in the process of getting divorced and the house is on the market.'

'Does she have a forwarding address for him?'

'Claimed not to, but she's happy to talk to us further. I've arranged for us to go round there tomorrow morning and get a statement from her in person.'

'Excellent. Looks like that's us done here for the day then. But ...' He paused, as if he wasn't quite sure what he wanted to say. 'But everybody take care this evening. Something's going on, and I'm not sure what. So, stay safe.'

'See you tomorrow, Guv.'

7

Lucy was waiting outside the Traverse theatre. 'I wasn't sure if you would make it!' She flung her arms round him.

Bernard luxuriated in the hug. 'Of course I made it. It's our one-week anniversary.'

'Is it?' She looked surprised.

'Yup. One whole week since our first date.'

'So, that must make it nine days since you saved my life at the museum.'

'I'm not sure that I actually saved your life ...'

'I think you did.' She squeezed his hand. 'My hero.'

The past week may not have been the single best one of Bernard's life, but it was certainly a frontrunner. Before he'd met Lucy it had been a long, long time since he'd experienced anything resembling affection. He didn't blame his wife for that. They'd lost their baby son to the Virus and bereavement had hit them like a truck, wrecking their marriage. They might – might – have survived as a couple, had it not been for Carrie's desire to have another child. Bernard was of the opinion that he would rather die than bring a little one into the world to take its chances with the Virus, but, then, as Carrie was fond of pointing out, time was on Bernard's side, not hers.

When they'd finally gone their separate ways he had felt a slightly shameful sense of relief. He'd found the adjustment to living on his own a difficult one, and after several long and lonely months of singledom he was delighted that he'd now finally found someone. He would let nothing, especially not Maitland, interfere with his newfound happiness.

'So, it wasn't too frantic at work today? I heard there was a shooting at the Parliament, and I wondered if it would affect you,' said Lucy.

Bernard considered telling her that as he had been standing next to the person who was shot it had affected him a great deal. Such a comment would add to her somewhat misguided view of him as a daredevil man of action. However, it would also lead to all kinds of questions that he really didn't want to get into right now. He opted for bland. 'It wasn't too bad. Tomorrow's going to be busy though.'

'You work too hard.'

'Says the woman who runs a museum single-handed!'

She laughed. 'I have all my volunteers. Shall we go in?'

The show had been billed as a challenging piece of experimental theatre: Lucy's choice. He loved the theatre, but he had to admit his tastes were on the conservative side. He was more a fan of Shakespeare, or a well-performed Gilbert and Sullivan, but it was way too soon in their relationship to admit that his tastes differed from hers in any way.

'I hope this is good,' whispered Lucy. 'It got wonderful reviews.'

One hour later Bernard wondered if the critics had been having some kind of joke at his expense. It had fully lived up to its experimental billing, but whatever the experiment was he wasn't sure it had succeeded.

He stole a look at Lucy, who was engaging in a

vigorous round of applause. Oh God, was she going to want to analyse the play afterwards? He wasn't entirely sure what had taken place on stage so he was going to have to bluff it.

'Did you enjoy it?' Lucy asked.

'I thought it was ...' He struggled for a word he could safely use. 'Deep.'

She nodded. 'Yes, I thought so. What did you think it was really about?'

He was a man skating on thin ice. 'I interpreted it to be an allegory likening the experience of a woman in love to the slow decay of Scotland caused by the Virus.'

'I didn't get that at all.' She stopped walking. 'Bernard, you are so insightful.'

He breathed a silent sigh of relief. 'Drink in the bar?' he suggested.

Lucy squeezed his hand. 'Or we could go home?'

Bernard's heart rate started to climb alarmingly. This was his fourth date with Lucy. They were already well into the zone where he should be sweeping her off her feet, seducing her, bringing her back to his bedroom and giving her everything he had to offer.

It wasn't that he didn't want to. Contrary to the commonly held view of some of his HET colleagues, he was a heterosexual man. He was a man who liked women, a man who liked sex, and a man who liked Lucy very, very, much. Unfortunately, he was also a married man.

His marital status was a fact that he just couldn't get past. When he'd married Carrie he was sure it was for life. Of course, he knew that couples break up all the time, and that both parties move on. However, he was old-fashioned enough to feel that he could not do anything with Lucy until he had at least regularised his affairs with his ex. He'd been a little bit vague with Lucy about his past relationships, hinting that there had been something long term, which hadn't ended happily.

Well, no more. Tomorrow, before he went on another date with Lucy and disappointed her again, tomorrow he was going to sort things out with Carrie, and tell Lucy the full truth of his situation.

'Perhaps just a quick drink tonight,' he said. 'Busy day tomorrow.'

A little smile played around her lips. 'OK.'

8

Mona's mother was in the huff. Not that she would come out and say that she was grumpy, but Mona knew from the huffing and puffing going on that she was annoyed.

Mona had been trying to eat her tea while flicking through Bryce's report on Blair Taylor; she could tell this was irritating her mother.

'It's work, Mum, we are really busy.'

'Yes, but I don't see why that means you can't take five minutes after being at work all day to talk to your mother.'

Living back at the family home was meant to be for her mother's benefit. She had had a fall which, added to the cancer she was already suffering, had meant that she was too frail to live on her own. Mona had moved in temporarily to see her back to health, but after her recent head injury the tables had turned. Dr Sangha had advised it was best if she didn't live alone.

Mona had run through all the possibilities of who might step up to the plate and let her move in, before concluding that she should have worked harder at maintaining the friendships she'd made at university. She couldn't think of a single friend she could ask to help her out. Even Bernard seemed to have better things to do these days, what with his new girlfriend. Her mother, on the other hand, didn't need asking twice, and had taken to this new arrangement of looking after her with undisguised glee.

'OK, Mum, what do you want to talk about?'

'Well, not that this will be of any interest to you, but . . .'

Her mother then spoke for five minutes, without drawing breath, on the changes that the council had made to the bin collection. Mona kept half an ear on the conversation, while with the rest of her brain she thought over the events of the day.

'Mona.'

She jumped, as she realised her mother expected an answer. 'What?'

'What should I do? Should I phone the council or not?'

'Ehm, not, probably?'

Her mother sighed. 'You weren't even listening, were you?' She picked up the *Evening News* and started leafing through it, her lips pursed.

'Sorry.'

'No, no. Just like your father, your one and only interest in life is police work. I expect you'd prefer it if I just talked about whatever crime is going on in Edinburgh . . .'

'Mum . . .'

'Yes, let's see. We've got a shooting at the Parliament, but I expect you know all about that, anyway.' She stopped to turn over the page. 'NHS Lothian is still complaining about the theft of anti-viral drugs from hospital pharmacies.' A further flick of paper. 'A murder trial at the High Court has collapsed.'

For the first time this evening, Mona gave her mother her full, undivided attention. 'Which trial?'

'I don't know.' Her mother was continuing to leaf through the news. 'Some drug dealer or other.'

'Well, can I have a look at it?'

'Oh, for goodness' sake!' Her mother thrust the paper

60

at her. 'I was right. Murder and mayhem is all you are interested in.'

Mona grabbed it and ran up the stairs to her room. Her mother's hurt feelings would have to wait. She spread the newspaper out on her bed. Her mother was right, an Edinburgh drug dealer by the name of Scott Kerr had walked free from the High Court after the case against him had collapsed. Several key witnesses had withdrawn their statements.

Mona was amazed that the case had actually made it as far as it had. She knew Kerr, and witnesses to his endeavours tended to find that their memories of the events in question couldn't be relied upon, or that they inexplicably didn't turn up for their day in court.

Mona had come across many drug dealers in her time at CID, and had been appalled and horrified by the lengths they would go to to protect their territory. A certain professional distance was required to keep yourself from going mad. She'd lost some of that distance at the HET, and had foolishly assisted Bernard to enable a trafficked prostitute called Alessandra Barr to escape Kerr's clutches. Once she'd reflected on what they'd done she realised that if Kerr ever found out about it, he would, without a moment's thought, have them killed. The one saving grace for her had been that it looked like Kerr was going to be locked up for an unrelated murder. Now that hope was gone.

She closed her eyes for a moment. Without the background chatter coming from her mother, she was free to acknowledge the low-level ache at the back of her head. This led on to a series of thoughts about what was a normal healing process, and what might actually be a sign of something more serious.

Would Bernard know about this? She'd heard him on the phone arranging a theatre trip after work, so it might well be that he hadn't seen the TV bulletin, and she was pretty sure he wasn't a regular reader of the *Evening News*. Her hand hovered over her phone, then she pulled back.

Bad news could wait until morning.

9

Bernard woke with a sore neck and a strange metallic taste in his mouth. So much for his early night. His dream had left him extremely anxious and he struggled to remember its focus. It might have been the dream that he was starving; he'd had that one a lot recently, prompted by the continuing price rises of perishable goods, and the fact that he was running out of food. He'd spent months stockpiling tinned goods, against all the advice from the government, but his current financial difficulties, caused by paying both his own rent and his wife's mortgage, meant that he'd been dipping into them regularly, and definite shortages were appearing in his larder. Despite his financial constraints, the need for chocolate sometimes overcame him, and the day before he'd had no change from £2.50 when purchasing a Mars bar. No wonder he was anxious. No wonder he had bad dreams.

There was a sudden loud clatter from the living room. Bernard sat bolt upright. His first insane thought was that he had brought something evil back from his dream, which was now corporeal and causing havoc in his bijou living space. His second, much more rational, thought was that it was a human being who was stumbling round his home, the kind of human being who didn't ring the doorbell, or shout a cheery hello through the letterbox, but instead saw fit to enter uninvited, and with the homeowner unaware. In many ways this was an even more terrifying scenario.

Two years ago he would have struggled to think of a single person who might wish him actual physical harm. At the height of his career as a professional badminton player there might have been the odd opponent who wished a sprained ankle on him, but even then, to be honest, his fairly modest talents hadn't brought him many disaffected rivals. Since he had started work at the North Edinburgh Health Enforcement Team, however, there was a list of people who might wish to hurt him. It wasn't even a particularly short list.

Who had he annoyed recently? There had been harsh words exchanged with the woman in the local shop regarding her confectionery pricing policy, but it was a bit of a stretch to imagine her tailing him home and sending someone round to exact an apology (which, to be honest, she would be getting next time he was in the shop anyway). No, he was working on the assumption that anyone willing to engage in a spot of breaking and entering had a fairly serious grudge.

He listened intently, hoping for an audible clue. Bernard's flat was not big; the bedroom opened directly on to the living room/kitchen. The lady from the rental agency had made much of its compact charms, but had failed to point out its lack of defensible space. The intruder was one door handle away from walking in on him.

There was another small thump from the living room. Whoever was out there was making a pretty limited attempt to keep quiet, which meant either they were too clumsy to do so, or they really didn't care if they were heard.

This last thought prompted a horrible realisation about

exactly *who* would feel no compulsion to stealth. Scott Kerr, Edinburgh's leading drug dealer, could be next door throwing Bernard's possessions to the floor one by one. He did, after all, have good reason to be annoyed. If it was Scott Kerr who was in his living room, there was nothing left to do except hope that his affairs were in order.

Which, of course, they were. His not-quite ex-wife would inherit the lot, such as it was. She'd get the equity tied up in their marital home, the mortgage of which was being paid by Bernard on the grounds that Carrie's grief-induced alcoholism meant that the chances of her holding down a job and paying her own accommodation costs were slight. She'd also inherit the £3,000 in his instant access ISA, money that he'd been hanging on to in case life at the HET got so bad that he really couldn't bear it any more and jacked the job in. That particular reason for saving was now obsolete, since the HET Powers That Be had invoked the clause in their contract which meant they couldn't leave even if they wanted to. The only hope there was a successful conclusion to Carole's legal proceedings.

He heard a cough, deep throated and growling. It had to be Kerr. No-one else would be that blasé about being heard. A common or garden burglar would have been in and out by now, with whatever meagre haul he'd secured. Kerr, however, could afford to take his time. His approach was to do what needs to be done, with whatever noise that involved (gunshots, sound of bones breaking, desperate cries for mercy) then intimidate any potential witnesses into keeping their mouth shut about whatever they thought they might have heard. Already he felt quite sorry for Mrs Peters next door. He hoped she slept through it all.

As he contemplated his imminent death, his memory threw him a lifeline. Scott Kerr was in prison, awaiting trial. It couldn't be him. He breathed a quick sigh of relief, before starting to consider the other possibilities. There was one other person who wanted to inflict some degree of hurt on him, might even want to kill him, but may not yet be 100 per cent committed to having him dead. Someone who may yet be bargained with. A further thump reverberated through the wall leading him to think that clumsiness was indeed a factor. Could it be the inelegant gait of a man who had, not two weeks earlier, suffered a number of injuries at Bernard's hands, namely, his colleague Ian Jacobsen? He sincerely hoped so. If Bernard had to defend himself against a home intruder with murder on his mind, the former colleague with a broken arm and only one working eye was definitely his favoured option.

Defend himself! What was he doing, worrying about who was in his living room, when his first concern should be how he was going to protect himself? He should definitely phone the police – but then he remembered his mobile had been charging in the kitchen and he'd left it there, carefully unplugged, of course. Safety first. If he couldn't call in the cavalry, he'd have to deal with this himself. He contemplated shouting loudly enough to wake Mrs Peters and have her phone the police instead, but decided it was too risky. She'd have had a couple of sherries, and the only thing that would wake her now would be her bed bursting into flames.

He swung his feet round and placed them gently on the floor. In the darkness he reached for his shoes and pulled them on. After reviewing the contents of his bedroom for a potential weapon, he realised that the most offensive weapon he could muster was a stout wooden coat hanger, which didn't feel like much to go into battle with. He stood up, stubbing his toe against one of the tins of tomatoes which were piled on his bedroom floor, for want of any better storage space.

An idea hit him, and he dropped the coat hanger and grabbed a couple of the tins. If he could get two direct hits to the intruder's head that might buy him enough time to make a break for freedom. The slight flaw in this plan was that he still needed a hand to open the door. He shoved a tin under his arm, then quickly pulled the door open, and stood, tins aloft, trying to get his bearings. Almost immediately his nostrils were hit with a familiar aroma of stale tobacco and dog hair.

A short, sturdy figure walked towards him.

'You feeling hungry, son?'

Bernard slowly lowered his weapons.

'Anyroad, son, I need a favour.'

TUESDAY

GOSSAMER
CATCHBASIN

I

Maitland was in pain and Bernard was enjoying it.

'Make it stop, for God's sake.' He slumped forward, pulling his long legs up onto his chair, his hands placed firmly over his ears.

'What's wrong?' asked Bernard. 'Don't you like music?'

'I do, but whatever that appalling sound is, it is not music!' He pointed in the direction of the YouTube video currently playing on Bernard's PC.

Bernard responded by turning the volume up a notch. 'But Arthusian Fall were experimental progressive rock at its finest.'

The new musical experience brought Paterson storming out of his room. 'For God's sake, turn it down!'

'Sorry,' said Bernard, rapidly shutting down the site. 'It was a bit of research on Arthusian Fall.'

'Well, take your "research" somewhere else. What are you planning to do today?' He stared at them suspiciously, as if the burst of music was an indication that they might be planning to skive off to a rock concert.

'Actually, we're just off to see Blair Taylor's flatmates again, Guv.'

Paterson grunted. 'Make sure you come back with something useful.'

Maitland started pulling his jacket on. Bernard looked at his watch. Where was Mona? He really, really wanted to speak to her about his nocturnal visitor. He needed advice, he needed it soon, and she was the only person who could help.

'Come on, loser.'

'Ehm ...' Bernard looked at his watch again.

Paterson stuck his head out of his office door. 'Why are you pair still here?'

'Just going, Guv.'

Mona and Carole arrived, the cups of coffee in their hands explaining their late arrival.

'Morning, ladies!' Maitland grinned at them as he headed out. 'Enjoy your rock star. Just don't let the ex-wife play you any of his music.'

Bernard sidled over to Mona. 'I really need to talk to you.'

She seemed to have been expecting this. 'I know, we do need to talk.'

'As soon as possible. Something happened last night that—'

'Bernard will you get out of here and actually do some work!' Paterson's voiced roared from his office.

Bernard made the international hand sign for *I'll call you* to Mona, and ran after Maitland.

'I wish we were going to a rock star mansion instead of a scabby student flat.' Maitland looked wistful.

'I think I can live without meeting Colin Karma. Anyway he won't be there. They're just meeting his ex-wife.'

'Hmm. Rock star wife. I bet she's really fit.'

'Maitland! You're about to get married—' Bernard stopped himself just in time from saying 'to the lovely Kate.' Kate *was* lovely, and far, far too good for Maitland.

72

'Calm down. I'm still allowed to look.' Maitland pressed hard on the buzzer. 'These girls better be here and not mucking us around.'

'Yeah, well, remember we're not the police, and we're not to behave as if we are. Paterson was quite clear about that.'

'Stop being such a girl, Bernie.'

'That's sexist.'

'You're right. I'm being unfair to the ladies. You're more of an amoeba, or maybe a jellyfish. Or am I being unfair to the invertebrates?'

Fortunately, the door opened at that point as Bernard didn't have a comeback. He ran up the stairs, silently fuming.

Kirsten stood in the open doorway to her flat, accompanied this time by a young woman with long straight blonde hair, wearing a navy blue business suit. Her expression suggested she would much rather have been at work.

'You must be Veronica.'

'Come in.'

They trooped through to the living room, and declined Kirsten's offer of refreshments.

'I don't know what I can tell you,' began Veronica. 'I haven't seen Blair for months.'

'Perhaps you can tell us a bit about the circumstances of his disappearance?' asked Bernard.

'He just left,' she said. 'I woke up one morning and he wasn't there. I didn't think anything of it at the time, I mean, it's not like all his stuff had gone, or anything like that. He just went out, and then never came back.'

'Did you report him missing?'

'No.' She shook her head. 'I wasn't actually sure he

was missing. He was just my flatmate so I wasn't really keeping tabs on him. After a couple of days I did kind of wonder where he'd gone, and when I hadn't seen him for a week or so I had a look around his room until I found a phone number for his parents. I rang them and they phoned the police.' She frowned. 'Are you saying I did something wrong?'

'No, of course not,' said Bernard. 'That was a reasonable course of action. You said Blair was "just your flatmate" – did you get on well with him?'

'No.' Her answer was immediate and emphatic. 'I really didn't like him.' She pulled a face, as if at an unpleasant memory. Bernard glanced over at Kirsten who was wearing a similar expression.

'In what particular way – perhaps you could expand a little?' he suggested gently.

Maitland suddenly leaned forward, obviously annoyed at the softness of the questioning. 'Yeah, what was wrong with him? Didn't do the washing-up? Dropped his towels on the floor?'

'Blair – do housework?' She gave a bitter little laugh. 'He was far too up himself to do anything like that. He never hoovered, never cleaned the bathroom, he didn't even wash up his own dishes. I used to leave a big pile of the cups and plates he'd used with a note on them to say he needed to deal with them, and he'd just ignore it. I was out working all day, and coming back to that was so annoying.'

'That wasn't the worst thing about him though,' added Kristen. 'It was the things he used to say—'

'Oh, God, yeah. He said some appalling stuff about women. Thought he was really superior to girly idiots like us. Him and his creepy mate.'

'Aaron Mitchell?'

She shuddered. 'Aaron, yeah. He was even worse.'

'Have you seen him recently?' asked Bernard.

'No,' said Veronica. 'I've not seen him since Blair disappeared. He's certainly not been round here. Can't say I've missed him.'

Bernard decided to move things on a little. 'Kirsten told us that you threw out a load of things belonging to Blair.'

Veronica shot her friend a dirty look. 'Not things, just papers and leaflets. I stuck them all in the recycling bin at Asda.'

'Wasn't really your place to do that, was it?' said Bernard. 'Those papers were his private property.'

She shrugged. 'I know, but the leaflets were really, really awful, and his parents were coming and I just felt so sorry for them. They sounded like really nice people on the phone.'

'You know what I think? I think you two girls are talking shit.' Maitland bounded back into the conversation with his customary finesse. It didn't appear that the talk about not pretending to be the police had been listened to. 'Your flatmate and his friend went missing, and you've thrown out a load of his possessions. Sounds to me like you might have been involved in his disappearance. What happened? An argument about his awful views? Fight over him being a slob? Let me guess, you pushed him, he fell and hurt his head.' He looked at each of them in turn. 'Come on, girls, what have you done with the body?'

To Bernard's surprise, Kirsten started to cry. Surely Maitland wasn't actually on to something?

'Get real.' Apparently Veronica was made of sterner

stuff than her friend. 'We argued with him plenty but it never came to blows.'

'I'm not saying it was intentional...'

'WE DIDN'T TOUCH HIM!' Veronica glowered at Maitland. 'I hated him, I hated living with him, I was glad when he pissed off and didn't come back, but I did not kill him!'

'Although you have done *something*, otherwise your friend wouldn't be bawling her eyes out.' Maitland sat back, his arms folded. 'Now, if I take your word for it that the last time you saw him he was alive and well, what could your pal be so upset about? When you were rifling through his possessions did you decide to keep a few bits and pieces for yourself? Did you strike it lucky and find a wad of cash in his sock drawer?'

Kirsten sniffed. 'Just tell them, Roni.'

Veronica glared at her friend, glared at Maitland, then gave in to the inevitable and started talking. 'Blair's parents are still been paying for his room. They wanted to keep it in case he comes back. I think they're deluding themselves but... Anyway, Kirsten's just started her new job and she needed somewhere to stay. It's an internship, but paid next to nothing, so Kirsten, well, she's been living here, rent-free.'

'Oh,' said Bernard. 'I see.' The revelation was something of an anti-climax. He'd been steeled for a story of a fight that had got out of hand, or some drunken accident that had been covered up by the girls. A bit of squatting wasn't exactly the crime of the century.

'Well, that's fraud, isn't it, Veronica?' Maitland sat bolt upright. 'I think you both better come down to the station with us.'

'No!' They both looked distraught. Bernard resolved

that he was going to report Maitland to Mr Paterson the second he got back to the office. He couldn't have been doing a better impersonation of a police officer if he'd been sat there dressed head to toe in black and sporting a flat peaked cap with a chequered band round it.

'It wasn't hurting anybody,' said Veronica, sulking.

Maitland tutted. 'Except you were conning those nice people that you were just talking about, you know, Blair's parents? Right, I want you to get a bit of paper and a pencil, and write down everything that you can remember that was in his stuff that you dumped.'

'Actually, we could probably do better than that.' Kirsten wiped her eyes with the back of her hand. 'When I moved into Blair's room I found a box at the back of a cupboard that we'd missed.'

Bernard was intrigued. 'You still have some of his leaflets?'

'I'll get them.' She stumbled out of the room.

'Do we need to get a lawyer?' asked Veronica.

'Not yet,' said Maitland. 'But I suggest you are very, very helpful with our enquiries. Starting with the phone number of Blair's parents.'

She pulled out her mobile and scrawled down a number onto a piece of paper. As a half-hearted show of defiance she flung it in his direction rather than passing it to him. He picked it up with a grin.

'So, do you think Blair is dead then, or what?' Veronica directed her question to Bernard.

'We don't know, but there's nothing to suggest he's come to any harm. Please let us know if you do hear anything from him.'

She gave a curt nod.

Kirsten reappeared with an armful of leaflets, which she dropped on the floor. 'Here you go. I'll get you a bag for them.'

Bernard picked one up and flicked through it. 'Oh,' he said, his eyebrows raised. 'I wasn't expecting this.'

2

'Stuttle is not going to like this at all.' Mona had her knees pressed up against the glove compartment of Carole's car, *The Scotsman* spread across her legs. 'He's totally being hung out to dry over the shooting.'

'Why is he getting the blame?' asked Carole. 'Surely it was a security issue for the Parliament, not him?'

'I don't know, but they've got Carlotta Carmichael on record as saying she thinks it's his fault.'

'Seems unfair. Not that I'm exactly a Stuttle fan.'

The feeling was mutual, ever since Carole had decided to sue.

'How is the court case coming along? Have you worked out a way to escape the clutches of the HET?'

'It's on hold.'

'Really?' Mona turned towards her in surprise. 'You're giving up?'

'Absolutely not.' Carole looked outraged at the idea. 'It's a complete disgrace that we're being forced to stay at work. But there's a HET officer in the Forth Valley team who's beaten me to it. We're waiting to see the outcome of his court case before my lawyers proceed.'

'Oh, that makes sense.' She stared out the window at the fields. 'Do you think we're heading in the right direction? It's been a while since I saw any houses.'

As if in answer to the query, the Satnav spoke. *In five hundred metres turn left.*

'Where?' Carole slowed the car down. 'All I can see are hedges.'

'Oh, I see it.' Mona pointed. 'There's a *For Sale* sign just over there.'

Carole turned left, and they drove along a narrow lane, the car bouncing along the rough track.

'I still don't see the house.'

They drove on in silence for a second or two, until a pointed roof appeared on the horizon.

'I think this is what you call splendid isolation,' said Carole.

'You certainly wouldn't have any arguments with your neighbours.'

A few seconds later Carole pulled the car up next to the solid Victorian farmhouse, which looked as it had been extended a number of times over the years. A further *For Sale* sign was nailed up next to the main entrance. The sound of their wheels on the gravel had alerted the occupant to their arrival and she stood in the doorway. Mrs Karma looked more or less exactly as Mona had expected the wife of an ageing rock star would look: tall, slim, elegantly dressed in casual but pricey leisurewear, and with long, blonde hair pinned up in a chignon. She waved to them.

'Mrs, ehm.' Mona realised she didn't actually know the correct form of address for the women she was speaking to. 'Karma?'

'Mrs Murray, actually.' There was a soft American drawl to her voice, with a twang that suggested a Southern state. Now that Mona was close to her she could see that she was older than she had first thought, probably close to forty. 'Karma is his stage name, and there was no way on God's earth I was changing my name to that. And I'm soon to be the ex-Mrs Murray, anyway, if my lawyers ever get their overpaid asses into gear. So, probably better all round if you just call me Lana. Come in.'

They followed her down a wood panelled hallway into a large drawing room. It must have been magnificent in its heyday, when it could have been decked out with several three-seater sofas and still have had room left over for a grand piano. The magnificence of the room was somewhat diminished by being furnished solely with two garden chairs.

'Are you still living here?'

'Just,' she said. 'The last of the furniture went into storage yesterday. Apologies for the lack of seating.'

'No problem. We just wanted to ask you a few quick questions about your husband.' Mona corrected herself. 'I mean ex-husband.'

She smiled. 'You were right first time. He'll still be my husband for a few more months. The law works slowly. Can I ask why you're interested in him? Has he done something?'

Mona couldn't quite read the expression on her face. She was curious, obviously, but there seemed to be something else. Maybe she was hoping there was something she could use in her divorce settlement.

'We just have a few routine questions for him. Nothing to worry about. We're finding it a bit difficult to catch up with him. When did you last see him?'

She thought for a moment. 'Two or three months ago. We communicate through the solicitors nowadays.'

'How did he seem when you last saw him?'

'Furious. We are in the middle of a divorce after all.'

'We know your husband had a few run-ins with the police in the height of his rock star days.'

Lana threw her head back and laughed. 'Rock star – that's a laugh. His music was totally unlistenable to. Have you heard Arthusian Fall?'

Mona and Carole both shook their heads.

'Try it some time. I guarantee it will give you nightmares. So, Colin and the police? What can I tell you? He did have a few run-ins with them. My husband is a very angry man. Everything annoys him. Every*one* annoys him. But I'm not aware of him getting into trouble with the police recently.'

'Does your husband have a job?' asked Carole.

'No. He just lives off the royalties from his wonderful career, not that he makes much in the way of music these days. Oh – the only other thing he ever did was write letters to the newspaper. They stopped publishing them after a while.'

'What exactly was he angry about?'

'Everything irritated him. Young people, the NHS, parking, you name it he'd complain about it. What I think he was really annoyed about, though, was just the fact the he wasn't famous any more. The more people didn't care about his thoughts, the more loudly he had to shout them.'

'Is he a violent man, do you think?'

'No.' She shook her head. 'Maybe once upon a time, but not now. Colin's a spent force.'

'And you've no thoughts at all about where he might be?'

She shrugged. 'Abroad, perhaps? He was always saying that he thought Britain was finished.'

'Well, if you think of anything.' Mona handed over her card.

'The Health Enforcement Team,' read Lana. 'So, are you guys like the police?'

82

'No. We look for people who have missed a Health Check, nothing more serious than that.'

She frowned in confusion. 'But he's immune. He doesn't need to go for a Health Check.'

Mona didn't have an answer to this, so decided to wrap things up. 'Thanks for your time. We'll update our records. Will you be around for a while if we need to speak to you again? Or are you heading back to America?'

'Yeah, I'm afraid so. I've no family or anything over here. I was only over because of Colin so, you know.'

'You'll miss the NHS,' said Carole. 'Taking your chances with the American health care system and the Virus can't be easy.'

She shrugged. 'I've got insurance. I'll be OK.'

She showed them back to the door, and stood watching as Carole turned the car around and negotiated her way back out of the gate.

'What did you make of that?' asked Carole, giving a final wave to Lana Murray as they left.

'Well, no love lost between her and her hubby, but I still got the impression that she wasn't actually giving us a full picture of him. Unless, of course, he is just the world's most boring man.'

'Certainly some claim to be the world's most angry man. That's definitely something he's got in common with Bryce. They're both very, very angry about something.'

'So, where now?' Carole waited at the junction.

'Well, we've seen the current Mrs Karma. Time to go and see the former one.'

3

'I don't get it,' said Maitland.

'Get what?' Bernard was concentrating on his driving and on watching the road signs. Maitland was supposed to be navigating but his mind clearly wasn't on the job.

'The point of the leaflets. When the girls said Blair Taylor had a bad attitude to women and a cupboard full of stuff they didn't want his mum to see, I assumed he had a massive porn collection. Didn't you?' Maitland grinned at him. 'Or does that kind of thing never cross your mind?'

Bernard sighed. 'No, Maitland, that's what I thought they meant too.'

'Did you?' Maitland grinned. 'I thought maybe your convent schoolgirl upbringing meant your mind didn't work on that level. What with you seeing Lucy for weeks now and not having got her into bed yet.'

Bernard gripped the steering wheel a little more tightly. 'Please stop talking about Lucy and focus on the investigation.'

'OK.' Maitland returned to looking at the leaflets. 'But if you have any questions about what men and women do in bed you only have to ask.'

'I was married for over a decade!'

'Course you were.' His colleague smirked. 'To a woman none of us have ever met. My offer stands – if you need any advice about how to satisfy a woman in bed, I'm your man.'

'Maitland, I guarantee I will never need your advice about sex or anything else.' Bernard took a deep breath; one of these days he really was going to snap. 'Anyway, the leaflets are all about eugenics.'

Maitland's expression could charitably be described as blank. 'Eugenics?'

'It's about trying to create a master race of perfect human beings.'

He flicked through the leaflet again, still looking puzzled. 'Which would be a bad thing because . . .'

Bernard sighed. 'OK, let's start from first principles. In ancient Greece and Rome they used to kill babies if they thought they weren't perfect, leave them out on a hillside to die. You know, if they were disabled or something. Then in modern times that viewpoint developed into trying to discourage certain people from breeding.'

'Some people don't need help not to breed. Like you, Bernard.'

'Shut up, Maitland! So, for example, the Nazis were big into this. They killed a lot of people that they thought didn't measure up to their Aryan ideals. It wasn't just totalitarian states, though. Even in less repressive regimes there's been some pretty horrible things done, like sterilising women if doctors thought they were mentally ill.'

'Oh, right.' He put the leaflets back into his bag. 'It does sound pretty grim when you put it like that. Nobody thinks like that any more though, do they?'

'We're a bit more concerned about human rights these days. Although I don't think the views have ever entirely disappeared in certain quarters. The Far Right's philosophy is pretty much underpinned by the superiority of the white race.'

'So these guys are white supremacists?'

'I don't think so.' Bernard mulled this over as he changed lanes. 'I think it's a bit more nuanced than that. The people who wrote the leaflets have updated eugenics principles to take account of the Virus. They think the Virus is part of natural selection. That the people most likely to die are the weak, and the people who remain will breed some kind of master race.'

'Well, that's bollocks, isn't it? You're more likely to die of the Virus if you are really fit.'

'Yep. For once you are quite right, Maitland.'

It was one of the quirks of the Virus that the flu affected people's immune system by overstimulating it to the point where their body couldn't cope. Young people with healthy immune systems were most likely to die. The teenage eugenicists must have been quite wilfully blind to miss that particular flaw in their argument.

'There is absolutely no science underpinning what they're saying. But then there never has been a strong scientific basis for eugenics.'

'His flatmate said he had a really bad attitude to women. Is that a eugenics thing, or is he just a common or garden arsehole?'

'Don't know. I don't think eugenics has ever worked particularly well from the point of view of women. My money is on him just being a bit of an a-hole though. The nonsense these guys have been writing is just good old-fashioned misogyny dressed up as ideology. You know – women are the weaker sex, should get back into the kitchen, stick to having babies, that kind of stuff.'

'So they do talk some sense then?'

'I'll tell Kate you said that.'

Maitland laughed. 'Right, turn off here. This is the exit for Inverkeithing.'

The door was opened by a man in his fifties. At least his face indicated he was in his fifties, but his hair was completely and totally white. Maybe this was what having a missing child did to you.

'Hi, Mr Taylor?'

The man nodded.

'We're Bernard and Maitland from the Health Enforcement Team. We spoke on the phone.'

'Yes, yes.' He lingered in the doorway, without inviting them in. 'Can I just say that my wife is—'

They didn't find out what he was about to reveal about his wife, as a door flew open and she appeared. Like her husband, she seemed to be in her fifties. She didn't share her husband's whiteness of hair, but her face was lined, and there were dark shadows under her eyes. She held herself stiffly, as if it was taking all her energy just to walk. She brushed past her husband. 'Do you have news? Have you found him? Have you found my boy?'

'Ehm . . .' Bernard thought of the most tactful thing to say, but took too long.

'You must have found him. You wouldn't have driven all this way out of Edinburgh just to tell us that you hadn't found him. What happened to him? Is he alive? Does he want to see us?'

'Isabel, calm down and let the man speak.'

She grabbed hold of Bernard's arm. 'We had words, you see. I didn't mean anything by it, we just didn't like that boy he was hanging around with. All those funny ideas; he was turning Blair's head. Blair could be anything. He could be a lawyer he is so bright. Have you found him? Found my boy? Do you know where he is?'

Maitland took control. 'I'm very sorry, Mrs Taylor, we don't have any new information about your son's disappearance. We just wanted to ask you a few questions.'

She was crying now, holding tightly onto Bernard's arm. It was beginning to hurt, but he couldn't bear the thought of trying to remove her.

'You *must* have some new information to be here.'

'Isabel.' Her husband's tone was firm, though not unkind. This obviously wasn't the first time he'd experienced such a situation. 'You need to go into the kitchen and have one of your pills.' He turned to them, and pushed open the door which led on to the living room. 'Please go through. I'll just be a minute.'

Mr Taylor was substantially longer than a minute. They could hear loud voices in the kitchen, then the sound of him helping his wife up the stairs.

'Do you think that's Blair?' asked Maitland in a low voice, pointing at a picture of a school boy on the mantelpiece. The teenager in the photo was slight of build, wearing large glasses and with a smattering of acne across his cheeks and forehead.

'I guess so.' Bernard looked round the room at the other pictures. They all appeared to be of the same child, at different stages of development. 'It looks like he's their only child. You've got to feel for them.'

'I do.' Maitland nodded. 'But God in Heaven help us if he's going to be the start of a master race. '

'Shut up.'

Mr Taylor reappeared. 'Sorry about that. My wife hasn't worked since Blair's disappearance. She spends a lot of time on her own and gets into all kinds of negative thoughts.' Almost sheepishly he continued, 'I don't suppose you do have any news about Blair?'

'I'm really sorry, but no, we don't. We're just re-examining an investigation that was made into his activities around...' Bernard paused for a moment, wondering if Mr Taylor knew about his son's activities.

'You mean the eugenics nonsense.' His face was a mixture of irritation and slight embarrassment. 'He was never into all that kind of stuff until he met that Mitchell boy at university.'

'Yes,' said Maitland. 'We're looking into their activities again, to see if they are linked to other activity that is related to our area of work.'

To Bernard's ear this sounded unconvincingly vague, bordering on nonsensical. Mr Taylor didn't pick them up on it.

'I'm not sure that they did a great deal beyond the printing of propaganda. Have you seen the leaflets?'

'Yes, they're an, ehm, interesting read,' said Bernard. 'Do you know what they did with them?'

'They handed them out at the university. I understand they were repeatedly told not to, but I only found that out after Blair went missing. If I'd known what he was up to I could have done something about it. He was a bright boy. He had a great future...' He stopped and turned away from them, making a show of rearranging the pictures on the mantelpiece.

Bernard looked over at Maitland, who nodded in the direction of Mr Taylor, and mouthed *keep going*. He thought about mouthing back *no you keep going*, but decided this wasn't the time or the place to address Maitland's unwillingness to do difficult tasks.

'I'm so sorry to drag all this up again, Mr Taylor,' he

continued. 'Could you tell us a bit about what happened when he disappeared?'

'I don't really know. As my wife said, we had had words with Blair about his attitude. I really didn't like the way he was speaking to us, particularly to my wife. We were concerned about his friendship with another boy.'

'Aaron Mitchell?'

'Yes.' He looked momentarily surprised. 'You know him?'

'We know of him.'

'Well, Blair got very annoyed with us when we suggested he should try to make some other friends. So we weren't all that surprised when we didn't hear from him after he went back to university. As time went on we did start to get worried, though he sent us a few texts when my wife threatened to call the police if he didn't contact us. It was actually the girl that he lived with that let us know he was missing. Have you spoken to her?'

'Veronica, yes.'

'A nice girl.' Mr Taylor nodded. 'There doesn't seem to have been anything to indicate he was about to go missing, although we do know now that he was on the point of being thrown out of the university.'

'Because of the leaflets?'

'Yes, and the number of classes he'd missed.'

'At the time, what did you think had happened to him?'

There was a long silence. 'Are you the police?'

'No. The Health Enforcement Team is a completely different agency.'

He seemed reassured by this. 'At first I thought he was just, I don't know, hidden away somewhere because he was embarrassed about being kicked out of the university. His mother texted him about a million times telling him that we weren't angry, he just needed to get in touch. But when we tried to speak to the police—' a look of anger came over his face '—we couldn't get them to accept that Blair might be missing, that something might have happened to him.'

'They didn't look for him?'

He shook his head. 'I don't entirely blame them for that. I know it looks bad that he'd fallen out with us, and was about to be kicked out of the university. I know that he doesn't seem to be vulnerable. But I knew my son. He was bullied all the way through school. This Mitchell character had something about him that appealed to Blair. Something about his views that meant that even after all the hassle he'd had at school, Blair could still come out of it being a winner, just by dint of the fact that he was a man.' He looked embarrassed again. 'A white man. I know the police are stretched, and I know they don't have the resources to investigate everyone that goes missing. You'd have to be a fool not to realise how many other priorities the police had, but still . . .' He clenched and unclenched his fists. 'It was the way they spoke to me that still sticks in my throat. You've seen how fragile my wife is, yet the police officer turned round and said she would just have to accept that my son may not want to be found.'

'What do *you* think happened to your son?'

'I would love to think that he's out there in a bad mood with us, not wanting to get in touch. If that's his choice I can live with it, although it may yet kill his mother.' He sighed. 'In reality, I think something has happened to him. I accept that he could be . . .' He tailed off, leaving the word unspoken.

'Do you have a particular reason to think that?' asked Bernard, as gently as he could.

91

He nodded. 'Blair's bank statements still come to the house – he never bothered updating his address with them. We've been opening them, I'm sure we're not supposed to but . . .'

'Under the circumstances . . .'

'Yes. His bank account was emptied over the period of a week. Someone withdrew the maximum amount they could every day until the money ran out. I don't know why Blair would do that, but I can think of plenty of reasons why someone else using his bank card might. I think that Mitchell boy knows what happened. Will you be speaking to him?'

'We certainly hope to at some point,' said Maitland.

Maitland appeared to have decided they were done, and got to his feet. Bernard was less convinced that they'd asked everything they should have, but reluctantly followed suit. 'Thank you for your help, Mr Taylor, and again I am very sorry for the situation you're in. If we find out anything that would be useful to you we will be sure to let you know.'

'I would be extremely grateful.'

He showed them out. Bernard noticed his hands trembling as he held the door open for them both. He suspected that as soon as it closed behind them, Mr Taylor was going to fall apart. A lump formed in his throat. He knew what it was like to lose a child, the pain and the powerlessness he'd felt when his baby son had died; he could only imagine the horror of not knowing if your child was alive or dead.

Maitland strode on ahead, down the garden path and into the car. He didn't speak until they had returned to the motorway.

'You're very quiet,' said Bernard. 'It's not like you.'

'Just thinking about the possibilities of what could have happened to Blair. I need to have another look at the case notes that Bryce left us.'

'Bryce's notes certainly gave the impression that they were harmless and there was nothing in this.'

'Yeah, I know, but I was getting the vibe back there that Aaron Mitchell wasn't entirely harmless, although I suppose that it's in Mr Taylor's interest to blame Mitchell for anything that went wrong. Easier than accepting that your son might actually have just disappeared off without a backwards glance.'

'I hope we can leave the Taylors in peace now,' said Bernard.

'Do you?' Maitland sounded surprised. 'Because I hope we're back here in a week's time with some answers for them. I don't think that mound of crap we're wading through is going to tell us one useful thing about what Bryce is up to, but I do think we've got a real chance of reuniting that spotty white supremacist freak with his parents, or at least finding out what happened to him.'

'I suppose you're right.' He couldn't help feeling that whatever happened, it wasn't going to be a good outcome for the Taylors.

4

'Do you really think this is it?'

Mona checked the address she'd noted down. 'Yep. Sharon Murray's Green Card gives her place of residence as Wester Hailes.' She double-checked the paper again. 'And this is the right block.'

Carole stared up at the high-rise. 'Bit of a contrast with his second wife's home.'

'I'm guessing the first Mrs Karma's lawyer wasn't as good as the second's.'

'Do you really think she's going to be able to shed any light on things?' asked Carole. 'If his current wife doesn't know where he is, what are the chances of his ex knowing?'

'I'm just hoping from a bit of brutal honesty about what kind of man he is, and what he's likely to have been up to. I thought Lana was being a little bit cagey with us. Here's hoping the ex-Mrs Karma is bitter and keen to dish the dirt.'

Mona pressed the buzzer. No-one responded, but after a second the door opened with a metallic clunk.

'Stairs or lift?' asked Carole.

'It's only four floors.'

'Only?'

Mona grinned and ran up the stairs, Carole climbing

sedately behind her. She held the door to the fourth floor open.

'Which flat do you think it is?' asked Carole, surveying the four available options.

'Four.' Mona spun round looking at the options. 'One, two, three . . .here we are.' She knocked loudly.

'Who is it?' A female voice, soft and low, spoke to them from within the flat.

'Mona and Carole from the HET. We spoke on the phone.'

The door opened slightly. There was a large chain keeping it shut.

'Have you got some ID?'

Mona held up her HET card.

'Can you bring it closer?'

She pressed it into the crack between the door and the door jamb. As she removed it, Sharon Murray finally saw fit to let them in. Despite being dressed in jeans and a long, baggy cardigan, there was no disguising the beauty of the woman. She was slim, with large dark eyes, and long brown hair that was pulled back from a set of high cheekbones. Her eyes darted around the landing as she held the door open. 'I don't have any tea or anything in. Would you like a glass of water?'

'No. We just have a few questions about your ex-husband.'

'Colin? What's he done now?'

'What makes you think he's done something?'

'Nothing.' She turned away abruptly, and walked down the corridor, disappearing through a door at the far end of it. Mona and Carole exchanged a glance then followed her. They found themselves in her living room; Mrs Murray had settled herself into an armchair, her cardigan pulled tightly around her.

'You won't be telling Colin that I spoke to you, will you?'

'Not if you don't want us to,' said Mona. 'Are you scared of your ex-husband, Mrs Murray?'

'No, of course not.' She looked down, her hand tapping the side of her chair. As denials went it was pretty unconvincing. Mona glanced over at her colleague, who was staring intently at Sharon Murray.

'Mrs Murray, I think we've met before.' Carole leaned forward. 'At the Western General.'

There was no response to this.

'I used to work at the Western about, maybe, a dozen years ago.' Carole tried again. 'You worked on a dementia ward there, didn't you?'

Sharon Murray shook her head, her eyes still downcast. 'You must be thinking of someone else.'

'Oh, right. You're not a nurse then?'

'No!' She spoke firmly, obviously irritated. 'I work in the community, with people with learning difficulties.'

Carole stared at her. 'Sorry, you just look really like someone ... Anyway, it's not relevant.'

Mona picked up the thread. 'So, when did you last see your ex-husband?'

'It's been ages.' She chewed at her fingernails. 'Years. I've got no reason to be in contact with him.'

'No alimony arrangements to discuss, or anything like that?'

Sharon Murray glared at her. 'I don't see that that is any of your business. As I said, I haven't seen Colin for years, so I don't think I can help you any further.' She got to her feet and opened the living room door. She stood there, waiting.

Mona and Carole took the hint. As they followed her

back to the door, Mona took the opportunity to have a discreet look at the surroundings. Although Sharon had ducked the question about alimony, it was pretty obvious she wasn't living a life of luxury.

'Thanks for your help, Mrs Murray.'

'I wasn't much help, I know. I'm sorry I couldn't be more use.' She hesitated. 'Is Colin still with that American woman, the one that makes films?'

'Lana?' Mona opted for discretion. 'I'm not sure.'

'Oh, OK, bye then.' She shut the door behind them.

They walked slowly back down the stairs.

'We didn't get much out of her, did we?' said Carole.

'I don't know. Sharon Murray might not know where Colin Karma is, but I think she definitely helped us develop our picture of him.'

'Yeah, that's true.' She nodded. 'I can't say I'm warming to Karma – he's obviously got the poor woman scared. Do you think he was violent?'

'I don't know. When we get back I'll get his police record checked out. See if he was done for domestic abuse at any point.'

'My money is on him being abusive. We used to see this all the time when I was still in nursing.' Carole shook her head, angered by the thought. 'His second wife said he was Mr Angry, and Sharon Murray was pretty on edge back there.'

'Let's not jump to any conclusions.'

Carole frowned at her. 'I'm not jumping to conclusions. There were signs.'

'I agree Mrs Murray was nervy but it could be that she's paranoid about everything, not just her husband.' Mona shrugged. 'Could be she has mental health issues that contributed to them splitting up.'

'Maybe.' Carole conceded the point.

Mona walked down a few steps in silence. 'Something else is bugging me. She claims not to have seen him for years, yet got really worried that he'd find out about us talking to her.'

'He could have been so awful to her that she's still terrified of him years later.'

'Entirely possible. Or she could have seen him much more recently than she's admitting to, and if that's the case, I'd like to know why she's keeping it to herself.'

'Well, whatever the real issue I feel sorry for her.' Carole frowned. 'I was so sure I recognised her from the Western. I think I remembered her because she was so pretty.'

That fact hadn't escaped Mona's notice. 'Yeah, but why would she lie about where she worked? It's not like it's something anyone would be ashamed of. People are generally pretty well disposed toward nurses.'

'I know, doesn't make sense. I must have confused her with someone else.' Carole pushed open the door to the block, and they were out in the fresh air again. 'Back to the office?'

'Nope. I have a better idea.' Mona called up a search engine on her phone. 'Let's go and visit Jepson Bartlett Artist Management.'

'Who?'

'Karma's agent.'

5

Bernard was hungry. Melanie Mitchell, Aaron's mother, had agreed to meet them in the bakery where she worked. It was a small family-run affair in Corstorphine, which seemed to specialise in cakes and pastries. The smell was overwhelming sugary, but to a man who hadn't eaten anything since a breakfast bar on his way to work, it was delicious.

They were shown into a small room lined with chairs, with a kettle and sink in one corner. A cork noticeboard on the wall declared it to be the staffroom.

'This is a bit out of the blue,' Melanie Mitchell said, taking off the cap that prevented stray hairs making their way into the baked goods, and shaking her tresses loose. She was much younger than the Taylors; she must have had Aaron when she was still a teenager. 'I assume you haven't found him?'

'No, I'm afraid we're not here with good news, or in fact, *any* news about your son,' said Bernard. 'We were hoping you might be able to help us with some background information about his disappearance, but I appreciate that might be very upsetting for you.'

'I'm not sure I could be any more upset.' She took a seat and motioned to them to join her. 'I've made my peace with the fact he's not coming back any time soon.'

'When did you last hear from him?'

'About a year ago, but to be honest we weren't really speaking by the time he disappeared.'

Maitland sat forward. 'Why not?'

'My son had developed a very negative attitude towards women. I was fed up of the way he was speaking to me.'

So far, so very similar to Blair Taylor. Bernard pressed on. 'Were you aware of your son's campaigning activities?'

'Not until after he disappeared.' She gave a bitter little smile. 'That other boy's parents phoned up. They seem to be holding Aaron responsible for their son's disappearance as well. They said that their son had never been in trouble over anything until he'd met my Aaron.'

'What do you think?'

'I think that Aaron gets the blame for a lot of things, and not all of them are actually his fault.'

'Was Aaron in trouble a lot?'

She grimaced. 'Unfortunately, yes. His dad left when he was very small, and it seems like his whole life has been a quest for some kind of meaningful masculinity. There was bullying at school and things like that.'

'Why was he bullied?'

'He wasn't. He was bullying other children. As I said, he struggles with the concept of masculinity and what it means. He isn't great with any kind of authority figure, to be honest. He hates anyone telling him what to do.'

'Have you any idea where your son might be?'

She shook her head. 'I didn't know my son by the time he disappeared.'

'Did you contact the police at the time he went missing?'

Again, there was a shake of her head.

'If you don't mind me asking, why not?'

She stared at the floor for a few seconds before answering. 'Please don't think less of me for this, but

I was glad to have Aaron out of my life by that point. I'd worked two jobs for most of his childhood to try to give him what other children had. He was keen to go to university, so I paid for a tutor for him to make sure he got the grades.' She looked up, defying them to judge her. 'In return, I was hauled into the school every second week about some incident he'd started, usually by some comment to one of the girls in his class. Then just when I get him into university and think he might finally do some growing up, he starts on with all this nonsense about master races and survival of the fittest. Then he drops out of uni, totally throwing everything I'd worked for back in my face. I know you'll think I'm a terrible mother...'

'We don't,' said Bernard, hastily.

She smiled. 'Thank you. But by the time Aaron took off, I was glad to see the back of him. I hope he's happy, and I hope he comes back into my life someday, when he's matured a bit. For the moment, though, I think I deserve a bit of a life of my own.'

Bernard stood up, and nodded to Maitland to do likewise. 'We'll leave you to it. Thank you for your time.'

She showed them back to the front door, sadly without offering them any pastries en route, and they walked back in the direction of the bus.

'So, we appear to have one teenage bully, and one bullied teenager,' said Bernard.

'Yeah.' Maitland nodded. 'Blair Taylor strikes me as pretty easily led, and I didn't get the impression that Melanie Mitchell had entertained for a minute the idea the Aaron might be dead. I say they're both still alive, well, and up to something.'

'If they're still out there promoting their crazy ideas

101

they shouldn't be too difficult to track down. Maybe we will be able to go back to the Taylors with some good news.'

'Let's hope so.' Maitland walked straight past the bus stop.

'I thought we were going back to the office?'

'No way. I'm starving now. Let's get something to eat.'

6

Artemis Bartlett was very pleased to see her. In fact, he was more pleased to see her than Mona could ever remember anybody being since she started working for the HET. She wondered if he understood what it was they did; he didn't look as if he was particularly well connected to the modern world. She'd place him as late fifties, with curly blonde hair which stuck out like a halo around his head. He was wearing a purple velvet jacket, paired with what looked like tartan trousers, although she was pretty sure there wouldn't be a clan in the land rushing to claim that particular check.

'We're the agency that looks for people who have missed their Health Check,' she said, trying to extract her hand from Artemis's vice-like grip. He was wearing a ring on every finger, and all of them were now digging into her.

'Yes, yes, I know. I'm delighted to see you ladies. You've found Colin, haven't you?' Artemis's loud Home Counties voice echoed around the room.

'No, I'm afraid not,' she said. 'We're actually looking for him, and we thought you might know where he is.'

Mona's hand was immediately released. 'Oh, I must have misunderstood what you said on the phone. I thought you lot had arrested him or something.'

'We don't do that,' said Carole. 'We don't arrest people.'

'Well, this is a disappointment I've got to say.'

'Can I just clarify, Mr Bartlett, that you are still the manager of Arthusian Fall?'

'Yes. And also lead vocalist, along with Colin on guitar, Eldon Smarts on drums, and the late Mr Nigel O'Hara on bass, God rest his soul. Anyway, come through.'

He gestured to them to follow. The room they went into was some kind of lounge. Artemis threw himself down on a chintzy sofa and picked up his abandoned cup of tea. It was rather less rock and roll than Mona had anticipated.

'I take it then that you are also looking for Colin Karma?'

He nodded vigorously. 'Yep, he's got some money of ours, I mean Eldon Smarts' and mine, which we would very much like to see again,' said Artemis.

'This is money he stole from you?' asked Carole.

'*Borrowed*, love. But seeing as it's not looking like we're getting it back, it's mostly the same thing.'

'Have you been to the police about this?'

He laughed heartily. 'Nobody in their right mind would report Colin to the police.' Artemis was still chuckling as he spoke.

'Why not?'

'Have you seen his gun collection? The guy's a nutter.' He patted his head to emphasise the point. 'If I set the police on him I'd be scared of waking up with a shotgun pointing at my head. You ladies want to look after yourself around the likes of him.'

Mona was starting to think that this was good advice. 'How long have you known Colin?'

'Ooh, we're going back a while. Eldon and I were at school together, boarders, and we sneaked out to the pub one night in the sixth form, and met Colin. So, probably '78?'

'You formed the band while you were still at school?'

'Yup. Not that we were at school for long after we met Col. We'd only known him two months when he managed to get us expelled. Suddenly we went from life at a minor public school to living in a squat in London. We'd never have survived without Colin. Although...' Artemis looked thoughtful. 'In fairness we'd probably never have been expelled if we hadn't met Col.'

'When did you last see Mr Karma?'

'That I can answer,' said Artemis, confidently. 'We had a thirtieth anniversary relaunch of *Gossamer Catchbasin*, our biggest album.'

Mona decided Bernard and Marcus could fill in any gaps in her Arthusian Fall knowledge later. She'd be telling them to keep it brief though; she could do without Marcus educating her on every development in rock music since Elvis picked up a guitar.

'The launch was about six months ago. That's when Col presented us with, as he put it, a business opportunity. We've not seen Col or our money since.'

'What was the business opportunity?'

'Col wanted to buy a building and turn it into a recording and film studio.'

'Where were the premises?'

'He was a bit vague.' Artemis scratched his head. 'We'd all drunk quite a lot by this point of the evening. But we shook on it and agreed we'd invest £200k...'

Two thousand pounds?'

'Each,' he clarified. 'From both me and Eldon.'

There was a brief silence. 'I don't mean to be rude, but that's a lot of money to invest on very little information.'

'I know,' Artemis flung his hands up, 'but that's what the demon drink does to you.'

'Couldn't you just say you'd thought better of it?' asked Carole.

'We shook on it! You don't go back on something like that with Col. He'd skin you alive.'

'Do you think he did actually buy a building with your money?'

'Don't know.' Artemis shrugged. 'According to the agreement his lawyer sent over, our names were supposed to go on the title deeds, but as far as we're aware we're not co-owners of any disused factories.'

'That's what he was planning to buy? An old factory?'

'I think so. Like I said we'd had a lot to drink ...'

Mona hoped that someday she'd have so much money she could invest two hundred grand while drunk and forget what she'd spent it on.

'Could you give me the name of his lawyer?'

'Sure.' Artemis started scrolling through his phone. 'Have you spoken to his wife? The American woman?'

'Soon-to-be ex-wife.'

'Oh.' He looked surprised. 'He never mentioned they were splitting up. He spent a lot of the evening ranting about the state of the UK, and how the USA had a much more sensible view of life, so he's obviously not been put off Americans.'

'What was he upset about?' asked Carole.

He gave another shrug. 'Don't remember the details. He's always complaining about something or other. I don't usually pay much attention. He's got another ex-wife, you know. Sharon.'

'We know. We spoke to her.'

'You spoke to Shaz?' Artemis looked delighted. 'How is she?'

Mona opted for a white lie. 'She seemed OK.'

'Good.' He nodded to emphasise how positive he thought this was. 'She was a lovely girl in her day. She'd have been better off if she'd never met Colin – maybe we all would be. We'd have been accountants or lawyers or something. Although I supposed we'd have missed out on a lot.' He smiled. 'We've had a myriad of adventures, girls. Anyway, here's the lawyer's number.' Artemis pulled out a pen and scribbled the number on a scrap of paper. 'But like I said, ladies, look after yourselves if you're going anywhere near Colin.'

They took their leave and headed back out onto the street.

'Well?' said Carole.

'OK, I think you might have a point. Mr Karma does not appear to be a very nice man.'

'He sounds like a complete psychopath, and I'm sick to the back teeth of dealing with people like that. Don't tell Paterson, but I'm phoning my lawyer as soon as I get in. I'm fed up searching for people who may want to hurt me or mine.' She let out a little squawk of frustration. 'I didn't sign up for this. They said it was a health care job!'

'Well, good luck fighting the Scottish Government and its emergency powers.' Mona smiled. 'In the meantime, we just have to work out where the hell Colin Karma actually is.' Her phone pinged. 'That's Bernard looking for me again.'

'Are you going to call him back?'

Mona looked at her phone and guessed that the six missed calls indicated Bernard had also seen the article about Scott Kerr's release. 'I suppose I'd better.'

7

It was turning out to be quite a long lunch in Corstorphine. In fairness, it could truthfully be described as a working lunch. Maitland had spent most of it on the phone discussing the case with various former police colleagues, usually with his mouth full of ham and cheese panini while he talked. It was not a pleasant sight.

Bernard finished his salad, and decided to give Mona another ring. She'd ignored his first five messages but this time he might just strike it lucky and she'd actually pick up.

As usual, providence was not on his side. 'Hi, Mona, just me again, Bernard, that is, can you give me a ring when you get this? I really need to speak to you about something that happened last night. Kind of urgently. At least definitely before the end of work today. Anyway, bye.'

'This is total bullshit.' Maitland slammed his phone down on the table.

'What is?'

'I must have made four, no make that five, calls to mates at Police Scotland, and not one of them will talk to me. Either they're allegedly not in the office, or they can't wait to get me off the phone.'

'Maybe none of them like you?'

'Shut up. I think it's the Cameron Stuttle thing. He's in trouble so now we're all outcasts. All I wanted them to do was run Aaron Mitchell's name through a couple of databases, but it was all, *sorry, Maits, but it's more than my job's worth.* We're, what's the word?' He snapped his fingers in Bernard's direction.

'Pariahs?'

'Yeah, probably. Anyway, we might as well get back to the office.' He got to his feet, showering Bernard with bits of panini which hadn't actually made it into his mouth.

'Crumbs, Maitland!'

'"*Crumbs?*" Don't you ever want to swear like a proper adult?'

'I meant *actual* crumbs which you've just covered me with ...' He realised that Maitland wasn't listening, and picked up his coat to follow him.

'Hurry up,' said Maitland. 'We've got things to do. Golly gosh, darn it.'

As they approached the door of the office they could hear the sound of tuneless singing.

Maitland pulled a face. 'What's Marcus doing here again?' he whispered. 'Isn't he supposed to work out of Fettes?'

'He was.' Until recently Marcus had shared a basement office with Bryce at Fettes, Police Scotland's HQ. 'They closed down his office after they found out about Bryce, so they could check it for bugs and stuff. I suppose he's homeless now.'

His colleague did not look particularly charitable. 'Why do we have to get landed with him?'

Marcus stuck his head out of the doorway. 'Thought I heard the sound of returning troops!'

Maitland grunted and pushed past him. Marcus looked surprised, but not particularly put out.

'Joining us again?' Bernard smiled as sincerely as he could. Much as he liked Marcus, he did find that his productivity declined considerably when he attempted to work with Marcus chattering away in the background.

'Indeed! Today I have mainly been working as a secretary to Maitland, answering phone calls ...'

'Who phoned?' yelled Maitland.

Marcus returned to the desk he had borrowed – Carole's – and consulted his notes. 'A Matt Sugston returned your call – I believe he works in the Counter Terrorism Unit?'

'Yes, I know that,' said Maitland, making a grab for the piece of paper that Marcus was holding. He turned it over in his hand. 'Where's his phone number?'

Marcus looked surprised. 'He didn't offer one. I assumed you had it already.'

'No! I phoned his office looking for him and they said he no longer worked out of there, but they wouldn't give me his mobile.'

'Ah. Whoops. Well, if it is any consolation, Matt and I had a long conversation.'

Maitland's expression suggested he was quite far from being consoled.

'Anyway, Marcus,' said Bernard, hastily. 'What did this Sugston chap have to say?'

'Well, he asked what the young men you had referred to in your message to him were involved in, and I explained the whole eugenics angle. He got quite excited about that.'

'Why?'

'Apparently it's a trend they're monitoring – you know, wackos who think the Virus is some form of natural selection. They're keeping tabs on it in case anyone decides to help Mother Nature on her way with some violence toward Virus sufferers, attacks on hospitals etc.'

'I thought *you* kept tabs on the wackos on the internet?' asked Bernard. 'Hadn't you heard of them?'

'Ah, Bernard, so many crazed people and so little time! I'd not come across this particular ideology, but dear Matt has given me a steer in the right direction, and while you boys were out I've had a fine old time surfing the Facebook page of the cryptically named Operation Manacle Lap.'

'Did you find anything useful?' asked Maitland, peering over Marcus's shoulder at the screen.

'Possibly. I had to go back a long way, we're talking over a year ago, but look at this post.'

Someone had posted a link to a BBC article about the Virus. Beneath the link there were several paragraphs of what Bernard could only describe as nonsense. He shook his head at the spelling and grammar, but ploughed on manfully. From what he could make out through the swearing and inexplicable capitalisation, it outlined the theory that the Virus was a method of the Earth cleansing itself of the weak.

'Was there something in particular we were supposed to be looking at?'

'Look who posted it – eh, Bernard? Eh?'

He stared at the screen. 'DarkLordEdel? I don't get it?'

Marcus's surprised expression at Bernard's lack of knowledge gave way to one of disappointment. 'Arthusian Fall album *Auroria* – side two, track one – "The Dark Lord Edel Will Rise"?'

'Of course, how did I miss that?' Bernard would not have recognised the Dark Lord Edel if he sat next to him on the bus, but he didn't want Marcus to think he hadn't listened to the albums he had suggested. 'You think that's been posted by an Arthusian Fall fan?'

'Oh, no.' He shook his head. 'I think it's been posted by the Dark Lord himself – Colin Karma. And if you scroll down through the many comments that Lord Reith would find highly offensive, you find a big thumbs up from a boy too young and naïve to use anything other than his real name . . .'

Maitland read the name aloud. 'Aaron Mitchell.'

8

'I'm not sure this is a good idea, Bernard.'

'Well, what do you suggest we do? Annemarie broke into my house last night. If we don't meet with her she'll only come back tonight.'

'I suppose.' Mona looked round the pub, checking out the other clientele. None of them looked particularly dodgy. The last thing she wanted was an associate of Scott Kerr's seeing them have a quiet drink with Annemarie. 'I'm just not sure that getting involved with Annemarie is a good idea. I was kind of hoping never to see her again. The stuff we helped her with wasn't exactly legal.'

'It's not sure it's a good idea either,' he said, frowning. 'She says her brother is missing, and if that's all there was to it, I'd say I'm sorry, but we can't help. That's not what we do.'

'Although you can see why she might be confused about our boundaries.' Mona had given up trying to work out what the HET's boundaries actually were; the border seemed to run directly through whatever it was Cameron Stuttle needed them to do. Although at least when he ordered them to do something, he could take the blame when it went wrong. Their entanglement with Annemarie was all their own doing. If there was blame to be apportioned here, it was heading straight for her. And Bernard.

The pub door opened, and Annemarie stood there. Five foot tall, if that, she was as broad as she was long, and sported a grey flat-top that was so similar to the Guv's that Mona wondered if they shared a barber. Mona had known her for several years, since her earliest days in the police. Back then Annemarie had run a project supporting prostitutes in Leith, a gig she'd held for the best part of four decades. Her relationship with the police, or any government authorities for that matter, had been fairly fraught, but she'd accepted Mona and Bernard's help to make Alessandra Barr disappear.

'Yes, but she's worried that . . .' Bernard broke off as Mona pointed over his shoulder. 'Oh, she's here. She can tell you herself.'

'Hello, son, hen.' She nodded to both of them.

'Would you like a drink?' asked Bernard. 'They do a very nice house red in here.'

'Just a ginger beer for me, son, I don't drink. Thirty years of living with an alcoholic puts you off the stuff.'

'Yes, people do some stupid things when they're drunk,' said Mona. *Two hundred grand. That was a whole house-worth of stupidity.*

Bernard returned with a ginger beer and two glasses of the nice house red. Mona took hers with gratitude. She had a feeling this was going to be the kind of conversation that required a drink.

'So, Annemarie, tell Mona what you told me last night after you, you know, broke into my flat.'

Mona tried not to smile at the slight bitterness in his voice.

'Your door wasn't locked properly, son.'

They both stared at her, and she laughed.

'Anyway, you know I was telling this one,' she hoiked a

thumb in the direction of Bernard, 'that Alec, my brother, is gone.'

'On a bender?'

'That's what I thought at first. Cursing him, I was. I thought he was getting better in his old age, or if not better, at least less able to take off. But that's him gone a week, and the thing that's really bothering me is I had a visitation.'

'Who from?'

'Somebody that claims Alec owes him money.'

'A loan shark?' Visions of baseball bats and big dogs on leads leapt into Mona's mind.

'Worse than that, much worse. I recognised the laddie as one of Scott Kerr's.'

'That's not good,' said Bernard. 'That's really not good.'

'It could be genuinely all about moneylending,' said Mona.

'If we're lucky.' Annemarie took a large drink of her ginger beer, then burped. 'Sorry. It's not beyond the realms of possibility Alec's just done something really stupid. These guys are in the pub all the time offering money to people who can't pay it back.'

It wasn't a very cheerful best-case scenario.

'Although,' Mona added, 'it is a bit of a coincidence that Kerr gets released from prison, then this happens.'

'What?' Bernard's jaw dropped. 'He's out of prison?'

Mona exchanged a glance with Annemarie. 'It was in yesterday's paper.'

'Did you not know that, son?'

Bernard answered by taking a large gulp of his wine. 'If it's not about moneylending ...'

'Well, then, Scott's found out about that dirty great lie

we told him. If he has, then we're all in serious trouble.'

'So, what do we do now?' asked Bernard.

They both looked at Mona, who felt her irritation level rise. Why did everyone always expect her to sort things out? 'I don't know.' She thought for a minute. 'How are you supposed to get the money paid back?'

'I'm on strict instructions to turn up to the Duke's with the money on Friday.'

'The Duke's?' asked Bernard.

'It's one of Kerr's pubs,' explained Mona. 'He does a lot of business out of it. What happens if you don't turn up?'

'I don't fancy Alec's chances. But if I do turn up . . .'

'I don't fancy yours.' Mona took a thoughtful sip of her wine. 'You could talk to the police?'

'They're not going to bother themselves looking for an old jakey. They know Alec, and they know what he's like. Anyway, they're not going to put themselves out for me, are they? Not with everything else they've got on their plates.'

'You could call in a favour, Mona?' said Bernard. 'Explain the real situation to your former colleagues?'

'Explain the situation? Which bit do you suggest I start with? The bit where we forged HET paperwork? The bit where Scott Kerr has photographs of Carole's son selling drugs? I mean, we could explain to them that Kerr set Carole's lad up, and point out that we only created the paperwork to give a woman trafficked into prostitution a fighting chance of not being killed by Kerr, but . . .' she paused to let that sink in, 'you have to admit we'd all be in a lot of trouble.'

'Yeah, good point.' Bernard's glass of red was wobbling slightly as he took in the full complexity of their situation.

'I need to think it over.' Mona resigned herself to being the one to sort out this particular mess. 'Annemarie, you probably shouldn't stay at your flat.'

'All right, doll, I'll stay with this one.' She pointed at Bernard.

To Mona's surprise, he nodded.

'You're OK with that?'

He nodded again, without looking her in the eye, and she realised the reason for his co-operation. He was scared.

He was probably right to be.

9

Bernard ran along the street in the direction of his estranged wife's flat. He hoped that he was doing the right thing.

He was pretty sure he'd made some questionable decisions already that evening. He'd given his house key to Annemarie, only to realise when they were leaving the pub that Sheba was also going to be moving in with him. Much as he loved animals, he drew the line at living, however temporarily, with the slobbering, stinking hound that Annemarie doted on.

'See sense, son,' she'd said, as she unhooked the beast's lead from the lamp post she'd tied it to, 'I can't leave her home alone.'

She'd hurried off before he could argue the point further, so now he could kiss goodbye to getting the deposit back on his rental flat, after Sheba had done her worst. The only slight consolation was that she probably was the kind of animal you needed on hand if Scott Kerr appeared on your doorstep.

His second questionable decision was to phone Lucy and cancel the vague plans they'd made to meet up that evening. She'd said reassuringly that *just going out for a drink would be fine*, which led him to believe she was interpreting his behaviour as sexual performance stage fright. There'd been quite a long silence on the phone as he thought of a polite and non-creepy way to communicate to her that he'd like to have sex with her *very much indeed*, which had ended when she'd said she'd better let him go and hung up.

He'd calmly put the phone back in his pocket, and then sprinted the mile or so to his former residence at a record-breaking pace. If he could wrap things up with his wife this evening, by tomorrow night he could be sweeping Lucy off her feet. At her place, obviously. Far, far, away from Annemarie's chain-smoking and Sheba's dog breath.

He still had a key, but as a courtesy pressed the buzzer, crossing his fingers that she was in.

'Hello?'

She was in. *Thank God.* 'Hi, it's Bernard. We need to talk.'

He stared expectantly at the intercom, which remained silent.

'Carrie?'

'This isn't a good time, Bernard.'

'I don't care, Carrie. It's really imp—'

He was cut off mid flow as she hung up. He dug into his pocket for his old keys, and let himself into the building. He took the stairs two at a time and knocked on the door of his marital home. 'Carrie, don't be silly. Let me in.'

'Go away.'

Should he leave? He'd taken her by surprise – maybe if he gave her a couple of days to get used to the idea she'd be more receptive. He could come back at the weekend...though by Saturday, Lucy really would have given up on him. She was probably sitting at home this very minute considering the possibility that he was some kind of eunuch. It was time for action. He lifted up his key, put it into the lock, then hesitated. He wasn't really the type to force himself into an ex's flat, albeit one that he was paying for. Sighing, he stuck the keys back in his pocket.

'Carrie, I just want to talk.'

'I'm not ready. Come back in three or four months.'

He leaned his head against the woodwork. 'This is ridiculous. We're going to talk, even if it has to be through a door.'

'Fine, have it your way, as always.' The door opened.

'Thank you.'

Bernard looked into Carrie's eyes, and his stomach turned over. They'd been married ten years, and probably would still be together if it wasn't for the death of their son. There would always be a part of him that cared for her very deeply. He swallowed. 'You look well.'

She didn't say anything, but took a step backwards. He looked at her again, taking her in from head to toe, noting her new hairstyle, what looked like new shoes, and the large and prominent belly in between.

'You're pregnant.'

She glared at him.

'Is it . . .mine?'

WEDNESDAY

FIRE AND DEATHSTONE

I

'Morning.'

Mona had been standing on the doorstep of Carole's family home for five minutes, waiting for someone to answer the door. She'd rung the bell twice, decided that it obviously wasn't working and had hammered loudly. This had provoked a shouted conversation inside the house about someone getting the door, but the heated discussion hadn't actually concluded with anyone taking responsibility for this, and it had taken a further pounding on the woodwork to persuade anyone to finally reach for the handle.

'Oh, sorry, Mona.' Carole was attempting to tie up her hair as she talked. 'I thought it was one of Andrew's pals calling for him. Are you early or am I running late?'

Mona made a noncommittal sound, which Carole interpreted correctly. 'I am running late, aren't I? Just give me two seconds while I get this one sorted.'

A tall young man in a school uniform pushed past Carole, gave her a brief nod, and headed down the path.

'Do you have your lunch?' Carole shouted after him.

'I'll get something from the shop.' He didn't turn round.

'Have you got any money?'

He gave a wave of his hand which could have meant anything, and kept walking.

'I'm sure he won't starve, Carole.'

'No, just fill up on a whole load of empty calories.' She pulled the door shut behind her. 'I think he is doing it just to annoy me. He blames me for his little brother being down in England.'

This seemed harsh to Mona, but she supposed being blamed for things that weren't your fault was part of being a parent. 'Are you going to transfer him back up here?'

'I'd rather move down there myself, to be honest. I want him as far away from that Scott Kerr person as possible. Unfortunately, I can't do anything about that until this bloody court case thing with the HET is settled.'

Mona wondered whether to mention last night's conversation with Annemarie. Did Carole have a right to know? Had she seen the newspaper report about Kerr being out on bail?

'You OK?' asked Carole.

'What?' Mona hoped she didn't look too guilty.

'I said are you OK?' Carole was looking at her with a concerned expression. 'You were deep in thought – is something on your mind?'

Should she say something? Maybe Carole needed to be aware of what Annemarie had said; after all, Kerr knew where she lived. Yet Carole was already dealing with living apart from one son, and coping with the fall-out of that on the other family relationships. She decided not to dump this on her as well, at least not until they knew for certain that Kerr was gunning for them.

'Just thinking about the investigation. Come on, let's go. We can't be late.'

The lawyers' offices were in a large modern building, just off Lothian Road in the city centre. She'd been worried they wouldn't get parked, but they had arrived before the morning rush and had grabbed a short-stay parking place on a back street.

'So, this was the only time the lawyer would see us?' asked Carole.

'It was either today, or three days from now, if she was being honest about her diary commitments. I went for the "today" option, although I'm pretty sure from the way she was speaking on the phone she's not planning to tell us anything useful.'

'Are you sure the building will be open?' Carole looked at her watch, as they climbed the stairs to the front entrance. 'It's only just gone eight.'

Mona looked around. 'There seem to be enough people already heading in to work.' She pushed open the glass door, and they went into the reception area.

'We have a meeting at 8am with Gillian Grahame.'

The receptionist consulted her computer, scowling as she did so. For a moment Mona thought there had been some mistake with the appointment, then the tapping on the keyboard stopped, the scowl turned into a polite smile, and two minutes later they were sitting in a small but comfortable meeting room. After a further moment or two waiting, the door opened and a young woman in a beautifully tailored suit walked in.

'I can't give you long. I have another meeting at eight thirty,' she said, by way of introduction. 'What was it you wanted?'

'OK, thanks for taking the time to see us, Ms Grahame,' said Mona. 'We are trying to trace Mr Colin Karma, also known as Murray, who we are led to believe is a client of yours.'

'Do you have a warrant?'

This wasn't the start to the conversation she had hoped for. 'No, we were hoping we could keep this informal.'

Mona's phone rang. She turned it off.

'I'm not sure that I want any informal discussions, thank you.'

'Can you at least confirm—'

Carole's phone also began to ring.

'—that Mr Karma, or Murray, is actually a client of yours?'

'Do you need to get that?' asked the lawyer. 'It sounds like somebody is trying to get in touch with you urgently.'

'Sorry,' said Carole, hastily turning her phone off. 'It's just our boss. We'll get him later.'

'So, can you confirm that Mr Murray is actually a client of yours?'

Ms Grahame leaned forward. 'Can you explain why the North Edinburgh Health Enforcement Team is looking for Mr Murray, who is immune to the Virus, and therefore does not come under the scope of the Health Checks regime, and therefore your investigations?'

There was a silence.

She stood up. 'If you'll excuse me, I have another meeting to go to. But for the record, yes, I am happy to confirm that Mr Colin Murray is a client of ours and has been for some time. Which is why I will be writing to the head of your organisation to ask why you are harassing him.' She stood up. 'I'll show you to the stairs.'

'Well, if you could mention to Mr Murray that we are keen to speak to him, I'd be really grateful.'

Ms Grahame didn't respond. She stood watching them as they descended back down the shiny chrome staircase. As they reached the main door, Carole turned and gave her a wave, which was not reciprocated.

'Well, that went well, don't you think?' said Mona, as they walked back to the car.

'Is that just standard lawyer behaviour, or was she concerned about us talking to him?'

'Who knows? Although I can't say I'm surprised that a man as angry at the world as Karma appears to be has an aggressive lawyer.'

'Suppose not. Anyway, we'd better phone Mr Paterson back and see what he wanted. I've missed another three calls from him since I turned my phone off. It must be urgent.'

'I'll do it,' said Mona.

He picked up the phone on the first ring. 'Mona, is Carole with you?'

'Yes, we're—'

'I need you both to come back to the office immediately. Don't go anywhere, don't talk to anyone, just get straight back here.'

'Why?'

'I think you may be in danger from Bryce.'

'Bryce? What has—?'

Paterson had already hung up, surmising correctly that the fastest way to get her back to the office was to leave her questions unanswered.

'This is us,' said Carole. 'The car's parked down this one. What was Paterson after?'

'He wants us in the office pronto. Says he's had intelligence that we're in danger from Bryce.'

'What?' Carole looked furious. 'More danger? I hate this bloody job!' She stormed off in the direction of the car. Mona hurried after her, only to bump full tilt into her when she stopped abruptly.

'Look!' Carole pointed to the car. The tyres had been violently slashed.

'Shit.' Mona spun round to see if anyone was watching them. The street was deserted. 'Let's get out of here.'

2

'Where the hell are Mona and Carole?' asked Paterson, looking out of the office window.

'Calm down, Guv, you only phoned them, like, five minutes ago.'

Bernard held his head in his hands, and wished for the umpteenth time that morning that he hadn't downed a bottle of wine last night. Annemarie had tried to talk him out of it, and he'd responded by storming off to his room and drinking it in bed, like a sulky teenager. After two and a half glasses he'd emerged and explained to her his sudden need for oblivion.

She'd been surprisingly supportive. He shouldn't really have been surprised. She had, after all, worked with the prostitutes of Leith for forty years, so there probably wasn't much of the human condition that she hadn't already encountered. She'd listened sympathetically, if with some degree of confusion, as to why he thought a woman whom he hadn't had sex with for two years might be carrying his child.

'She could have stolen a condom back when we were still, you know, and kept it frozen. She's been going on about having another child ever since our son died. She could have prepared for this.'

'Aye, son. Or she could have got herself a new man.

129

And pardon my French, but that sounds a frigging sight more likely.'

He hoped Annemarie was right. Carrie had refused to discuss the issue of paternity, or anything else, with him. The door had slammed shut, and he'd hightailed it back to his flat stopping only to visit his local off-licence. He rubbed his head again, wondering if anyone would notice if he rested it on the desk.

Paterson was pacing up and down the room. 'They said they were on Lothian Road, and it shouldn't take them this long to get back. Marcus, any change on that damn website?'

'No, Mr Paterson. Just exactly the same wording. "Meet my demands or I kill one public servant every day."'

Bernard tuned back into the conversation. 'What do you think Bryce means by public servant? Do you think he means civil servants, or *anybody* who works in the public sector like teachers, road sweepers ...'

'HET officers,' added Maitland.

'I don't know what the bastard meant, but I'm guessing he's starting with HET officers. After all, it's us he's pissed off with.'

'Unless he's started already,' said Bernard.

'What?' They all stared at him.

'I mean, Paul Shore works for the Parliament. Wouldn't that make him a public servant?'

'He was aiming for Paul not Carlotta? That's brutal.' Paterson mulled this over. 'I need to talk to Stuttle.' He disappeared into his office, closing the door behind him.

'Do you think Stuttle's writing his resignation letter even as we speak?' asked Maitland, his voice low so that Paterson didn't hear.

'I still don't think any of this is his fault,' said Bernard.

'Yeah, but if Carlotta was planning to throw him under the bus because of one shooting, think how much she's going to need a scapegoat for multiple shootings.'

'Of course,' said Marcus, 'the one thing we *don't* know is what Bryce's actual demands are. We don't know what he's upset about or who he is holding responsible. My money is on Carlotta Carmichael, whether he was aiming directly for her or not.'

'Yeah, I agree,' said Maitland. 'I think we can assume that Carlotta knows exactly what it is that he wants. Question is, is it something she can deliver on?'

The clattering of footsteps could be heard in the hallway, and Mona and Carole rushed into the room.

'What's going on?'

'This.' Marcus spun his laptop round to show them.

'What does it mean by "public servant", and what *are* his demands?' asked Mona.

'Been through all that,' said Maitland. 'Nobody knows.'

Paterson appeared. 'Mona, Carole, thank God. What kept you?'

'Somebody slashed all four tyres of our car while we were in talking to the lawyer.'

There was a silence as Paterson thought this over. 'Bryce?'

'Don't know.' Mona looked at Bernard, then quickly looked away. He got the message. Bryce wasn't the only one who could be in the frame for this. His stomach turned over, and he was hit by a wave of nausea. He wasn't going to make it through the morning without throwing up.

'Could be unrelated, I suppose,' said Paterson. 'Just kids or something?'

'Eight thirty in the morning, Guv? I can't imagine there are any kids messing about at that time.'

He nodded. 'Fair point. I take it nobody shot at you or anything?'

'No, and we didn't see Bryce, or anyone else in the area. I'm afraid we had to abandon the car and get a taxi back.'

'I wouldn't worry about it. They aren't going to be many traffic wardens out and about once that message is public.' He frowned. 'Actually, when is it going public? Stuttle is supposed to be making a statement.'

'Any minute now,' said Marcus. 'They're trailing it on the BBC website.'

'Stuttle? Shouldn't it be one of the politicians?' asked Bernard.

'Yes, Bernard, it probably should be, but nobody wants to touch this one with a barge pole. Ms Carmichael apparently takes the view that as the message was posted on the Health Enforcement Team's website, it should be Stuttle's responsibility to co-ordinate. And by co-ordinate I mean go on telly and to be the public face that's going to be hated by everyone about this.'

'Mr Paterson, I think that's it starting now.'

Marcus turned up the sound on his laptop. Stuttle appeared to have aged about ten years since the start of the week. He was reading from a prepared statement on the BBC News website.

'There has been a credible threat made to people working in the public sector. We do not have details of who is being targeted, therefore we are taking the widest possible response to this. As of this moment, schools will be closed and we are asking parents to pick up their children as soon as possible. Hospitals will continue providing their usual emergency services, although elective surgery will be cancelled. The army will be posted in all hospitals, and there will be searches made of people entering the building. Public sector staff in all non-emergency services are being asked to go home directly and remain there until further notice. That is all I can say on the matter at this moment.'

A forest of hands went up. 'Who is behind the targeting? Is a terrorist organisation?'

'Is this an official curfew?'

'What if people in the public sector don't want to go home? What if they want to remain at their posts?'

'I'm afraid I can't answer any further questions at this point.' Stuttle got to his feet. The camera followed him as he left the room and the commentary picked up.

Bernard muted the sound. 'Poor Mr Stuttle.'

There was a murmur of agreement.

'Do you reckon that's him sacked then, Guv?' asked Maitland.

'Not yet. They'll let him deal with all this mess then they'll ask for his resignation afterwards. No-one else is going to step up to the mark on this one, otherwise they'll end up sharing the blame. Anyway, pack up your things. Bob Ellis is heading over with some counter terrorism blokes to pick up the files.'

'Are they taking over the investigation?' asked Mona.

'Yes, they are.' Paterson's face betrayed a certain annoyance with this turn of events. 'They will probably want to speak to you again, Marcus.'

'Oh dear. I really have told them everything that I can remember about Bryce already.'

'So, what do we do now?' asked Mona. 'Are we supposed to go home?'

'I'm not going to stop anyone going home, as we have just been instructed,' said Paterson. 'However, if any of you do want to stay, we can keep our heads down and start looking for some junkies or alcoholics that have missed a Health Check ...' He paused.

'Or?' asked Maitland.

'We dig both the HET and Cameron Stuttle out of this mess, and try and stop public sector staff being picked off one by one.'

'All in favour of that, Guv,' said Mona, 'but how?'

'Well, we know that Carlotta is worried about something coming to light, and we know Bryce is upset with her about something. I'm guessing they're probably the same thing. If we can find out what it is that Bryce is outraged about, we could pass Stuttle some pretty strong ammunition. And, if by some miracle we can persuade Carlotta to address whatever it is that Bryce is upset about, we might even stop some poor bastard civil servant getting shot.'

Paterson sounded more passionate than Bernard had ever heard him before. Unfortunately, the members of the HET staff responded to his address with an extended silence, and four pairs of eyes staring at the floor. After a few seconds Bernard couldn't bear it any longer, and spoke up. 'But we still have absolutely no idea what Bryce is upset about.'

His boss swivelled round to face him. 'You must have some idea? What have you been doing for the past two days?' He tutted. 'Have you even established if he could have been turned by either of the groups?'

'We've got a lot of white noise in the paperwork from Bryce,' said Maitland, 'which indicates to me that he wanted to look as if he had done a thorough investigation, without actually admitting to finding anything incriminating. I think he did find *something* he could relate to in all this.'

'Any thoughts which of the groups he was interested in?'

Maitland continued. 'Don't think it's the students, who really do come across as a couple of losers. They're into eugenicals ...'

'Eugenics.' Even though he was suffering, Bernard couldn't let that one pass. 'I think Bryce is an unlikely eugenicist.'

'Our rock star guy sounds pretty charismatic,' said Mona. 'Also a bit of a bastard if his ex-wives are to be believed.'

'Never judge a man by his ex-wives,' said Paterson.

'I'm sure the ex-Mrs Paterson speaks very highly of you, Guv.'

Marcus coughed. 'If I might put my tuppence worth in, I think the students and Colin Karma might be linked. They move in the same circles, at least on the internet. And of course, Bryce is a common link between them.'

'Interesting,' said Paterson. 'Let's focus on this rock star to begin with.'

Mona picked up the thread. 'Our best lead so far is that according to his bandmates, he seems to have bought some disused factory. Nobody knows where it is, but to me if you were bunkering down to prepare for some terrorist acts that would be the kind of place you look for.'

'The lawyer you were seeing this morning, did she shine any light on this?'

'It was Colin Karma's lawyer, and she threatened to sue us if we didn't stop harassing him. She certainly wasn't rushing to put us in touch with him.'

'Well, good luck to her trying that one with the counter

terrorism goons when they land on her doorstep. Right, let's focus here – what's our next move?'

'Can we just take a bit of a step back, Mr Paterson?' asked Carole. 'Do you think Bryce is intending to target us? It might have been him that slashed our tyres.'

'We can't rule it out,' said Paterson. 'Obviously he does have some beef with us.'

'Then shouldn't we also be at home trying to stay safe?' she asked.

'As I said, I'm not going to stop you, if that's what you want to do,' said Paterson.

There was a silence while Carole looked round them all. 'Bernard, what do you think?'

'I think I don't want to die ...'

'Especially as you've got your best chance of a shag in years.'

'Shut up, Maitland. I don't want to die, but I do think that we're probably the people best placed to find Bryce. Even though I know he's not who we thought he was, I still can't imagine Bryce shooting one of us. Except possibly you, Mr Paterson. Sorry.'

'Thanks for the words of comfort, Bernard.' Paterson smiled. 'Well, if anyone wants to leave, leave now. Otherwise we've got a factory to find.'

Mona got to her feet. 'I'm going back to see his ex-wife, see if she knows anything about this factory.'

'Which ex-wife?' asked Maitland.

'The one who's allegedly a film star.'

'I'll help out.'

'Why? Just so you can get an eyeful of a film star? You're getting married, Maitland.'

'I'm just going to be looking.'

Marguerite appeared in the doorway, her coat on.

'That you heading home, Marge?'

'Yes, Mr Paterson. Just wanted to let you know there were people for you downstairs. They were just going to march straight up here, but I told them to wait.'

'Manning your post to the last. Very impressive. Send them on up.'

Bob Ellis appeared in the doorway, flanked by two other men in dark suits.

Marguerite tutted. 'It looks like they've followed me up, Mr Paterson.' She squared up to them. 'I told you lot to wait downstairs.'

'It seems to have escaped your secretary's notice that there's a major incident taking place.'

'All the more important that I don't let *just anyone* into the building.' Marguerite turned on her heel and hurried out the door.

Bernard tried not to laugh at the look of annoyance on Bob's face.

'Who was that?' Bob asked.

'Security,' said Paterson. 'We weren't expecting you quite so soon. We've not got the files together yet.'

'We're here to talk to Marcus.'

'Oh no, not again.' Marcus looked round the room in despair. 'Tell them, Mr Paterson. Tell them, I've already said everything that I know about Bryce.'

'We'll be the judge of that,' said one of the men.

'I'm not doing it.' Marcus crossed his arms. 'I'm not being interrogated again.'

'It's not an interrogation!' Bob let out a sigh of exasperation. 'We only want to ask you a few questions. Can you come with us, please?'

'I'm not going anywhere. If you want to ask me anything, ask me here. In front of witnesses.'

'Oh, for—'

'It might be quicker,' said Paterson.

Bob thought this over. He looked at one of the men in suits, who gave the slightest of nods. 'Right, what we want to know is—'

There was a chorus of electronic beeps, as all three of their visitors received a message. Bob pulled out his phone. He stared at the screen, then his face broke into a smile. 'We need to go.'

'What about the interrogation?' asked Marcus.

The men were halfway out the door already. 'Later.'

'And the files?'

'We'll call back for them.'

Paterson watched them leave. 'What was all that about?'

3

'What's this bird of Colin Karma called?'

'She's not his "bird", she's his wife.' Mona was already regretting allowing Maitland to come with her. She was also starting to regret not letting him drive, as the ache behind her eyes wasn't getting any better. 'She's called Lana Murray.'

'Is that her stage name?'

'I don't know. Why do you care?'

'I want to look her up on the international movie database to see if she's fit.'

She tutted. 'Maitland! You're getting married.'

'So everyone keeps reminding me. Is there some rule that you have to lose the use of your senses when you put on a wedding ring? I can still look, can't I?'

'Why don't you run that theory past your fiancée?' Mona laughed. 'Anyway, I don't think Lana's going to be Mrs, for long. I think they're on the point of getting divorced.'

'Why?'

'Why?' She was surprised by the question. 'How would I know? Do you think it makes a difference to our investigation?'

'No. Just with Kate and me getting married I'm interested in why it doesn't work out for some people.'

She glanced over at him. 'Cold feet?'

'Absolutely not.' He looked offended. 'Kate and I will be together forever. I just wonder why other people mess it up.'

'I suppose it's different for each couple. Lack of compatibility ...'

'Not a problem for Kate and me. We've loads in common.'

'There could be pressures at home, you know, if the two families don't get along ...'

'Kate's parents love me.'

'Ha! Lack of judgement there. I guess some couples split up because they rush into things.'

There was an unexpected lack of response from Maitland. She looked over at him. 'Well, you and Kate aren't rushing into things, are you? I thought you were waiting a couple of years until she'd finished her degree?' Plenty of time, thought Mona, for Kate to come to her senses.

'Actually, it won't be that long. My wife-to-be is keen to bring the wedding forward.'

'Really? What's the rush to get married? Can't you just live together?'

'Sadly, no. I'd be happy with that, but remember the whole Christian thing, no sex before marriage, blah blah blah. Kate won't do a thing until she's legally wed, and she just can't wait to get her some Maitland-loving.'

Mona pretended to dry-heave. 'I think I'm going to be sick.'

'I'd be offended by that if it wasn't for the fact that your sexual orientation makes it impossible for you to see quite how attractive I am.'

'I'm a lesbian, I'm not blind! Or deaf. Believe me, I'm perfectly capable of judging your attractiveness.'

Although, annoyingly, she would have to admit that he was inexplicably alluring to otherwise sane women. 'Aren't you nervous at all about this whole marriage thing? It's a lifetime commitment.'

He returned to his phone, the question unanswered. 'I'm going to try searching for Lana Karma.'

'I think this is us. Oh ...' She broke off at the sight of a man taking down the *For Sale* sign.

'Looks like it's sold,' said Maitland.

'Excuse me.' She slowed the car down next to him. 'Is the house now off the market?'

''Fraid so. You'll have to speak to our head office if you want to try and get a last-minute bid in.'

'Is Mrs Murray still in the house?'

He shook his head. 'She left first thing this morning in a taxi. I've been here all day boarding up windows. Want to keep the place secure until the new owners move in. Again, try the head office if you want to try and get in touch with her.'

'OK, thanks.' She turned the car around. 'Back to the office, I suppose.'

'No, 'fraid not. We've had our warning as well.' He read aloud from a message on his phone. 'All HET staff are to return home immediately and await further instructions.'

'Well, this sucks.'

4

It was remarkably quiet in the office after the departure of the men in suits. Marcus had returned to his own room, and Paterson was in his office. Bernard should have been working on the case, but couldn't bring himself to stop checking the BBC website. When he wasn't refreshing the live news feed, he was on Twitter looking at the comments from outraged public servants across the country. He couldn't remember a time when the Virus had been so comprehensively relegated to the back pages.

'Right, that's me.'

He jumped, then relaxed when he realised that Paterson was not remotely interested in what he was doing.

'Are you going out, Mr Paterson?'

'Yes. Somebody needs to rescue our pool car. I'm meeting a mechanic on Lothian Road to see how we get the tyres repaired. Hold the fort here.'

Bernard nodded and decided that this meant he was being given *carte blanche* to monitor the situation via the World Wide Web. He dug around the issue for twenty minutes or so, before deciding that no-one actually had any new insight to offer on the subject. He opened a private browsing window, and typed in the words 'establishing paternity'.

'Paterson in?'

He hadn't heard Bob Ellis come into the office. He

rushed to hit the X in the top corner of the screen.

'No, he's...out.' Bernard was never sure what he was supposed to tell people regarding the goings-on at the HET. Maybe slashed car tyres were something he should be keeping quiet about. 'Here is the paperwork you wanted.' He pointed at the pile of files his colleagues had rounded up for onward transmission. He couldn't help but notice that it wasn't as large a pile as it had been when it had first arrived in the HET office. Had Mona and Paterson held on to a few of the more useful documents?

Also, now he stopped to think about it, shouldn't they have additional material to pass on, seeing as they had been investigating the two groups for days now? Shouldn't his colleagues be briefing the counter terrorism squad about the potential sedition base in a disused factory? Shouldn't they have...oh, he gave up. He never knew what he was supposed to admit to. Why did Bob have to turn up when he was the only one in the office? Paterson would kill him if he said the wrong thing.

Fortunately Bob didn't pursue the conversation, just scooped up the folders. 'Thanks. I wasn't sure if there would be anyone here. I thought you'd all have been e-mailed and told to go home.'

'No, I've not received...' He noticed the little envelope indicating he had mail in his inbox and clicked on it. 'Oh, right, yes, I have. *All HET staff are to return home immediately.* I probably ought to get going.' He was very keen to get away from Bob Ellis as quickly as possible. Any friend of Ian Jacobsen was definitely someone he did not want to be around.

'Well, you can cool your heels.' Bob grinned. 'We found Bryce.'

'He's in custody?' said Bernard, surprised.

'Not yet, but we tracked him down. Got him on CCTV using a cashpoint.'

Bernard's surprise was rapidly turning to disbelief. 'That seems a stupid mistake for him to make. He must know you'd be tracking his cashpoint card.'

'It wasn't his own card, it was an alias that he was using. He's not smart as he thinks he is, because we were on to him.' Bob grinned. 'We've known about his alter ego for quite some time.'

'It was definitely him?'

'The camera doesn't lie, Bernard. Full-frontal close-up of him.'

'Here in Edinburgh?'

'Obviously I can't tell you exactly where it was, but let's just say it was north of here. Well north.' He winked, then frowned. 'What?'

'Sorry, what do you mean "what?"'

'You're staring at me like you still don't believe we've got him.'

'I'm just surprised, that's all. He's run rings round us all so far.'

'Round you lot maybe, but we were on to him.' He looked round the empty office. 'Is Mona around?'

'No, she's out as well.'

'OK. Pass the message on and tell her to get in touch with me when she gets back.'

5

'Are you sure we should be going back to the office?'
Maitland stared out the window, while the car idled at a
red light. 'It's getting a bit fraught out there. Look.'

To their left was a primary school, where among the
climbing frames and oversized toadstools in the playground there seemed to be some kind of altercation going
on. Maitland wound the window down, and they listened
to an irate parent shouting at a teacher that she was
taking her child home whatever it said on the school's
paperwork. Unusually, the teacher was shouting back,
pointing out not unreasonably, that she was as keen as
anyone to get home because there had just been a death
threat made, but nonetheless she couldn't release the
child because she wasn't authorised to ...

The car behind them beeped, and Mona saw the lights
had changed. With an apologetic wave over her shoulder
she drove off.

'Should we get out and help?'

'Nope. It's a matter for the school, or the police if it
comes to that.'

'Yeah, but ...' He twisted round on his seat. 'Oh, she's
thrown a punch. The teacher is down. We totally need
to stop.'

Mona pressed the accelerator. 'Variations on that
theme are going to be going on in every playground in

Scotland, Maitland. The entire country has just had its day turned upside down. Tempers are going to be flaring all over.'

'I suppose.' He reluctantly turned back. 'So, you really think we should go back to the office?'

'You go home if you want to, but I'm not leaving work until we track Bryce down.'

Maitland's phone rang, and Mona was treated to a one-sided conversation that related to Maitland getting himself home *right now* and out of the possible line of fire.

He made a number of noncommittal noises and hung up. 'My fiancée worries about me.'

'That's very sweet. So, are you coming back to ...?'

The metallic ring tone of Maitland's phone sounded again. Mona listened as he, once more, made a number of not exactly excuses for not heading home.

'Kate still worried?'

He looked sheepish. 'No. My mum.'

'Strange to think that these people care so much about you.'

'Not hearing *your* phone ringing off the hook here,' he replied. 'No significant other out there looking for you? What happened to that woman from the radio station?'

'There was never anything going on there.' She really didn't want to discuss her love life, or lack of it, with Maitland. 'Anyway, I'm sure my mother will be on the phone in a minute.'

There was a brief silence before a phone started to ring. Maitland's phone.

'Yeah, OK, I'm on my way home now, right.' He sighed. 'Kate and my mother have spoken to each other, and are both insisting that I go home immediately.'

'Where can I drop you, Mama's boy?'

'Back at the office, obviously.' He grinned.

The front door to the Cathcart Building was firmly closed when they approached. The fact that there was no one left working inside was emphasised by the elderly man knocking loudly on it and receiving no answer.

'Can I help you, sir?' Mona called to him.

He turned and she could see that the man was younger than she'd first thought, maybe only in his fifties. He was carrying a large cardboard box, which triggered a slight feeling of alarm in Mona. Anything out of the ordinary today needed to be treated with caution.

'Oh, Mr Taylor.' Maitland stepped forward, obviously recognising their visitor, and Mona relaxed a little.

'Sorry you didn't get any answer there. As you may have heard there have been some, ehm, difficulties, and we've all been sent home for the day.'

'Yes, it's been all over the news.' He hesitated. 'Is it connected to Blair?'

The pieces fell into place in Mona's head. She wondered what might be the quickest way to get rid of him. Blair was not the focus of her current attention; they needed their dwindling staff resources to be concentrated on finding the factory. She started to make an excuse, then caught sight of his face. His skin was grey and lined, as if he hadn't slept in weeks. He was the father of a missing child; even under the current circumstances, she could spare him five minutes of her time.

'Perhaps you'd like to come inside, Mr Taylor?'

They grabbed the first meeting room they walked past. 'Can we offer you a cup of tea or coffee?'

'No. I know how busy you must be at the moment.' A look of embarrassment, mixed with determination appeared on his face. 'Is all the stuff on the news anything to do with my son's disappearance?'

She'd seen that look on people's faces before when someone had gone missing, the horrible tension playing out between wanting to know what had happened to your child, and the fear of actually finding out.

'We don't think so, Mr Taylor,' said Maitland. 'We've concluded the part of our investigation involving your son.'

Mr Taylor sighed wearily.

'I'm so sorry that we didn't find any news for you,' said Maitland.

'No, no, it's not your fault. It's just that when you turned up out of the blue like that, it's the most hope that we've had for I don't know how long. My wife . . .'

Maitland nodded. 'I know, sir, it must be extremely upsetting for her.'

'It is, and she's sent me down here on a bit of a fool's errand, I'm afraid.' He patted the box. 'Some of Blair's old things. Notebooks, writing, bits and pieces. Rubbish, probably. Some of it's appalling, I have to say; I really don't know how he came to have these views. Please don't think that my wife and I think any of these things.'

'We don't, sir,' Mona reassured him.

Mr Taylor held out the box. 'Could you at least have a look at it? There might be something in it that's relevant to whatever it is you're looking for?'

'I really don't think there is, sir,' said Maitland, politely.

She saw the look of desperation on Mr Taylor's face. 'We'll have a look, sir. Is it OK if we keep it for a few days?'

He nodded, gratefully. 'Take as long as you like.'

'I'll show you out.'

She locked the door firmly behind him. The image of the playground fight came back to her, and she thought, not for the first time, how much easier it was to navigate the world without children. She really didn't know how parents coped with the horror of their children being at risk from the Virus, and as for Mr Taylor's suffering? She would rather face a million life-threatening situations at the HET than end up like that.

Maitland was flipping through the stuff in the box. 'What are we supposed to do with this?'

'In reality, nothing. But at least Mr Taylor can go home and tell his wife that we're looking into it.'

'I'd love to give them news about Blair.' Maitland frowned. 'Although maybe we're just prolonging their agony by pretending this stuff is useful?'

'Oh God, I don't know. Let's get upstairs and see if there are any other rats that haven't deserted the sinking ship.'

Bernard was the sole occupant of the office. He stood up when he heard them walking in. 'We're all supposed to be at home,' he said.

'Yes, we know.'

'So, should we go home?' Bernard's face was a study of indecision. 'I mean, if we keep working after we've officially been sent home we're probably no longer insured, are we?'

Maitland dropped the box he was carrying onto Bernard's desk. It landed with a thump. 'Yes, that's what I've been worrying about. Not the fact that we might get shot going about our daily business, but the fact that we might not be insured when we cop it.'

'It's not just about us.' Bernard looked annoyed. 'What about our dependants?'

'Last time I looked, none of us had any dependants,' said Mona. 'The only member of our team with kids has had the good sense to go home and make sure she doesn't get herself killed.'

'Actually, I'm not sure we're in any immediate danger,' said Bernard. 'Bob Ellis came in to collect the files, and he said they've tracked down Bryce, and he's not in Edinburgh.'

'Really?' She stared at Bernard. 'They've got him locked up?'

'No, they haven't actually got him in custody yet, but Bob said they'd tracked him down on CCTV at a location, in his words, "well north of here". He's looking for you, by the way, Mona. He said for you to get in touch when you got back.'

She snorted. 'That's not going to be happening. So, they've really tracked him down? I'm surprised he let himself get caught on CCTV, though.'

'Yeah.' Bernard looked similarly bemused. 'It was the camera at a cashpoint. Using a card in the name of an alias that Bob and his colleagues were aware Bryce used. I wouldn't have thought he would be that careless.'

'He wouldn't,' said Mona. 'The kind of training Bryce has had, he should be able to stay hidden for months.'

'Maybe he wants to be found?' said Maitland.

'But why? Why go to all these lengths, then let yourself be caught?'

Maitland shrugged. 'Don't know. I'm having difficulty thinking myself into psycho Bryce's frame of mind.'

'What is this stuff?' Bernard peered into box. 'And why is it on my desk?'

'Because it's completely unimportant, and I can't think of anywhere more appropriate to put it.'

'Shut up, Maitland,' said Mona. 'Blair Taylor's dad brought it in.'

'Mr Taylor? Was it him knocking earlier on?'

'Yup.'

'I thought we'd kind of ruled Taylor and Mitchell out of the investigation?' Bernard frowned.

'Well, not entirely ruled them out. Marcus might have a point that they moved in the same circles, I just think that Colin Karma is the more likely to be an effective facilitator of whatever Bryce has planned. Either way, I didn't have the heart to turn Mr Taylor away.'

Bernard began leafing idly through the box. He picked up a notebook with a drawing of an asymmetric triangle balanced on a plinth. 'I've seen this picture somewhere before.'

'Where?'

'I don't know.'

'You probably saw it at the Taylors' when we were there.'

'Maybe. It's probably not important anyway.'

They heard footsteps clattering up the stairs. 'I think it's happened again!'

Marcus's voice. Obviously he had decided to ignore the instruction to go home as well. He flung himself into the room, holding his laptop aloft. 'There's been another shooting! At least according to Twitter there has, so maybe take it with a pinch of salt?'

In unison, Mona said 'Who?' and Bernard said 'Where?'

'It doesn't say who's been shot or where. The info is coming from the CounterplotWorld website. They're an odd bunch of conspiracy theory nutters, but they're often quite accurate. They were right about the government having a secret stockpile of medicines in a warehouse at Bellshill, and that the Minister for Food was—'

'And this time, Marcus?' Mona redirected his attention to the present moment. 'What are they saying about a shooting?'

'Not much in the way of facts, but they claim there has been a firearms incident in Aberdeen, and they're pointing out that the Minister for Virus Policy is visiting Aberdeen today.'

'Aberdeen is well north of here,' said Maitland.

'Yes, it is,' said Marcus. 'About a hundred and twenty-five miles north of here.'

'It's on the BBC website now as well,' said Bernard. 'Breaking news, saying there's unconfirmed information that there has been an incident involving a firearm. I'll keep refreshing this, there's bound to be—' He broke off, and pointed at Marcus. 'Your T-shirt?'

Everyone including Marcus stared at his stomach, which was covered by a picture of an asymmetric triangle on a plinth.

'What?' asked Marcus, holding the edges of the T-shirt out at an angle so he could get a better look at it. 'It's an old Arthusian Fall T-shirt. This was the artwork from their third album.'

Mona picked up the notebook from Bernard's desk, and held it next to the T-shirt. 'That's got to be more than a coincidence.'

'What has?' asked Marcus, struggling to see what everyone else was looking at. Mona had the distinct impression he was trying to smell her hair as she leaned in towards him, and took a swift step off to the side.

'They're pretty unlikely Arthusian Fall fans,' said Bernard. 'Marcus aside, I'm not sure anyone in their fan base is under forty. Maybe it's worth another look at them – I know they're not our focus, but they might be able to lead us to Colin Karma.'

'Yes, but—' She was interrupted by her phone ringing. 'The Guv. I better take this.'

She held a brief conversation with her boss, which due to the decibel level at which Paterson spoke, the entire office heard.

'Paterson's at the hospital?' said Maitland.

'Has he been shot?' asked Bernard.

'Well, obviously not through the head. You heard the conversation, you know as much as I do. He just said get ourselves to the Royal. Marcus, you should probably go home and continue monitoring this from there.'

'OK.' He started packing up.

'I might just, ehm, swing past home, and, you know, catch up with you later.' Maitland sounded if not exactly embarrassed, certainly considerably less bullish than usual.

Mona grinned at his discomfort. 'Aw, Kate still worried about you?'

'Actually, I'm going round to my mum's.' He stood up and headed out the door before they could ridicule him further.

'What about you, Bernard?'

'I think I'll just get on with stuff here. I should check out what else is in this box.'

She nodded. 'Later.'

6

'He shot a catering assistant?' Paterson was pink with outrage. 'I mean, it's bad enough shooting the likes of Paul Shore but at least he's a highly paid exec. What has somebody who works in the kitchen ever done to Bryce?'

'This is just what it says on Twitter,' said Mona. 'It may or may not be true. More information is coming out all the time.' She checked her phone. 'Actually it's confirmed on the BBC website now as well. He appears only to have shot her in the leg though. Is his aim getting worse or is he being nice?'

'Not sure that *nice* is the right word,' said Paterson. 'Why was she even at work?'

'According to the Beeb, she previously worked for the Scottish Government in Edinburgh, then moved to Aberdeen, where she works for a private catering firm.'

'Subcontracting Government work?'

'Perhaps. I'm sure all will be revealed over the next few hours. How is Paul?' asked Mona.

'I don't know. They won't let me in to see him.'

'Then why are we here?'

'Because a woman claiming to be Paul Shore's mum phoned up and asked me to come over. Apparently he's in with the doctor at the moment. I'm not sure if that's true, or if they're just stonewalling, but I'm hoping we get in to talk to him at some point.'

'Why does he want to see us, and not Stuttle or someone from Carlotta's team?'

Paterson laughed. 'I'm guessing we weren't his first choice.'

'Are you the gentleman who was looking to speak to Mr Shore?' A young doctor with a stethoscope round her neck strode towards them.

'Yes. Are you done with him?' asked Paterson.

'Well, we don't have any more immediate tests to do on him, but I have to say if it was up to me I wouldn't let you in there. It's been a very traumatic time for Mr Shore, and I don't want him further upset.'

'But it's not up to you?' asked Paterson. He was unable to keep a hopeful note out of his voice.

The doctor spoke through pursed lips. 'Mr Shore is not a very good patient. He's threatening to drag himself out of the hospital if we don't allow him to have visitors. So I'm OK-ing it, but you will still have to speak to the police officer on his ward.'

'Thank you.' He nodded to Mona to follow him. 'OK, let's give it a go.'

The policeman on the door was younger than Mona had anticipated, and didn't appear to be armed. Any threat to Paul had obviously been downgraded, and he now seemed to have the level of guarding that a minor criminal on an unscheduled stop to have his appendix removed would warrant. Paterson marched up to the officer on the door who blinked nervously at Paterson's gaze. 'Hello, Inspector Paterson.'

'I knew it was you! Miller, isn't it?'

'Millen, sir.'

155

Paterson turned to Mona. 'Millen here was one of my last new recruits before I moved over to the HET.'

Mona smiled. She suddenly understood why the PC was looking so nervous. Having Paterson as your first boss would be fairly terrifying.

'Right, son, my colleague and I are here to see Paul Shore.'

The PC's top lip was covered in a layer of sweat, which Mona assumed was not solely due to the hospital temperature. 'I'm under instructions that I'm not to let anyone in who isn't family.'

'I'm not just anyone, though, am I? I'm a pretty unlikely terrorist threat, and most importantly, I've been invited in by Mr Shore himself.'

Paterson and PC Millen stared silently at each other for a second or two. The constable opened his mouth to speak, but no words came out.

'Thank you, PC Millen. Your assistance will be remembered.'

He pushed open the door and gestured Mona through. She hoped whatever Paul had to say to them he could make it quick, because PC Millen was already reaching for his radio.

A grey-haired woman was sitting by Paul's bed, every inch of her face conveying worry.

Paul attempted to sit up, slowly and, it appeared, painfully. 'Give us a minute, Mum, would you?'

Mrs Shore shot them a venomous look. It would appear she was of the same opinion as the doctor, which was that Paul should be left alone to recuperate in peace. Mona wondered if she was holding Carlotta responsible for what had happened to her son; it would probably help their case if they made it clear that they weren't fans.

'Mum?'

'OK, OK, I'm going.' She dumped a pile of possessions on the floor, and stood up. 'I'll be in the cafe. Please don't tire him out.'

Paterson waited for the door to close behind her. 'You look like shit.'

'Thanks. Being shot does that to you.'

'How are you feeling?' asked Mona

'Weary, mainly. Please thank Bernard for breaking my fall. Apparently I'd have been a lot worse off if I'd gone straight down onto the concrete instead of landing on him en route.'

Mona smiled. 'I'm sure he was delighted to be of assistance.'

'So,' said Paterson, 'what can we do for you? Not that we aren't delighted to visit, but I sense there might be a purpose for us being summoned here.'

'Stuttle isn't answering my calls.'

'He is very busy at the moment, what with trying not to take the blame for the entire fiasco at the Parliament. Anyway, Carlotta's your boss. Shouldn't she be your first point of contact?'

'Also not taking my calls. Although at least she had the decency to send some flowers.'

'And very nice they are too.' They regarded the giant bouquet. 'Has anyone from the Parliament or SHEP been down to see you?'

'No. Although from what I overheard in the corridor there's been some strict instructions that no-one except my mother is to be allowed into the room. Well done in braving the extensive security arrangements.'

Mona looked over to the internal window. The extensive security arrangement still seemed to be on his radio, probably bitching about his former boss.

'Since we are your only lifeline to the outside world, what do you want to know?' asked Paterson.

'Let's start with why I was shot? I'm assuming Carlotta was the actual target. Have you any idea which of the many, many people she's pissed off over the years actually tried to kill her?'

'We'll come back to the "why". Let's start with the "who" shot you, because we've a pretty good idea of that.'

'OK.' He tried to sit up. 'Name names.'

'Bryce Henderson. He worked in the IT department at the HET. Northern Irish guy.'

Paul shook his head. 'Not ringing any bells.'

'We think he was actually embedded there by, well, we're not quite sure. That bit of the Government's security services that never show their face in public.'

'Shit.' Paul's face contorted.

'Are you OK?' asked Mona.

'Yes,' he gasped, and moved over a little to make himself more comfortable. 'Just thinking things over. So, what else can you tell me?'

'Ms Carmichael was very keen that nobody except her was around when you woke up,' said Mona. 'Seemed very concerned that you were going to give away state secrets as you came round from the anaesthetic.'

'Cue to share what that might be, Paul,' said Paterson, 'seeing as we're doing swapsies here.'

'I hear a lot of top-secret things in my job.' His eyes flicked away from them, and Mona thought that he knew exactly what it was that had Carlotta so worried.

Paterson stared at Paul for a moment, before accepting he wasn't going to be any more forthcoming. 'Anyway, moving on to the "why" of the shooting, Bryce is targeting civil servants at random – you'll have seen that much on the TV.'

'They're not letting me have a TV in my room in case it overstimulates me.' He thought for a second. 'So, I could have been the target, not Carlotta? Just a random victim?'

'Try not to take it personally. We had assumed Bryce was aiming for your boss and missed and you got caught in the crossfire, but it turns out that you were just a public servant in the wrong place at the wrong time. Not *totally* arbitrary, I guess. I suppose Bryce wanted to send a message out to your boss.'

'How do you know he's targeting people at random? Is this all supposition on your part?'

'He's put a message on the HET website, which nobody seems to be able to remove, which says he's going to shoot a public servant every day until his demands, whatever they may be, are met.'

Paul opened his mouth to speak, but Paterson got there first. 'If your next question is what are his demands, don't bother because we have no idea, although the fact that he hasn't felt the need to spell them out suggests that Carlotta knows exactly what it is he's upset about.'

'Shooting public servants at random.' Paul mulled this over. 'There must be panic on the streets.'

'Yep, there is. The next victim after you was some poor catering assistant up in Aberdeen, if Twitter is to be believed.'

'A catering assistant?' Paul closed his eyes.

Mona and Paterson exchanged a glance. Paul looked extremely pale, with large dark circles under his eyes. 'We're tiring you out,' said Mona. 'We should go.'

'No, don't.' He opened his eyes. 'This catering assistant is a woman?'

'Yes, I think so.' Mona pulled out her phone to check on updates.

'What's her name?'

'According to the BBC, her name is Emily Keith.'

Paul's eyes closed again. He was looking even worse than he did when they'd walked in, his pallor edging ever closer to the colour of his bed sheets.

'Are you sure you're OK? Do you want us to call someone?'

Paul said something very softly.

'What?' They leaned in to hear him.

He tried to sit up, but was defeated by pain. 'This isn't random.' He spat the words out.

'I don't understand?' Paterson looked at her in confusion.

'This Bryce Henderson person isn't shooting at random.' Paul was looking increasing frustrated, and redoubled his efforts to sit up. 'I know why I was shot, and I know who's going to be next.'

The monitor next to his bed let out a loud beep. After a second or two delay the door flew open and a nurse and doctor came rushing in.

'I need you all to leave now.' The doctor waved his hands in the direction of the corridor.

'But . . .'

'Out, now!'

Mona felt a hand pulling her out of the room, as the frightened-looking PC emptied the room.

'We really need to speak to him,' said Paterson, as the door closed on him.

'Sorry, sir, but that won't be happening.' The police

officer was firmly back in front of the door. 'I shouldn't have let you in in the first place.'

'What's going on?'

She turned to see Paul Shore's mother standing in the hallway. 'Did you tire him out?'

'Something like that. We're really sorry.'

7

Bernard eyed the cardboard box. He was glad to have something to do that didn't involve leaving the office, although this was only fifty per cent due to the threat of shooting. The other fifty per cent was his worry that if he went home Annemarie would be waiting, ready to make good use of the free time that had been thrust upon him.

He reached in and pulled out a handful of papers. Even if the contents of the box turned out to be completely useless, if he spent some time cataloguing its contents, at the very least Mr and Mrs Taylor could see that they had looked into it. He spread the items out then paused when he heard someone approach.

'I thought you went home.'

Marcus shrugged. 'Well, I thought about it, then I decided that I'd be better off staying here.' He put his laptop down on Bernard's desk. Bernard wondered why everyone thought that his desk was fair game for dumping things on. 'I can monitor the situation just as well here, and I thought you might need my insider insight into Arthusian Fall.'

'Did Bryce listen to Arthusian Fall?'

'Not particularly.' He shook his head. 'I mean, we were both generally fans of progressive rock, at least I thought we were, but who knows what his real feelings about the genre were, seeing as he was no doubt adopting some persona while he was undercover. Anyway, he seemed to like most of the bands active in the 1980s, like Yes and Pink Floyd, and Marillion, of course. He was less of a fan of the more out-there 1970s stuff like Egg or Gong ...'

'Anyway ...' Bernard was beginning to regret asking.

'So, anyway, I assume if he listened to the other stuff, he'd also have listened to Arthusian Fall.'

'Do young people listen to this kind of stuff?'

'You mean like teenagers?'

'Well, twenty-somethings.'

Marcus screwed up his nose. 'They've kind of fallen out of fashion. The lead guitarist's views don't help.'

'His views?'

'Yeah. He gave a few fairly controversial interviews back in the early noughties about his opinions on the superiority of men and of the white race.'

'Interesting. Fits in well with our theory that the students are linked to Karma in some way. They've got a very similar world view.' He thought for a second. 'I'm a bit surprised he'd voice those opinions publicly though. It must have lost Arthusian Fall a lot of black and female fans.'

Marcus laughed heartily, slapping the desk at Bernard's apparent joke. 'You'd think, but no. Prog rock has a fairly homogenous fan base. White. Male. Surprisingly conservative, given the level of innovation and experimentation in the music. Do you want me to look for the interviews?'

'Yeah, that would be helpful.'

Marcus started tapping away on his keyboard, humming

away to himself as he did so. It may well have been an Arthusian Fall song, but Bernard wasn't going to ask for fear of a long explanation of its provenance. He turned back to the piles of paper, and decided to start with the notebook. He worked solidly through its contents, trying to ignore the delighted squeals coming from Marcus as he uncovered various articles on the internet.

'Oh, I'd forgotten all about this.' Marcus sounded excited.

'What?' Bernard gave up on the box, and rolled his chair over to his colleague.

'Arthusian Fall's American tour in 1998.' He turned his laptop round, so that Bernard could see the article he was looking at. It was illustrated with a picture of the band, all of them with luxuriantly backcombed hair, posing next to a big yellow taxi on what looked like Time Square.

'Were they big in America?'

'No. The tour was a bit of a disaster. They were promoting their *Fire and Deathstone* album, which, frankly, was their weakest work.'

Having heard the albums that Marcus considered their finest, Bernard shuddered to think what a weak Arthusian Fall album might sound like.

'But, and this is the bit that is probably relevant to your investigation, at the end of the tour, most of Arthusian Fall came home with their tails between their legs, but Colin Karma stayed on and recorded a solo album.'

'What was that like?'

'I don't know.' Marcus stared at him. 'To be honest, I never sought it out. I always regarded him as the least musically able of the band, and by all accounts he didn't have much of a singing voice, so ...'

He left the full enormity of this crime against music to Bernard's imagination.

'Anyhoo, he must have met some fellow travellers in the US, because he ended up doing a tour of the American Midwest, the theme of which was to oppose gun control. According to this interview, he found America to have a much more sensible approach to the right of citizens to bear arms.'

Bernard peered at the photo on the screen. 'Is that a Confederate flag he's draped in?'

'Yes. I wonder why he didn't stay in America?'

'Probably couldn't get a visa. They've got enough gun nuts of their own, without importing them from here. I wonder if that's when he met his second wife?'

'Could well be. And I have one last interview of note for you, Bernard. This one tells you all about his preparations.'

'Preparations? What for?'

He smiled, a slightly manic look in his eye. 'The end of times, Bernard. According to this one, he's a full-blown "prepper". Come the apocalypse, he's made sure that he's got enough tinned goods, fresh water, and I assume, firearms, to make it through alive.' He looked solemn. 'I do hope that you all are being very careful in your searching for Colin Karma. He sounds like he could, and would, do a lot of damage to anyone who attempted to ambush him.'

Bernard sincerely hoped that they were being careful, too. 'So, Karma's spent all this time preparing for doomsday. Do you think he maybe believes that the Virus *is* the apocalypse?'

'I think it's a very real possibility.'

'Do you think Bryce believes that?'

Marcus shut the laptop. 'I don't know which scenario I find scarier, Bernard, either that Bryce believes all this, or that he doesn't, but is using someone as obviously unstable as Colin Karma to further his ends.'

Bernard sighed and rubbed his eyes. 'Whatever those ends might be.'

8

'This better be murderously urgent.' Stuttle glared at them from the other side of his desk. Mona had been relieved to find that he was still Head of the Scottish Health Enforcement Partnership, even if it might not be for much longer.

'We're hardly going to bother you with something that isn't, are we?' Without waiting to be invited, Paterson sat down. 'Not given your current circumstances.'

This was the second time in an hour they'd had to fight their way in to see someone. There was a hospital doctor who was probably busily writing a strongly worded letter of complaint about them, no doubt with assistance from a certain rookie of Paterson's who would be desperate to cover his back. And that was to say nothing of what Paul Shore's mother would do if he didn't make a full recovery. The important thing was that they had made it to Paul's bedside, and he'd choked out a name.

'Oh, well, get on with it while I still have a job.'

'Why haven't you been returning Paul Shore's calls?'

'That's why you're here?' His eyebrows shot up toward the ceiling. 'Because I've hurt Paul's feelings? What am I supposed to say to him? He can take his place in the very long queue of people who want to sue me.'

'He doesn't want to sue you, he just wants to know

what's going on, and more to the point he's got something to tell you.'

Stuttle returned to the document he appeared to be marking up with a red pen. 'Mona, I've got no idea what your boss is moaning about. *You* tell me what's going on.'

Paterson shot her a filthy look, but she took over anyway. 'Paul says the two shootings aren't random. He says he knows the other woman involved.'

'Oh yeah?' He sounded sceptical, but his pen had stopped moving.

Now that Stuttle was actually listening, Paterson stepped back in. 'Paul organised a meeting for his boss, and Emily Keith provided the catering. While they were waiting to go in, they overheard Carlotta Carmichael and someone else, who Paul now thinks was probably Bryce, having a set-to.'

'What about?' The pen had been abandoned. They had the full, undivided attention of the Head of SHEP.

'He won't say. What he did say is that what they overheard was such a big deal that they've both now signed the Official Secrets Act, and are forbidden from speaking about it at any point.'

'But Carlotta knows what they were arguing about?'

Mona could see the cogs springing into action in Stuttle's head. He'd love to get his hands on this potentially embarrassing secret, whatever it was.

'Oh yes.' Paterson nodded solemnly. 'I think the shootings are Bryce's way of getting his message across to Carlotta. But the most important thing about all of this is there were *three* people waiting to go into the meeting. Two of them have been shot, so it's not a huge leap to guess who he's going to target next, if Carlotta doesn't do whatever it is she's supposed to be doing.'

'You know Bob Ellis's mob have located Bryce, don't you?'

'He said,' said Paterson. 'But that's all they've done. They've narrowed it down to him being in a particular bit of the country, at a particular time, but they haven't got him in custody yet, have they? Even if they have, there's nothing to say he's working alone.'

'In fact, sir,' Mona broke in, 'the investigation we've been undertaking into those two case files suggest that he might be working with some well-equipped associates.'

Stuttle sat staring into space.

'Why aren't you picking up the phone and getting some protection for this person?' Paterson was balanced on the edge of his seat. 'Every minute we're hanging around here there's a woman in danger.'

'I'm thinking.'

'What about?' Paterson's voice was breathless with frustration.

'About the fact that this has all happened a little bit easily, hasn't it? There was a crisis situation with Bryce, everyone rallied round really quickly to decide that this was my fault. I think I underestimated Carlotta. I think that bloody woman had this planned. Since Bryce took off she knew that he would do *something* and she knew that when he did, she could take the opportunity to blame me for it. After all, in theory he worked for me.'

'I know you're mad at Carlotta,' Paterson attempted a more conciliatory tone, 'but we need to move to get this person protected.'

'Who is this person anyway? Another civil servant?'

'Not any more, apparently. Her name's Catriona McBride. She was an intern, who was shadowing Paul Shore.'

169

'An intern? We're talking some twenty-year-old lassie here?'

'Yes.'

Stuttle threw his head back, and let forth the longest continuous outbreak of cursing that Mona had ever heard. Under other circumstances, she'd have been impressed.

'Enough of this, Cam, we need to move.'

'And do what?' He glared at Paterson. 'Whatever this woman knows could be very dangerous to Carlotta. Do we want to put her in the hands of Bob Ellis and his mates?'

There was a moment's silence while they considered this. Mona wondered what exactly the relationship was between Ian Jacobsen, Bob Ellis and Stuttle. Once upon a time she'd assumed that Stuttle was the boss, but every passing day nudged her towards thinking that he was as worried by them as she was.

'What's the alternative?' asked Paterson. 'For all we know, Bryce is on his way to find her even as we speak.'

'My colleagues insist they have Bryce in their sights.'

'But not in their custody, sir.' Mona could feel exasperation seeping into her tone too. 'And he may not be working alone.'

Stuttle started typing on his keyboard. A second or two later the printer sprang into life. He snatched the printed page and started scribbling something on it. She looked over at Paterson who shrugged.

Stuttle held the paper out to her. 'So, find her.'

'Us?' Paterson looked surprised. 'I'm not sure that we're qualified for protection duties.'

'You're not. But I've got fuck all other options. I've given you the information from her Green Card.'

'What do we do with her when we find her?'

170

'You take her to the address I've written on it. They'll be expecting her, and she'll be looked after. These are people I trust.' He waggled a finger at them. 'Do not tell anyone where she has gone, and don't let her mouth off to anyone about her situation.'

'What is this . . .?'

'Do not ask questions about the arrangement, Mona. Just accept that this is the best chance of staying safe that poor lassie has.'

'Is all this legal, Cam?'

'Seeing as I'm about three days away from being sacked, I don't much care. If you two are worried about the ethics of what I've asked you to do, now's your chance to opt out.'

'Let's just get the girl found.' Paterson got to his feet, and Mona followed his lead.

'If you don't mind me asking, sir, what will you do if they try to sack you?'

'Threaten to take them to an industrial tribunal, and bring all this nonsense into the public domain. At which point, if they've any sense, a meaningless but well-remunerated consultancy job will be created for me somewhere in the public sector. So, don't worry about me, Mona, I'll be fine. Unless Bryce or some other nutjob decides to shoot me.'

'We wish you well, Cam,' Paterson held the door open, 'in your new role as Chief Inspector of Lollipop Ladies.'

Cameron Stuttle's response was less than professional.

9

Bernard flicked through one of the notebooks, wondering how to categorise it. It was full of fairly random rantings, many of which were quite unpleasant, particularly about women.

Marcus, who somehow had still not headed home, picked up one of the other books, perused it for a second, and hastily put it back. 'Yuck. Some deeply unpleasant views there.'

'I know. What I'm reading isn't any better.'

'Do you think Bryce actually believed any of this?' asked Marcus.

'You'd know that better than I would. You were best friends.'

'Were we?' Marcus shook his head. 'I was best friends with a Northern Irish computer geek, who liked *Buffy the Vampire Slayer* as much as I did, and was well versed in Tolkein, Lovecraft and Pratchett. Except that person didn't really exist, did he? As for the real "Bryce", or whatever his actual name is, I didn't know him at all.'

He looked so miserable that Bernard felt obliged to attempt to cheer him up. 'I'm sure the *Buffy* stuff was real, Marcus. I heard the two of you discussing plot lines for hours at a time.' The weeks he'd spent sleeping on Marcus's floor were hard to forget. 'That took real depth of knowledge, beyond any mere job.'

'You're probably right.' He perked up at the thought. 'Can I help?'

'If you can stomach it, I'm trying to catalogue what we have in here to see if any of it is relevant.'

'OK.'

The two of them sat in silence, broken only by an occasional 'Dear Lord' from Marcus when he'd found something particularly objectionable. Bernard's attention was caught by a string of figures which had a box drawn round them. He wondered if it was a code.

'What do you make of this, Marcus?' He turned the book round so that he could see it.

'A mysterious code – just my cup of tea!' He stared at it for a moment. 'Except I don't think that this *is* a code. I think this is a much more prosaic ordnance survey point.'

'You think it's directing us to a place?' Bernard turned the book back towards him. 'Actually I think that's far more interesting than a code. Much easier to crack.'

Marcus pulled out his phone, turned the book round yet again, and tapped the numbers into an app. 'Does this look familiar?'

Bernard stared at the picture. The whole screen was entirely green. 'It's a field, Marcus, it looks like every field everywhere.'

'I think there's something there if we zoom in on it. Look! There's an old farmhouse or something. Let's go and explore!' Marcus's eyes glistened behind his little round specs. 'Let's do some "fieldwork".'

'I'm not sure. We're supposed to be keeping a low profile, and not getting shot.' Even under normal circumstances, he wouldn't have been keen to go exploring with Marcus. Marcus's skill set was far too similar to his own, and lacked the proficiencies that he tended to rely on

Mona or Maitland for. Like, for example, the ability to hit people, or make decisions.

'But our colleagues are quite sure that Bryce is north of here. This might be the best possible time to go and look.'

'Where is it?'

He referred to the app again. 'About three miles west of Edinburgh.'

Bernard had been hoping for somewhere a little bit further away, somewhere he could rule out in terms of logistical difficulty. 'I suppose there's no reason not to. If we're careful.'

'Caution will be our watchword!'

For the first time ever, Bernard had his pick of the pool cars. He selected his favourite Ford Mondeo, and they packed themselves, and Marcus's extensive set of laptops, into it. As was his habit, Marcus kept up a running commentary as they drove.

'I'll keep an eye on the situation as we go.' He glanced out of the window. 'Considering this should be rush hour, there's not much traffic on the roads.'

'That's because every public servant in Scotland apart from us is at home.'

'That's not entirely true. There's been a bit of a back-lash. Lots of frontline staff are refusing to leave their posts.'

'Like nurses?'

'Yes, nurses, teachers, carers, and lots of other people who feel they can't just walk away from their job. Ooh, I think we need to get into the other lane.'

Eventually Marcus ran out of conversation, and they drove on in relative silence, leaving the city behind them. He piped up from time to time with an instruction to turn left, or take the next right. Each turning seemed to take them on to a narrower, less used road. Eventually, after they had driven through nothing but fields for twenty minutes, he tapped decisively on the dashboard. 'We're getting close. In fact, we should probably try to park up somewhere soon, and continue on foot.'

'On foot?' This was a little more up close and personal than Bernard had been planning. He squeezed the car onto the verge, and looked round. 'I hope it will be OK here.'

'It should be. We've not passed much traffic.'

This was true. They'd seen very little in the way of other people on their journey, a fact that Bernard didn't find altogether reassuring. Marcus, on the other hand, seemed much more confident. He walked up to the fence, still looking at his phone, and put one of his long legs over the top. 'I reckon it's a mile or so in this direction.'

'A mile?' Bernard looked doubtfully at the horizon. 'We're not really dressed for a cross-country ramble. Also, this is private property. Won't we be trespassing?'

There was no heed paid to his concerns, and his colleague set off across the field. He sighed and followed him, watching very carefully where he put his feet. The field seemed to be fallow, so at least they weren't destroying someone's prize crop. He was, however, doing serious damage to a pair of Hush Puppies that had not been designed for countryside life.

The far side of the field gave way to a coppice of trees.

'We need to go through these,' said Marcus, looking at his phone.

'How? I don't see a path.'

Marcus's bravado knew no bounds. 'We'll just have to push on through somehow.'

Bernard mentally waved goodbye to a pair of M&S

cords that were going to be joining his shoes in the bin. Despite his misgivings, there was enough space between the trees for them to wriggle through, and they made it to the other side relatively unscathed. Bernard's one consolation in all this was that there were no signs of footprints or car tracks that made him think anyone else was here – or had been recently.

'I guess that's what we're looking for.' Marcus pointed at a couple of ramshackle stone buildings.

'They look pretty derelict.' Which, hopefully, meant there was no-one living there. Bernard definitely did not want to stumble across any of Bryce's friends, particularly the NRA fan Colin Karma, and end up planted in one of the empty fields.

'Shall we have a closer look?'

He took a final look around to reassure himself they were alone. 'I suppose so.'

The buildings were even more run-down than he had anticipated. They looked like they'd been bothies, or barns in a previous existence, but now they were now semi-derelict. As he walked round the buildings, he found that one wall had collapsed completely.

'It strikes me, Bernard, that this is exactly the kind of place Bryce might bunker down in between attempts to shoot people. It's very discreet. Nobody can see you from the road, and there's no-one else for miles around.'

'Yes, you're right.' Bernard's slight unease was turning into full-blown panic. 'For that very reason I think we ought to get out of here.'

'But we haven't looked around. We could be missing a vital clue!' Marcus gave a cheery grin, and stepped over the wall and into the building. 'In fact, I see something.' He peered into the gloom inside the building. 'I think someone has been living there. It's a sleeping bag.' He crouched slightly and manoeuvred his body into the ruin.

'Be careful.' His colleague seemed to be oblivious to danger, be it human or inanimate. 'You don't want to bring the roof down on you.'

'Oh, dear Lord!'

Ignoring Bernard's warning about being careful, Marcus retreated hurriedly from the building. He fell backwards, but continued his journey scrabbling like a crab.

'What's the matter?' Bernard helped him to his feet.

Marcus pulled out his phone, and hit the torch setting. 'See for yourself.'

Bernard followed the beam of light. It bounced off the heaps of fallen brickwork, which appeared to be littered with dried flowers of some kind. He looked past these, into the furthest corner of the room, his eyes travelling over a red sleeping bag before resting on the object that had so alarmed Marcus.

There, resting on its side, was the unmistakable sight of a human skull.

10

'This is the place.'

Mona looked up at the glass and chrome. 'Very modern, isn't it?'

'Very high end. I'm not sure that N-vsage, or however you pronounce it, is going to be too impressed when we disappear off with one of their members of staff.' He pushed the glass door open.

'What do you think they do here?' she asked. The foyer wasn't giving anything away.

'Marketing, PR, or some other load of bollocks. You can ask Catriona when we catch up with her.'

They were starting with Catriona's workplace. The mobile number they had for her was no longer working, and the landline number for her flat had rung and rung without being answered, leading them to suppose that she was probably still at work.

The receptionist was immaculately dressed in a vivid pink suit, with blonde hair that fell in complicated ringlets. She shot them a smile as they approached her desk. 'Welcome to N-vsage. How can we help you?'

Paterson scowled, his usual response to encountering extreme femininity. Mona's theory was that it both confused and unnerved him. 'We'd like to speak to Catriona McBride.'

'One moment, please.'

Paterson drummed his fingers impatiently while the receptionist called her colleague.

'I'm sorry, Catriona is not in the office today.'

'Is she out at a meeting, or did she call in sick? It's extremely important that we speak to her.'

'Is there a problem here, Elena?' A man strode across the marble floor towards them. He had glasses, very short hair, and was casually dressed in jeans and a checked shirt. Even at a distance, Mona could see that these hadn't been grabbed off the rack in a hurry on a Sunday afternoon shopping trip to Primark. As he walked past her to the desk, she took a discreet look at the back pocket of his trousers. *Armani.*

The receptionist looked relieved at the arrival of someone more senior to deal with the large, rather aggressive man in her foyer. 'Oh, Tye, this man was looking for ...'

'Catriona McBride.' Paterson repeated his request. 'We need to speak to Catriona McBride as a matter of urgency.'

Tye regarded them from behind a pair of yellow-rimmed glasses. 'And you are?'

'We're here from the Health Enforcement Team.'

He nodded. 'Thanks, Elena.' He gestured to them to move away from the receptionist, and they relocated to some black leather sofas near the entrance.

'Tye Evans.' He shook both their hands. 'I'm Catriona's boss. Is she ill?'

'We don't know.' She evaded the question. 'Your receptionist said she's not at work today?'

'She's not, and she hasn't phoned in to say she's sick, but ...' He looked a little embarrassed. 'I wondered if

179

Catriona was having health issues she hadn't told us about?'

'I'm afraid we wouldn't know, sir. Can I ask what makes you think that? Has she been off a lot?'

'No, not really.'

'So, what makes you think she was ill?'

'I wasn't thinking that Catriona was physically ill, maybe more under a bit of mental stress? Or problems at home, perhaps? She was keen as mustard when she started here, putting in the hours and everything, but lately she seems to be finding it difficult to focus. And this last week . . .' he shook his head in disbelief, 'it's like she's been on a different planet. She completely drifted off in a meeting with a new client, which he totally spotted. Nearly cost us the job. I should really have challenged her on it but she's a lovely girl, and I didn't want to pry. She was due for an appraisal meeting today, and I wondered if that was why she hadn't turned up, you know, nerves or something?'

Mona's anxiety about the situation was rising. Whatever Catriona had been worrying about, she was pretty sure it wasn't work. 'We should get going, Guv.'

'If you hear from her can you let us know?' Mona handed over a business card. 'Thanks for your time.'

As they left the building they both started to run.

'I hope we're not too late,' said Paterson.

Catriona McBride's home address was in the area of Stockbridge known as the Colonies. Mona had idly wondered one day in the office why they were called the Colonies, and had been rewarded with a ten-minute potted lecture on their origins from Bernard, and the offer of the loan of a book he possessed on the subject.

She'd not taken him up on the offer, and all she could remember was that they had once belonged to artisans. Now they belonged to aspirational young couples who wanted to live somewhere that looked like a village, but was within walking distance of Edinburgh city centre.

The Colonies flats were laid out in a one-up one-down arrangement. Catriona was on the upper floor, and Paterson clattered up the metal staircase with no thought for discretion. Mona hoped that Catriona wouldn't be put off at the sight of two complete strangers hurtling towards her front door. Assuming, of course, that she wasn't lying in her hallway in a pool of blood.

Paterson hammered on the woodwork. 'Catriona McBride? We're here from the Health Enforcement Team.'

They were answered with complete silence. He hammered again, with more force, the wood moving slightly under his weight.

The door next to Catriona's opened, and a small bird-like old lady stood at the top of the metal stairs that were the mirror image of Catriona's. 'She'll be at her work.'

'She's not,' Paterson snapped.

'Thanks for your help, though.' Mona smiled her brightest smile at the woman. The last thing they needed was a concerned neighbour phoning the police to complain about the aggressive behaviour of two potential housebreakers. She *could* explain what they were doing here, but she'd really rather not.

'Catriona.' Paterson was on his knees now, peering through the letterbox. 'Please let us know if you are in there. We're here to help.' He spun round to Mona, and lowered his voice. 'I saw something move in there. We're going to have to get in.'

181

'What are you doing over there?'

Mona flashed her ID card in the direction of the neighbour. 'We're here from the Health Enforcement Team. We're worried about Catriona, and I'm afraid we're going to have to break her door down. Please don't be alarmed.'

'Oh dear. Is Catriona unwell?'

'That's what we're afraid of.' It was a lie, but not much of one. They were, after all, extremely concerned about Catriona's health and wellbeing. 'Which is why we need to break in.'

'Or you could just use the spare key I have?'

After a frustrating five minutes while Mrs Sedley remembered where she'd put Catriona's key for safekeeping, they were finally in the flat.

'Catriona?'

By mutual consent they headed into different rooms. Mona's door led her into a bedroom. A half-filled bag lay on the bed, with clothes scattered all around, a speed packing that suggested someone wanted to leave town fast. Although there was no sign of Catriona, the unfinished nature of the packing supported Paterson's theory she was still in the house. She dropped to her knees and checked under the bed. There was nothing there except a couple of boxes.

The wardrobe caught her eye. It was a big, old-fashioned wooden affair, just large enough to hide in, if you were desperate. She moved softly across the room, and pulled the door open. It revealed a large, empty interior.

'Hoi!'

She shot out into the hall, just in time to intercept

Catriona as she made a break for the door. She grabbed her arm, and threw her back into the hall.

Paterson appeared, holding his head. 'Ms McBride packs a good punch.'

Catriona slid to the floor in between them and started to cry. She buried her head in her arms. 'I'm sorry. Please don't hurt me.'

Mona held her ID card down to the level of Catriona's head. 'We're here from the Health Enforcement Team. We're not going to hurt you, but we're pretty sure that someone else is intending to. Although I guess you already knew that.'

Catriona didn't glance at it. She seemed to be struggling to breathe.

'Are you asthmatic, Ms McBride?' Paterson was looking concerned.

'I think she's having a panic attack, Guv.' She stood back up. She shared her boss's concern. They didn't want to save Catriona from Bryce only to have her die of a stress-induced heart attack.

'We don't have time for this, Mona. We need to get her out of here.'

'How, Guv?' she whispered to him, so Catriona wouldn't hear. 'We can't take her anywhere in this state.'

'Have a womanly heart-to-heart with her,' he whispered back.

She tutted, but crouched down next to her. 'Catriona, listen to me. You are having a panic attack. I need you to focus on my voice. Can you do that?'

Her head lifted up a fraction.

'Now, I want you to focus on your breathing, slowly in, then back out again.'

Catriona attempted to comply, her breath squeaking as she tried to get it under control.

'In, and slowly out.' Mona was aware she sounded like a yoga instructor. She could sense Paterson's impatience. He walked over to the door and opened it a fraction to peer out.

After a couple more minutes, Catriona's breathing was returning to normal. With a huge effort she managed to speak. 'Are you here to kill me?'

'Again, no,' said Mona, as patiently as she could manage under the circumstances. 'Your life is under threat, but not by us. We're here to take you to a safe place.'

Catriona stared at her, uncertainty writ large on her face. Mona felt irritation that she wasn't moving, tempered by the knowledge that if two strangers turned up on her doorstep and insisted that she leave with them, she'd be equally unwilling.

'We know you overheard a conversation that you shouldn't have, and we know that you will have been put under a lot of pressure not to divulge what you heard.'

Catriona's eyes filled with tears.

'Unfortunately, as you are probably aware, the other two people who overheard the conversation have both now been shot.'

Catriona's breathing started to become uneven again.

She heard Paterson swear softly under his breath. She threw him a dirty look.

'Breathe, Catriona. Deep breaths.'

The girl took an extra deep ragged breath and started to speak. 'I knew we shouldn't have agreed to it. But I thought the Virus was just, you know, and this seemed like a really good way to protect my family. I mean, what would you do if you thought you could help to keep your parents and your sister safe?'

'I'd do exactly what you did,' said Mona, wondering what exactly she was on going on about. 'Likewise, I'm sure your parents and your sister would be very, very keen for you to be keeping yourself out of harm's way, which is what we're trying to do here. We need to get you out of your home, and into a safe house. And we need to do it quickly.'

Catriona looked around at the empty room, as if she was searching for someone who could tell her she was doing the right thing. Unfortunately, there wasn't anyone there that could help.

'I need you to stand up now, Catriona.'

There was a loud sound outside and voices shouting to each other. Catriona grabbed Mona's arm in panic.

'It's just the bin lorry,' said Paterson, from his position at the door. 'Nothing to worry about, but we need to go.'

Catriona got to her feet. She was shaking so much, Mona wondered if she could actually walk. The quickest way to the car would be for Paterson to throw the girl over his shoulder in a fireman's lift, but that would be less than discreet.

'Do you live with someone, Catriona?'

She nodded. 'Yes. I have two flatmates.'

'Leave them a quick note saying you've gone to your parents.'

'I need to speak to my mum.'

'We'll do that from the car.'

Mona picked up the first available piece of paper that she saw, which happened to be the envelope of a gas bill. Catriona did as she was told and scribbled a few lines on the paper.

'Grab your bag and let's go.'

Paterson and Mona looked at each other over the top of Catriona's head. They were both hoping the same thing. They'd no body armour, no guns, and a vulnerable witness, whom they needed to protect. *Please let Bryce be working alone.*

'Right, Catriona,' said Paterson. 'Let's go.'

11

'So, you just *happened* across this body?'

'That wasn't what I said.' Bernard was trying hard not to let himself be bullied by the police officer, who was of a similar vintage and persuasion as Paterson. 'I told you we were engaged in an investigation relating to a Health Enforcement Team operation when we came across the body.'

PC Blake snorted. 'Yes, I'm sure there's no end of health defaulters lying in ruined houses in the middle of nowhere.' His eyes wandered over the ruins. 'Please tell me you haven't been anywhere near the body?'

'No,' he lied, then remembered this was now an official crime scene and his footprints would be all over it. 'Well, not since we realised there was a body in there.'

The constable threw his hands up in despair. 'See, this is what you get with this HET nonsense. Civilians treading where they have no place to be. What are you lot up to anyway?'

Bernard had been up to a fair amount since Marcus had screamed and collapsed.

He had phoned the number they had for the Police Liaison Officer, thanking his lucky stars that Ian Jacobsen was still off on sick leave. Bob Ellis had not been available either, but the man at the other end of the phone seemed to know what to do. He told him to stay where they were and he would send out a police officer to survey the scene. *And on no account were they to trespass over the crime scene.*

Bernard had then turned his attention to Marcus. For a man who regularly posted about the number of people he had shot, stabbed, or exploded in a variety of computer games, he was not being particularly stoic when faced with an actual dead body. Once he had got Marcus a safe distance away from the skeleton, and had managed to stop him rabbiting on, he'd returned to the scene of their potential crime.

He'd walked into the building as far as Marcus had gone, careful to stand in his colleague's footsteps all the way, and shone his phone torch back into the room to have a better look at what was actually going on in there. The skull that Marcus had seen was definitely attached to a skeleton, and said skeleton was partially in a sleeping bag. He might have been laid there peacefully at one point but obviously wild animals had been in and had a full lunch at the free buffet that had been left out for them. It was not immediately apparent if the person had lain down to sleep and just never woken up or whether something more complicated had gone on.

Bernard leaned towards the complicated answer. He'd shone the torch slowly round the room again, stopping to take pictures as he went. Starting with the theory that this was someone, possibly completely unrelated to their enquiries, who'd just camped there for the night and passed away peacefully upon the midnight hour, where were his supplies? Aside from the sleeping bag, there was no rucksack, or primus stove, or remains of food, or clothing, or, in fact, anything you would need to survive.

If this was an acolyte of Colin Karma's, he was the least prepared prepper, ever.

Bernard's interrogation was interrupted by the sound of the SOC team arriving. He repeated the story that he already told to PC Blake, including all the apologies about walking on a crime scene, with a few extra *mea culpas* when one of the women who was climbing into a white suit had tutted particularly loudly at him. Finally, he was free to go.

'Come on, Marcus.'

'Oh, can we go? Thank God. I was worried that they were going to drag us back to Fettes for interrogation.'

'No, we're free to go, so long as we can make it back to the car before it's too dark to find the way.'

When they reached the car, Marcus surprised him by climbing into the back seat and lying down. 'I'm exhausted, Bernard.' There was a loud clicking sound. 'I've put a seat belt round me. It'll be quite safe to drive off.'

'OK,' he said, quite relieved that Marcus intended to sleep, rather than chatter the whole way back. 'I'll get going in a minute.'

He reached for his phone and scrolled through the pictures he'd taken of the potential crime scene, enlarging bits of them as he went. This wasn't some tramp's last resting place, he was sure of it. Something about the room felt ritualistic. Dotted around the skeleton there appeared to be the dying remnants of flowers that had been placed in jam jars. He zoomed in on them. The quality of pixellation wasn't great on his phone, but if pushed, he would declare them to be willow branches. The enlarged view also picked up something red on the far wall, as if someone had painted something onto it.

If someone had been bedding down here, perhaps all this could be explained away by them attempting to liven up their living accommodation with some flowers, and wall art.

Bernard stared at his phone. He didn't know if he was being melodramatic, too influenced by Marcus and his love of fantasy, but if he had to put money on what he thought was going on here, he would wager that this was a dead body that had been laid out for a ceremonial send-off to the afterlife.

12

The safe house was located in a block of modern flats, which were surrounded in turn by what seemed like acres of other flats, all made from the same brown brick design. If Mona had been asked to describe its appearance or exact location from memory half an hour later she would have struggled. She supposed that was the point.

'What's the buzzer number, Guv?'

'Nineteen.'

'I'm not sure about this,' said Catriona. She ground to a halt in the middle of the road, looking round at the buildings.

The girl been very quiet on the way over. She'd insisted on phoning her parents and giving them the registration number of the car. If that's what it took to get her onto the back seat, Mona thought it was probably OK. It was, after all, a HET pool car, not some top-secret military vehicle. She would rather not have the HET linked to Catriona at all, but if anyone dug into the situation to any degree, she was sure the North Edinburgh HET would be on the list of suspects anyway. She'd warned Catriona not to say anything about where they were heading, and, thus far, she had obeyed. Yet now that she was faced with going into a flat where she didn't know anyone, second thoughts were creeping in.

'What's the alternative, Catriona?' Paterson spoke

with as much patience as he could muster. 'You know you're in danger. Do you want to go to your parents' house and put them in danger as well?'

'No, of course not, that's the last thing I want. I'm not being funny, but I really don't know who you people are. Maybe *you're* dangerous. I mean,' she said, her expression changing from worried to suspicious, 'why didn't they send someone from the police to get me? Someone in uniform?'

Paterson was looking around to see if anyone was about. Mona hoped he didn't have any stupid ideas like throwing Catriona over his shoulder and making a break for it. She decided to have one more attempt to reassure the girl.

'Look us up,' said Mona. 'You can check on the HET website. Our picture is there, showing that we work for them. You can link to the Health Enforcement Team website from the NHS. We may not wear a uniform, but we are a legitimate branch of the public sector.'

'At least get her standing in the doorway or something, Mona, for God's sake.' Paterson's head was whipping back and forth as if he was at a tennis match. 'We're sitting ducks here.'

Catriona's bottom lip started to wobble again, but she saw the sense of this request, and moved into the doorway. She started playing around on her phone.

Mona held up her ID again. 'Look! The picture on my card matches my face, which matches the picture of us on the staff team of the North Edinburgh HET.'

'Oh, God,' said Catriona. 'I just don't know what to do.'

'I do,' said Paterson and held his finger long and hard on the number 19 button.

'Hello?' A crackling voice came over the intercom.

'We're here from the North Edinburgh HET.' Paterson spoke softly. 'You should be expecting us.'

There was a laugh at the other end. 'Yes, we certainly are. In you come. Third floor.'

They climbed quickly up three flights of stairs, and found an open doorway awaiting them. The man standing there was well past the official retirement age for either the police or the health service. He had short silver hair, and a very firm handshake. Despite his age he looked as if he could handle himself, and Mona felt slightly reassured at the thought of Catriona going into his protection.

'I'm Alfred, and I also answer to Alfie, Alf, and a whole host of other less pleasant names. Which one of you lovely ladies is Catriona?'

'That would be me.' She was holding her bag across her chest, like some kind of shield.

'I expect you're ready for a cup of tea after all this upset.' He grinned at her, his expression avuncular and reassuring.

Catriona's eyes filled with tears again, and she nodded mutely. Alfie was working some kind of magic, as she didn't put up any further fuss about going into the flat.

Paterson went round the property, checking out every room. 'Just yourself, then?'

'I was called in on short notice, but I can ensure you reinforcements are on their way. This young lady's not going to be short of company over the next few days.'

'A few days?' Catriona turned in their direction. 'Is that how long you think I'll be here for?'

'Hard to say at this point,' said Alfie. 'Could be a lot less if our colleagues are doing their job properly. But I can guarantee that you won't be bored while you're here.

I've got many years' experience of entertaining people in such situations.'

She gave a wan smile, and sat down on the living room sofa, her bag still gripped to her chest.

'So, Catriona,' said Paterson. 'You overheard a conversation. What was it about?'

Panic fleeted briefly across her face. 'I can't say.'

Paterson nodded. 'I appreciate that you don't want to break any confidences, but it would really help our investigation if you could let us know what we're dealing with.'

'I understand that, but I signed the Official Secrets Act.'

'As a direct result of that conversation?' asked Mona.

She nodded, her eyes darting nervously between the two of them.

'What was your role at the Scottish Government?'

'I was an intern. I was only supposed to be there on a six-week placement, learning about public sector marketing.'

'That was unlucky,' said Paterson.

She released her grip on her bag, and sighed. 'I thought the world of politics would be exciting.'

'Which it was, I suppose,' said Mona.

'No.' Catriona shook her head vigorously. 'It was horrible. After we heard, well, you know, what we weren't supposed to, all hell broke loose. This man came in that I'd never seen before, and started telling us, well, threatening us, really, that we couldn't say anything, and we couldn't leave the room.'

Was his name Ian?' asked Mona, a little too quickly.

'No. Bob, I think he said.' She pulled her bag back towards her again, cuddling it like a teddy bear. 'Maybe I shouldn't have said that. I've signed the Official Secrets

Act and I'm keeping my mouth shut, so stop asking me questions.'

'Now, now,' said Alfie. 'You heard the lady. Stop bombarding her with questions at such a difficult time.' He winked at them over Catriona's head, and Mona knew he would get some information out of her over the next few days, once he'd won Catriona's trust. Whether anyone other than Stuttle would be told what he found out remained to be seen.

She looked up at Paterson, who reluctantly admitted defeat. 'Right, we'll leave you to it. Come on, Mona, let's go.'

13

Bernard drove back to the office at what would usually be the height of the rush hour. The streets were noticeably quieter than usual. He attempted a calculation of how many people had been affected by the day's events; there was everyone who would consider themselves a public sector worker, obviously, every parent whose children had been sent home from school, everyone who used social care services that had been stopped at a moment's notice, the list was endless. In some ways it was a miracle there was anyone still at work.

Marcus hadn't said much on their return journey; he'd lain quietly on the back seat all the way into town.

'Do you think it was a homeless person?'

Bernard jumped at the sudden question. Marcus had propped himself up on one elbow, and was watching him in the mirror. 'Bunked down there for the night then took ill?'

'Possibly.'

'You don't sound convinced.'

'It would be a bit of a huge coincidence to find a set of coordinates in Blair's notebook, and it led to the body of a tramp who just happened to have bedded down there.'

Marcus, with what seemed a great effort, got himself back into a seated position. 'So, who do you think it is?'

'Well, given that it was Blair who got us there, I think

it's highly possible it was his "getting away from it all" spot. My money would be on it being Blair's body. Ties in with him being missing.'

'Oh God. How old was he?'

'Twenty.'

'Suicide?'

He thought it over. 'It could be. He certainly ticks a few of the risk boxes for that – young, male, experiencing bullying.'

'Oh, dear Lord. You know, Bernard, I don't really think I'm cut out for all this.'

'I know. Me neither. Shall I let you out here and you can go home?'

Marcus nodded, miserably.

Bernard had presumed he would have the office to himself, and was looking forward to a cup of tea, some peace and quiet, and a chance to digest all that had happened since he left the house this morning. He was disappointed to hear voices in the office as he approached, and opened the door to find Mona and Paterson drinking coffee. Neither of them looked particularly happy; whether this was because he'd arrived, or was a more general malaise he wasn't sure.

'What are you doing here?' asked Paterson. 'I thought you were at home protecting your no-claims bonus?'

'Thanks for updating Mr Paterson on my concerns, Mona.'

She grinned. 'You're welcome.'

Bernard turned his attention back to his boss. 'I need to tell you something, Mr Paterson. I followed up a lead in the box of stuff that Mr Taylor, Blair Taylor's father, brought in.'

'Oh, is that what that heap of crap is?' He glanced over at the dusty box. 'I thought someone had cleared out one of the cupboards in here.'

'Anyway, I went out and investigated it with Marcus ...'

'With Marcus? This isn't going to end well.' Paterson folded his arms and glared at him. 'Proceed.'

'I think we've found the body of Blair Taylor.' He briefly outlined the trail that had led them to the body, and sat back waiting for Paterson to say something, preferably along the lines of *good job, Bernard*.

In response, Paterson scowled. 'Have you let the police know?'

He nodded.

Paterson's scowl deepened a notch. 'And you didn't touch the crime scene in any way, shape or form?'

'Not once we realised it was a potential crime scene.' His boss's tone was *exactly* the same as PC Blake's had been earlier; did they teach them that at Police College? 'I told them who I thought it might be, and they said they'd be in touch with us tomorrow about identifying the body. What did Paul Shore have to say?'

'Nothing,' said Mona and Paterson, swiftly and in unison. They sounded extremely unconvincing.

Mona, at least, had the decency to look embarrassed. 'I mean, nothing of importance. He just wanted an update on what was going on.'

'Whatever.' He turned his back on them, and returned to Blair Taylor's box of tricks. He leafed through one of the notebooks, but failed to find what he was looking for. He pulled out another book and began turning the pages.

Mona appeared at the side of his desk. 'What are you scrabbling about for?'

'I'm not sure. There was just something in the way the body was laid out ...'

'Which you didn't touch, I hope ...'

'No, no, Mr Paterson, which I saw from a safe distance.' He turned a page of a blue, lined, A4 jotter, and found what he was after. 'This. Look!'

He turned the book round to face Mona and Paterson.

'It was a little difficult to get a clear idea if the body had been laid out because wild animals had been in and, well, eaten the body, but there had been an attempt to lay flowers out around the corpse, and there was daubing on the wall that looked not unlike this.'

'Suicide?' asked Mona. 'He had a perfect death in mind, then took himself off to try to enact it?'

'Possibly, very possibly, given the ritualistic preparations involved.' He nodded. 'What I'm wondering now is if this is linked in any way to Arthusian Fall? The other drawing was – you know, the plinth thing.'

'Can you look for them online?'

'I could, but it might be quicker to ask one of their fans.'

'Marcus?'

'Who else?' He reached for his phone.

'Bernard!' He picked up immediately. 'How sweet of you to check that I'm OK!'

'Yeah.' He winced; his friend's wellbeing was quite low on his current list of priorities. 'You *are* OK?'

'Yes. I'm not as hardened to this kind of thing as you are, but I'm just about coping.'

'I wouldn't say ... Anyway, never mind. I have a quick question for you. Does Arthusian Fall have an album cover with a body laid out surrounded by flowers and red painted symbols?'

199

There was a long silence. 'You don't think the body we found was laid out like the gatefold sleeve on *The Redemption Chamber*?'

'Probably not,' said Bernard and hung up. He googled *The Redemption Chamber* and two seconds later was looking at an image not dissimilar to both the pencil drawing, and to the scenario he'd seen earlier. He gestured to his colleagues to come over.

'That reflects pretty well what I saw.'

'What's this nonsense?' asked Paterson.

'The body had been laid out like a picture on an Arthusian Fall album called *The Redemption Chamber*.'

'*The Redemption Chamber*?' said Mona. 'Why did he need redeeming?'

Bernard shook his head. 'I think the bigger question is did he think that he needed redemption and kill himself, or did someone else think that he needed to be redeemed and kill him?'

'Or was he some kind of sacrifice?' asked Mona. 'An offering to the gods?'

'I think the biggest question of all,' said Paterson, 'is if Bryce is involved with these people, exactly how nuts is he?'

14

Mona lay on the bed, eyes wide open. She had called into her own flat to pick up some more clothing, and a couple of books she possessed on the subject of witness protection. The world of safe houses and bodyguards wasn't one that she'd encountered first-hand in the CID, and if she had to protect Catriona McBride, a little bit of brushing up of her skills was in order.

It had taken her a while to track down the books, which she'd finally traced to the bottom of a box stored under her bed, and, judging by the layer of dust on it, not opened again since she'd shoved it there when she moved in. She'd thrown the books into her rucksack, crammed in a couple of clean T-shirts, and topped it off with the heap of junk mail that passed for her personal correspondence these days.

At this point, she should have left and hightailed it back to her mother's, but the bed looked just so darn inviting. Mona had surrendered to its summons and here she was, half an hour later, still prostrate. She wished that she could just stay there, maybe get up and have a bath, and call out for a takeaway. Much as she loved her mother, it was nice just to enjoy the silence. Her mother kept up a constant stream of chatter, much of which seemed to require some kind of response from Mona.

So, all in all, it was nice just to lie there and reflect on the day. It had been a good one in some ways: getting Catriona McBride into a safe house had been a major result. On the other hand, it had been a distraction from the work of finding Bryce. Tomorrow she'd get on Bernard and Maitland's case and see if Bernard's findings could help them to locate the factory. They really couldn't be left to get on with things themselves.

The bed was incredibly comfortable. She could feel her breath slowing, and she closed her eyes. Almost immediately the dull ache she had felt in the front of her head turned in to something stronger. She turned on to her side, and a wave of pain coursed along behind her forehead. She opened her eyes, and decided that the pain was more bearable if she did her best not to focus on it. Company, even that of her mother, would take her mind off things.

She walked slowly to her mother's house. For the first few streets, every time she put her foot down a tiny bolt of pain went through her head, but by the time she was approaching the house the pain had more or less vanished. Maybe she should go for more walks; she certainly felt more relaxed now than she had all day. She turned into her mother's driveway and pulled up short.

The front door was open.

Her mother never left the door open. It had been a mantra of Mona's teenage years that you had to *pull the door firmly shut behind you.* She turned the handle of the internal glass door, only to find that it was locked. She didn't have a key. She didn't *need* a key because this door was never, ever locked.

To her relief, her mother appeared on the other side of the glass, and with a bit of difficulty turned the key.

'What's up with the door, Mum?'

'I only went out for half an hour to buy a paper and something for our tea. Then when I got back, this had happened.' She waved her hand in the direction of the door.

Mona tried to remain patient. '*What* happened?'

'Glue, Mona. Someone put glue into our lock. Who would do something like that?'

A potential culprit leapt into Mona's mind.

'Can't we get it fixed?'

'I phoned about six different locksmiths, but it was after five when it happened, and they were just quoting ridiculous prices to come out as an emergency. I'll try phoning again in the morning.'

She pushed past her mother. 'Give me the numbers, Mum. We'll have to get someone out tonight, whatever it costs.'

'Oh, well, whatever you think. You're probably right. I wouldn't feel safe all night with just a glass door to keep people out.'

In Mona's case it was going to take a lot more than a sturdy lock to make her feel secure.

15

Bernard could hear the television blaring. He was standing on the threshold trying to muster the emotional resilience to open the door and see what Annemarie and Sheba had done to the place. From the Northern vowels echoing round the landing she appeared to be listening to *Coronation Street*. Every time anyone on-screen raised their voice, Sheba let out a low growl.

He crossed his fingers and opened the door. Annemarie was sitting in the middle of his tiny kitchen area. It was a strange place to watch the TV from, and it took him a minute to realise why she had forsaken the sofa. Her right hand was stuck out of the kitchen window as she tried to minimise the amount of cigarette smoke she was creating in the flat. He was surprisingly touched at her efforts.

'Hello, son. Have you had a good day?'

Not really, but he didn't want to go into it. 'It was busy.' He suddenly became aware of a fragrance in the air. 'What's that smell?'

'Febreze. Every time the dog farts I give it a squeeze.'

Bernard wasn't sure that the overpowering synthetic perfume was particularly preferable to essence of dog, but again he was touched by her consideration.

The *Coronation Street* closing music sounded, eliciting another growl from Sheba.

'You're a fan of soap operas, then?' he asked.

'Beats the news, son. So bloody depressing. This evening the whole bulletin consisted of interviews with council workers who kept bursting into tears because they were so worried they were going to get shot.'

She didn't look particularly impressed by this, but then Annemarie's entire working career had been underpinned by the risk of being shot, stabbed, punched, or, as had actually happened last time they'd met, being locked in a burning building.

Annemarie turned the TV off and got to her feet.

'Anyroad, I've cooked.'

He joined her in the kitchen, and peered into the saucepan she was pointing at. It wasn't immediately apparent what the dish was, but it smelled delicious, even against the background aroma of chemical jasmine.

'It's stovies.'

Stovies! He hadn't had stovies since he was a boy. The smell evoked his grandmother's kitchen in Penicuik. A sudden doubt struck him. 'Is this vegetarian?'

'Are you a vegetarian?'

'Yes.'

'Then, yes, it is.'

'But—'

'You go and get a seat, son, and I'll bring it over.' She shooed him into the living area. 'There's wine as well.'

'Thank you,' he said, surprised. As a teetotaller he was surprised she'd even thought about getting a nice bottle of something in. 'You didn't need to go to all this trouble.'

'My pleasure, son.' She plonked a large plate of stovies in front of him, along with a very generous glass of red. 'It's the least I could do.'

The stovies were delicious, although he had his doubts

about their veggie credentials. He had a moment's guilt, before his taste buds overruled his head and he kept shovelling.

He threw back a large mouthful of the wine, and nearly choked. Whatever he was drinking, it wasn't a pick of the week from *The Sunday Times* Wine Club.

Annemarie grinned at him. 'It's a cheeky wee number, eh? A guy in the pub was selling them out of the boot of his car. I bought you a couple of bottles.'

He looked at the glass. The bass note he was sensing was probably anti-freeze. He wondered if the skin on his tonsils would grow back of its own accord.

'Anyroad, son, now that you're settled and that, I've a couple of things to tell you.'

Bernard put his fork down. So, this was what all the pampering was about. She had bad news for him, and all this kindness was just buttering him up to make it easier to swallow.

'I've been asking around Leith if anyone's seen my brother. Nobody's seen him for days. None of his drinking cronies, none of the bookies, no-one. I'm thinking he's gone.'

'You mean left town?' said Bernard, hopefully.

She shook her head. 'He's not got the organisational skills to do that. Every time Alec's had a problem in his life, man and boy, it's been up to me to sort it out. If he's not asking for my help, I think there's only one reason for that. I think he's dead, son.'

Bernard stared at her, trying to tell if she was upset. She remained inscrutable. The only thing he could read from her body language was that she was desperate for another cigarette. 'I'm so sorry.' He picked up his plate and wine glass and stood up. 'I don't suppose you'll be going to the police?'

'Nah. Anyroad, there's more.' She motioned to him to sit down again. He obeyed, his sense of foreboding rising as his body descended.

'I bumped into one of the lassies from the Project on my travels.' Bernard assumed 'the Project' was the charity Annemarie had previously managed supporting sex workers in Leith. 'She said she'd seen Scott Kerr in a pub on Salamander Street a couple of nights ago, which had surprised her, because he doesn't usually drink round here. He'd made a beeline for her and started asking if she'd seen me recently, and he wasn't being very complimentary, if you get my drift.'

He nodded.

'Then he started mouthing off to the whole pub about how people think they can get one over on him, but he's smarter than that. Said he's going to be settling some scores.' She lit up her fag, and made a token effort to blow the smoke in the direction of the window. 'I bet half the pub shat themselves when he said that.'

'But you think he was talking about us?'

'There's more.'

Bernard closed his eyes. He was feeling dizzy.

'Geri, the lassie I was talking to, was in a different pub yesterday. She sees Kerr's in there, and nearly backs right out again, but a couple of her regulars are in and she's got bills to pay, so she keeps a low profile and hopes he fecks off soon. She tunes in to what he's saying, and it's the same shtick as the night before, he's been wronged, he's on to them, and they're going to suffer.'

'Oh, God.'

'This time, but, he's going on about how he's going to toy with them first, play with them like they're mice and he's some God Almighty cat. Says he's going to have a bit of fun.'

'You think he's toying with us?'

'I think he could be.'

'But killing your brother – that's way beyond "toying".'

'I think Alec's dead, but I'm not 100 per cent sure he's been murdered. He could just as easily have taken a plunge into Leith Docks on his way back from the pub, and time will tell on that one. But I also think that somebody like Kerr *would* see that as toying. He's not like you and me, son. He doesn't put the premium on people's lives that we do.'

'We need to tell the police.'

Her jaw dropped. 'Have you got some kind of death wish, son? Kerr's got pals in the police. You go shouting your mouth off to them, you're putting yourself in line for a very nasty accident.'

'So, what do we do?'

She shrugged. 'Wish I knew, son.'

Bernard picked up his wine glass, and took a very big gulp of the anti-freeze.

THURSDAY

DEAD HUMMINGBIRDS

I

Bernard had half expected to get a text berating him about the fact that HET officers had continued to turn up for work, despite having been ordered not to, and to be strictly instructed to stay at home with the doors firmly locked. In some ways he would have welcomed that.

In other ways, namely Annemarie and her dog, he was very grateful to be heading into work. He anticipated that today could be highly productive, due to the absence of Maitland, Carole, Marcus, Marguerite, and everyone else who stood in the way of him getting his filing done on a daily basis. If only Mr Paterson and Mona had decided to stay safely at home he would be well on the way to developing his perfect working environment. And all he'd had to do to achieve this was risk being shot.

The office was promisingly empty. He doubted that Mona and Paterson really would take the day off, but at the very least they might have one of their important meetings that they never actually told him about and he would have an hour or two of peace. He stuck the kettle on, flung a teabag in a cup, and reached into the fridge, only to discover that there wasn't any milk. He considered venturing out to the shop, but decided this was an unnecessary risk, particularly as there was probably a full two-litres going off in the Admin department's fridge at that very moment.

He ran down the stairs singing gently to himself. The Admin department's fridge was considerably better stocked than the one in the second-floor kitchen. He considered whether to help them out by eating up anything else likely to go off in the next few days. Food prices being what they were, it seemed like a shame to—

'What do you think you're doing?'

He leapt at the sound of the voice and almost landed on top of Marguerite, who in turn took fright and screamed.

Paterson and Mona came running into the room, their coats still on. 'What the hell's going on?'

'Oh, dear God, Mr Paterson, I saw Bernard, and I got such a fright.'

'What are you doing here?' asked Mona. 'Didn't you get the message about staying at home?'

'I did.' She nodded. 'I went home yesterday like we were told to, but my dad went mental and said I was a wimp.'

Marguerite's dad had been in the army. From some of Marguerite's hair-raising stories about him, he may have been hit over the head several times in the course of his combat duty.

'My dad said that the only people who deserted their post in a time of crisis were babies and nancy boys, no offence, Bernard ...'

'Why would I be—? Oh, you know what, never mind.'

'So, I came back in. Not that I suppose there'll be much for me to do?' she asked, hopefully.

'Best you just man the phones down here.' Paterson patted her lightly on the shoulder. 'I'm sure they'll be ringing off the hook. And, Bernard?'

'Yes?'

'Bring the milk.'

One round of satisfying hot-drinks-with-milk later, Paterson was ready to get down to business. 'So, I was thinking,' he started, 'about the place where you found that body.'

Bernard nodded. 'Possibly Blair Taylor's body.'

'There seem to be some links between the two students and our missing rock star – we all in agreement about that?'

There were nods all round.

'So I'm thinking there must have been some reason why they chose that particular place to go.'

'Do you think it was significant to them?' asked Mona. 'Did it feature on a Arthusian Fall album or something like that?'

'Marcus didn't mention anything about it,' said Bernard. 'I'm sure if it had been significant he would have known about it. Although yesterday's horrible experience might have knocked him off his stride. I'll try asking him again.'

'Good,' said Paterson. 'Do we know who owns the land?'

'Nope, but I can find out,' said Bernard. 'Should be really easy to trace it through the Land Registry.'

A metallic sound rang through the building.

'Is that the doorbell?' asked Paterson. 'Who's going to turn up for a meeting on a day like today?'

'Someone who hasn't watched the news for forty-eight hours and doesn't know that everybody's supposed to be at home?' said Mona.

'Mr Paterson?' Marguerite's voice echoed up to them. 'I think there's somebody at the door. Should I get it?'

'No.' Paterson shot to his feet. 'Leave it to me.'

Mona and Bernard stood in the doorway listening to

213

a muted conversation drifting up from the bottom of the stairs. Paterson reappeared with a man with a mop of curly hair, dressed in a purple suit.

'Oh, Mr Bartlett,' said Mona.

'Arty, darling, or Artemis, if you must.' He bounded up the steps towards her. 'So, this is where it all happens then?'

'Well, not much happening today, to be honest.'

'I did wonder if there would be anybody here but I decided to take a chance.' Taking Mona's hand he raised it to his mouth and kissed it. 'Delighted to see you again, though, lovely.'

Bernard stifled a smile at the look on Mona's face. Surreptitiously, she wiped her hand firmly on her jeans.

'Mr . . . I mean, Artemis, was Arthusian Fall's manager, and singer.' Mona explained.

'Is, dear, is. We've not split up. We haven't recorded any new material since 1998, and our bass player died in 2002, but we're still technically a going concern.'

Bernard could see that Paterson was losing patience with all of this. Sure enough, his boss decided to move things along. 'What brings you in to see us, Mr Bartlett?'

'Well, I don't know if this is relevant or not, but I'd been thinking about what you said about our, ehm, investment with Colin and decided that I really ought to chase things up with his lawyer. So, I gave them a ring, and spoke to the young woman who deals with Colin's affairs, and she told me that they were no longer representing him, as of yesterday. Quite abrupt she was.'

'Really?' Mona said. 'Did she give a reason?'

'No. I did try to get some info out of her, but you know what lawyers are like. Paid by the hour and all that. My chitter-chatter was costing her money. I did get the impression that they weren't too pleased with him, which probably means he hasn't paid his bill. He's got a bit of a habit of that.'

There was a brief silence as everyone thought this over. Briskly, Paterson wrapped things up. 'Well, thanks for letting us know, Mr Bartlett. My colleagues have your contact details if we need to speak to you further.'

Artemis wasn't so easily moved on. 'So, you lot aren't supposed to be at work today then?'

'That's the general idea,' said Mona. 'Unfortunately there are urgent things to be done.'

Artemis proved impervious to hints. 'Fancy taking a bit of time off and coming out for an early lunch with me?'

'What a lovely thought,' said Mona.

'But we're all a bit busy here,' finished Paterson.

Artemis shrugged. 'Oh, well, when things calm down—' he put a business card down on the desk '—give me a ring.'

Mona gave him a smile that was all teeth and professionalism. Bernard noted she had both hands tucked firmly into her pockets.

'Right, better get off.' He turned to go, and then swivelled back. 'Oh, I meant to ask. Did you catch up with Sharon?'

'Yes, we did, thank you.'

'Is she OK? I always got the impression that it didn't end too well. One minute she was part of our circle, the next she was gone, and Colin was pretty tight-lipped about what had happened.'

'I think she's all right.'

'Good, glad to hear she's still alive and well, and Colin hasn't buried her in the back garden.'

Paterson's wafer-thin patience had completely worn

out. 'Good of you to raise these concerns several decades after you last saw her.'

Artemis appeared to have Marcus levels of immunity to sarcasm. 'Did she go back into nursing?'

'Nursing?' Mona seemed suddenly interested in Artemis's conversation. Bernard could see that Paterson was itching to get him out of the building, but Mona signalled to him to hold off.

'Yeah, she used to be a nurse. That's how we met her – an Accident and Emergency trip after Colin had one too many. I suppose she should have known what she was getting into. First impressions are rarely wrong.'

'So, you think she could still be nursing?'

He shrugged. 'I don't know. I haven't seen her for years but she was a lovely woman, so do remember me to her if you see her again. Colin wasn't the easiest to live with, so I reckon she's better off without him. Anyway, ancient history.' He grinned at her. 'Are you sure you don't want to discuss this further over lunch?'

'Unfortunately, Mona is required here,' said Paterson. 'I'll show you back to the door.'

Artemis looked put out at this but shrugged and blew a kiss to Mona, before following Paterson downstairs.

Mona frowned, deep in thought.

'What are you thinking about?' asked Bernard. 'Are you upset because Paterson ruined your chances of bagging a fading rock star?'

'Very funny. No, it's probably nothing but . . .'

She broke off as Paterson came back, walked straight past the two of them, and opened one of the windows. 'Stinks like a hippie festival in here,' he said, by way of explanation.

Mona carried on. 'It's probably nothing, but when I

spoke to Sharon Murray, Carole thought she recognised her from nursing, but Murray was absolutely adamant she's never been a nurse. Why would she lie about it?'

'I don't know, but I do know that everybody connected with Arthusian Fall seems to be fond of telling porky pies.' Paterson frowned. 'Worth checking out, do you think?'

'It just seems such an odd thing to lie about. Might be worth another chat with her? I'll head over now.'

'Not on your own you won't,' said Paterson.

Bernard looked up expectantly.

Paterson picked up this coat. 'I'll come with you.'

'What about Bernard though? He'll be on his own.'

'No, he won't.' Paterson grinned. 'Marguerite's here.'

Suddenly Paterson's eagerness to leave seemed clear.

2

'You know who it would be really useful to have with us, Guv?'

'I know who you are about to say, and I'm sure she won't do it. If Carole had wanted to turn up for work would have been here.'

'Yes, but she didn't know we'd need her specialist skills.'

There was a brief silence. She couldn't tell if Paterson was thinking it over, or just ignoring her. She decided to push a little further. 'We pass her house on the way there?'

Paterson sighed. 'All right, but you'd better do the asking. If I turn up on her doorstep I'll get my head to play with.'

'Mona.' Carole looked surprised to see her. 'Has something happened?'

'No, no-one's been shot or anything like that.' She updated Carole on the conversation with Artemis. 'I'm worried about Sharon Murray. When we spoke to her we both saw a few warning signs about domestic abuse, and I'm thinking if she's still in touch with Colin ...'

Carole nodded. 'I know, I share your concern. But Jerry will be raging if he finds out I've gone into work. He wasn't exactly well disposed towards the HET before people started getting shot. You see his point?'

'If it's any consolation I don't think we're in any real

218

danger. Bob Ellis and his mates seem to think they've cornered Bryce somewhere in Aberdeenshire.' She wondered about sharing the theory that the shootings weren't random, then decided against it. She still wasn't entirely sure where her colleague's loyalties lay.

Carole hesitated on the doorstep. 'I am really worried about Sharon. I'm sure she was a nurse and ...' She broke off, and her face scrunched into a frown. 'Is that Paterson in the car?'

'Yeah, sorry. I'm sure he'll be on his best behaviour.'

'Oh, God, let's just do it.' She disappeared into the house then returned carrying her coat and bag. 'Hopefully I'll be back before Jerry realises I've gone.'

'Mr Paterson.' Carole slid onto the back seat.

'Carole.' He didn't turn round. 'Thanks for helping us out here.'

'No problem.'

This was the longest, politest interchange Mona could remember them having in months.

Mona parked the car outside the multi-storey block where they had previously visited Sharon Murray. She'd tried phoning ahead, but the phone had clicked straight to answer-machine. She didn't leave a message.

'Just as well there are three of us,' said Paterson, surveying his surroundings. 'One of us can stay with the car.'

'Assuming that someone will be you, Guv?'

'Correct assumption.'

There was no answer to the buzzer. Mona tried a second, longer blast on the button, but to no avail.

'Try someone else?' suggested Carole.

'No need.' Mona nodded in the direction of the lift.

A young mum and buggy appeared. 'If she asks, we're Health Visitors.'

The woman shot them a suspicious glance, but obviously decided they didn't look like crazed gunmen. She gave them a curt nod of thanks as they held the door open for her to manoeuvre her buggy out.

'Lift or stairs?' asked Carole.

'Both, in case a phone call from a strange number, followed by someone at the door has spooked her, and she makes a run for it. You head up in the lift, I'll walk and see you there.'

Mona started up the stairs, and as she rounded the second-floor landing, saw a thin figure in a hoodie heading towards her. She took an educated guess and stepped in front of her.

'Mrs Murray?'

Sharon jumped a mile. She stared at Mona, an unmistakable expression on her face. Mona was surprised; of all the things she'd expected to see written on Mrs Murray's face, relief hadn't been one of them.

The look quickly passed. 'I don't know what you lot are doing here again. I told you everything I know.'

'No, Mrs Murray, you told us a load of nonsense. Can we go back to your flat to discuss?'

She looked at the stairs leading down, and then back in the direction she'd come from. After weighing up her options, she decided not to make a break for it. 'OK, but I've nothing more to say.'

Carole was waiting outside the flat. 'Hello again, Sharon.'

Sharon Murray didn't reply, but opened the door and hurried in. Mona followed closely behind, in case she was intent on slamming the door in their faces.

'Been doing your washing, I see,' said Mona. She wriggled past the clothes dryer that was taking up half the hall. 'Can't help but think that the tabard drying there looks awfully like a nurse's uniform.'

Sharon was in the living room, lighting up a cigarette.

'Why won't you admit that we worked together?' said Carole. 'Working in nursing isn't usually something people are embarrassed about.'

'I wasn't embarrassed, I just didn't think it was relevant. The only thing that nursing did for me was give me something to go back to when I left my husband.'

'Was Colin a good husband?' asked Mona.

There was a silence. 'I don't think that is any of your business.'

'Fair enough. But just answer one more question for me. When you tried to do a runner just now from your own home, who exactly did you think was looking for you? Because you didn't think it was us, did you?'

Despite her best attempts not to, Sharon started to cry, wiping the tears away with the back of her hand.

Carole put an arm around her shoulder. Mona was surprised when it wasn't immediately thrown off. 'If you are at risk of domestic violence, Mrs Murray, this is where we can help.'

She laughed, a small, bitter sound. 'If you can, then you would be the first people that could. I was married to Colin for four years when I was too young to know any better, and all this time later he's still ruining my life.' She stubbed out her cigarette. 'I'm sorry I ran off. I did think it was Colin out there.'

'You said before that you hadn't seen him for years. I take it that wasn't true?'

'It was true – I didn't see him for years and years.

Now I can't seem to get rid of him.' She stared at her hands. 'I was only twenty when we met, back in 1987. I was a student nurse, and Colin turned up in Accident and Emergency in a right state. I think he'd overdosed on something.'

Mona thought that Artemis had been right about one thing – this probably wasn't the optimum way to meet your life partner. At least, not if you wanted a life with a degree of stability.

'Colin was a bit older than me, maybe twenty-eight or twenty-nine, and way more worldly-wise than I was. And, you know, Arthusian Fall were at their height, and he was really handsome and, well, charismatic, I suppose you would say. I was totally star-struck. He seemed to be really into me too, kept saying how impressed he was that I was going to be a nurse. He said there was going to be a need for skills like that because things were going to go wrong in the world and the government had no way of making it right.' She pulled out another cigarette. Her hands were shaking. 'He wasn't entirely wrong, was he?'

'Did he think there was going to be a virus epidemic?' asked Mona.

'I don't know. I don't think he had anything specific in mind. He was always catastrophising that there was going to be some disaster that the government wouldn't be able to deal with. I seriously think the thing he liked most about me was that I was a nurse.'

'But you weren't together very long?'

'It was a whirlwind romance. We got married after six weeks, and my parents went absolutely mental. We were together for maybe four or five years in total, then I spent years trying to get him out of my life.' She looked up suddenly. 'I get no maintenance or anything from him. I

222

thought if I took none of his money I could just get rid of him, but he stalked me for ages.'

'Did you report him to the police?'

'They couldn't do anything. They tried, but Colin was so bloody minded he'd always find ways to track me down. It was always more about controlling me than physical abuse, so it was difficult to get people to take it seriously. It was the nineties.' She shrugged. 'Maybe they'd deal with it better now. Colin didn't have to be violent to get his way. I was scared enough of him without him having to raise his hand. Everyone's scared of him. Things did calm down a bit when he remarried. I didn't see him for ages, and I thought I'd finally got him out of my life.' She stopped, staring at the floor.

'Please carry on.' Mona tried to sound reassuring. 'I know this must be difficult for you.'

She finally lit her cigarette. 'You might not be so sympathetic when I tell you what happened. In fact,' she stopped to wipe another tear away, 'I think you're going to arrest me when I tell you what Colin got me involved in.'

'Have you been forced to do something under duress?' asked Carole.

She nodded. 'Colin turned up here a few months ago. My first thought was that his marriage had broken up and he was looking for a shoulder to cry on. I wasn't happy at that, but his real motive was so much worse. He said he needed my help and that I had to come with them immediately, and bring some medical supplies. I didn't want to get involved, and I tried to say no but ...' She wiped her eyes with the back of her hand. 'But you don't say no to Colin. He really had got himself into a mess. He drove me out into the middle of nowhere. I don't know exactly what they had been up to, but him and a young man, I think, had been trying to make . . .'

She stopped again. Mona struggled not to let frustration into her voice. 'Please carry on.'

'I think they'd been making bombs.'

'Bombs?' said Mona and Carole in unison.

'My ex-husband is nuts, in case you hadn't already gathered that. All this doomsday stuff has completely fried his brain, and he really does believe that the world is about to end because of this Virus, and that the only thing that we can do is try and protect ourselves.'

'Why did he need you?' asked Mona.

'He had cocked up, like Colin always does. One of the bombs had exploded. The poor kid had burns to the side of his face. He should have been in hospital, possibly even intensive care, but Colin wouldn't let him go. I patched him up the best I could, but there would be a really high risk of infection to his wounds.'

'Do you know what happened to the boy?' asked Mona, the vision of the body Bernard had found going through her mind.

'I don't. Colin eventually drove me back into town. I debated calling the police but it just sounded so insane . . . Then when you arrived looking for him I thought, this is it, it's all kicking off. They'll work out I'm a nurse, and that I've been involved with terrorists. I've been terrified that Colin was going to arrive on my doorstep.'

'But you've not heard from him?'

'Not a peep.' She looked up at Mona, her eyes large and tearful. 'Am I under arrest?'

'Not by us, that's not what we do.' She hurried on in case Sharon thought she was off the hook. 'We will, however, be liaising with our colleagues at Police

Scotland. It will be up to them to decide if they need to investigate whether a crime has been committed.'

Carole took Sharon's hand and squeezed it. 'This must have been terrible for you.'

'Do you know anything about the second Mrs Karma?' asked Mona.

Sharon Murray gave another mirthless laugh. 'When I read in the papers that Colin was getting married again, I thought good luck to her. There was even a tiny crazy part of me that thought I should get in touch with her and warn her about what Colin was actually like.'

'But you didn't?'

'No, which was just as well, because I think she's nuttier than he is.'

'In what way?'

'She's a card-carrying member of the NRA. She's into all that apocalyptic shit as well, believes that the world is going to destroy itself, and the only people who will survive are those who prepared.'

'How do you know so much about her views?'

She looked slightly embarrassed. 'I've been following her online. I think it's safer when I know as much as possible about what Colin is up to. Lana doesn't exactly make a secret of her views.'

'She's an actress, right?'

'No.' She shook her head. 'Not an actress. She's a behind-the-scenes person, something to do with pros-thetics. If you need to be made up to look like Churchill she's the kind of person that would do it. Lana Olsen – check her out.'

'That's interesting.' Mona needed to get away some-where quiet to think this through. *Prosthetics. The ability to make someone look like someone else.*

There was a knock at the door, and she heard Paterson's voice. 'Mona? Carole?'

'We need to go.' Mona stood up. 'Thank you for your time, Mrs Murray.'

Carole was still holding on to Sharon's hand. 'Are you going to be OK?' she asked. 'Is there somewhere more secure you could go? We could get you a refuge place?'

'I've done all that before. Colin always finds me.' She gave a bitter laugh. 'I wish you had arrested me. It's my best chance of being safe.'

'I still think it would be good to get you out of here.' Carole turned to her. 'I'm going to stay here for the moment, Mona. I'll do a ring round and see if we can get Mrs Murray a refuge place.'

'Are you sure?' asked Mona.

Carole nodded. 'Assuming that's OK with you, Sharon?'

Sharon nodded and buried her face in her hands. 'Thank you,' she whispered.

'OK, Carole,' said Mona. 'Phone Police Scotland or us at any sign of trouble. Lock the door.'

Paterson started knocking again. 'Mona?'

'Coming, Guv.'

She opened the door, and Paterson grabbed her arm. 'We need to go.'

'What's the hurry? Has something happened?'

'It certainly has. Catriona McBride has done a runner.'

3

Marguerite had not stopped for breath. Within minutes of Paterson and Mona leaving, she made her way up to Bernard's office, saying it was just *too spooky* to stay on her own downstairs.

Consequently, Bernard was finding it very hard to concentrate. He'd followed up, as requested, the owner of the land where the body had been found. His search had identified that the land was owned by a company. His search for the company details had identified two directors, neither of whose names rang any bells. He would have liked to follow up with a detailed search on both of them, but his attention was being severely undermined by Marguerite's stream of chatter.

He sighed, leaned back in his chair, and reflected that all the women in his life were causing him trouble, either by talking too much or too little.

His estranged wife wasn't talking to him at all.

His work partner didn't tell him half of what was going on.

And Annemarie couldn't be persuaded to stop talking about Scott Kerr.

He turned back to his work, then realised with a guilty start that he hadn't given any consideration to the one woman he did actually want to talk to. *Lucy*. He should call her. She was probably wondering what was going on ...

'Do you smell something?' asked Marguerite.

'No,' he said, firmly, annoyed at being distracted by another of Marguerite's fantasies.

'Are you sure? Hand on my heart, Bernard, I swear I can smell smoke.'

'Don't you have anything at all you can be doing downstairs?' An acrid smell reached his nostrils, seconds before the smoke alarm went off.

'I knew I could smell something. See, if I die in a burning building because I came into work today, I'm totally going to come back and haunt my dad.'

Bernard ran out into the corridor. There were clouds of smoke billowing up the stairwell.

'This isn't a joke, Marguerite. We need to get out of here.'

'Oh my God.' She joined him in the corridor. 'We really are going to die in here.'

'No, we're not, but we do need to get out. Come on.'

'Where are we going?' Marguerite grabbed his arm.

'The fire escape.'

'Good idea.' She intertwined the fingers of her right hand with his, gripping his arm with her left. 'I don't want to get separated,' she said, by way of explanation.

'We're about six feet away from the fire escape, Marguerite, I think we'll be OK.' He pushed the bar and threw his weight against it. It didn't move.

'Is it stuck?'

'It seems to be.'

'Give it some welly.'

He tried again, pushing even harder.

'Maybe you should kick it?'

228

'I don't understand. These things are supposed to open really easily.'

'You could hit it with the fire extinguisher?'

He looked at the extinguisher. 'I don't think that will make any difference. Where do you think the fire's coming from? If we could get down to the ground floor we could maybe get out through a window or door?'

'Hello?' A voice floated up through the smoke.

'Help!' shouted Marguerite. 'We're stuck in a burning building.'

'No, you're not,' it shouted back.

The voice was familiar. 'Is that you, Maitland?'

'Oh, thank God you're here, Maitland.' Marguerite dropped Bernard's hand. 'I was worried we were going to die.'

Despite the severity of their circumstances Bernard still felt put out by this. 'I have things under control.'

'Stay where you are,' shouted Maitland. 'I've got this.'

'Why does he not think we're stuck in a burning building, Bernard?' asked Marguerite. 'It looks like a burning building to me.'

Maitland appeared through the clouds of smoke, which seemed to be evaporating of their own accord. 'Somebody stuck a couple of smoke bombs through the letterbox.'

'Oh, thank God.' Marguerite threw her arms around Maitland. 'I am so glad to see you.'

'Why? Wasn't Bernard saving you?' He smirked.

'Actually I—'

'It was awful, Maitland. I thought I was going to die.'

Maitland grinned at Bernard across the top of her head. 'No worries. You've got a real man here to save you. You can let go now.'

She showed no signs of releasing him. It was Bernard's turn to grin. 'Yes, you stay safe there, Marguerite.'

Maitland gave up trying to extract himself. 'Why the hell is somebody putting smoke bombs through our letterbox anyway?'

'Who knows? We're always taking the blame for something.'

'We seem to have been targeted a lot in the last few days. Mona had her tyres slashed, remember.'

'Oh, yeah.' Bernard had forgotten about that in the excitement. A horrible idea was taking shape in the back of his mind, the horrible realisation that maybe Annemarie was right. Maybe this targeting was Scott Kerr's work.

'Are you all right, Bernard?' Marguerite had let go of Maitland and was staring at him with a look of concern.

'I'm fine,' he said, weakly. 'I think I'll just go and sit down.'

4

'I can't believe you just let her walk out the door.' Paterson's face was the peculiar shade of red it always turned when he was particularly furious. Mona worried it was the precursor to some kind of heart attack or stroke.

Alfie didn't look much happier. 'What was I supposed to do?'

'Stop her leaving!'

'On what grounds? Show me the piece of legislation, Paterson, which tells me why I can legally detain her here? Because when I spoke to Stuttle he was a little bit vague on that point. As far as I'm concerned, we're protecting Catriona for own safety, but if she decides she wants to take her chances out in the world, there is nothing I can do to prevent it, however much I'd like to.'

Paterson strode over to the window, as if he hoped to see Catriona winding her way back through the surrounding blocks of flats.

'Any idea what prompted her to go?' asked Mona. 'Did her phone ring or anything?'

Paterson spun round, even redder than before. 'You didn't let her have her phone in here?'

'Again, she's not under arrest, she can have whatever she likes. But to answer the lady's question, no, I'm not aware of her getting any phone calls. She can't log in to the internet from here, so she didn't see anything online

231

that prompted her to flee.' Alfie thought for a second. 'I can't guarantee that she didn't get a text though.'

'Did she say where she was going, or what it was she was upset about?' asked Mona.

'Nope, not a word about what the problem was, and before you ask,' he glared at Paterson, 'I did my level best to find out what she was scared of, but she wasn't giving anything away. She was very clear on her rights, though; she knew she could up sticks if she wanted to.'

Mona tried to join the dots. 'Was it an impulse thing, do you think, or had she always been planning to leave as soon as she could?'

'Could be either, but the poor lassie was bloody upset about something. She was in floods of tears when she went out of here.'

'Fantastic.' Paterson flung his arms in the air. 'She's mentally unstable, and we've no idea where she's gone.'

'Calm down,' said Alfie. 'I wouldn't say she was mentally unstable. She's upset right enough, but underneath it I think she had a plan. I think she was leaving here for a specific purpose.'

Mona thought this over. 'OK, let's assume the worst-case scenario and somehow Bryce has been in touch with her. What would he have said?'

'No idea.' Paterson turned back to his vigil at the window.

'If he wants to shoot the girl,' said Alfie, 'then he's obviously said something that would get her to wherever it is he wants her to be. She seems like a nice girl, and from the chats I had with her she seemed far more worried about her parents and sister than she was about herself.'

'You think Bryce could have threatened them?'

He nodded. 'I think that's probably the thing most likely to get her running out of here.'

'Do you think she's headed for her parents' house?'

'I doubt it, she said they lived in Shetland.'

'What about the sister?' said Paterson, without turning round.

'University – one of the English ones. I don't think she's gone anywhere very far, though, because she didn't take her bag. Her purse, her Green Card, her money are all still here.'

'She's gone somewhere on foot?' asked Mona.

'She might have had enough in her pockets for a bus fare, but I'd say she was planning to stay local.'

'The last two shootings, Guv, have been in places where Carlotta Carmichael was nearby. Do you know where she's supposed to be today?'

'No. Stuttle would know, though.' He pulled out his phone, then hesitated. 'I don't want to bother him with this unless we're sure.'

'I don't think we can be sure, Guv, but it's following the pattern.'

'If you're not going to phone him, I will,' said Alfie. 'He wanted to be kept abreast of developments here.'

Paterson pressed the number and hit the speaker button so they could hear the response.

Stuttle answered on the first ring. 'This better be murderously urgent.'

'Do you know Carlotta's movements for today?'

'What am I – her diary secretary? But seeing as you asked, she's at a demonstration of some fabulous new hands-free toilets. The glamour, eh?'

'Whereabouts?'

'Some primary school or other on the Southside of

Edinburgh. It's a brand-new building and state of the art, apparently.'

'A primary school?'

Mona and Alfie exchanged a pained glance.

'Yes, what's this all about?' Stuttle somehow managed to sound both impatient and interested.

'Catriona McBride's done a runner, and we don't know why. Worst-case scenario Bryce managed to get in touch with her and has lured her somewhere.'

'You think somewhere near Carlotta?'

'Would fit with the previous shootings.'

'Leave this with me. I'll warn her security detail. Half the Scottish police force is protecting her today.' Whatever her other thoughts about Stuttle, Mona had to admit he responded well in a crisis. They could hear the sound of tapping at the other end as he typed on his keyboard. 'They should have bloody cancelled this, in my opinion. Every other civil servant is at home, but she's "refusing to give in to terrorism", as she puts it. Right, got it. She's at Wincanton Primary School. Thank God there won't be any kids in class. Head over as soon as you can, and I'll meet you there.'

Paterson pocketed his phone. 'You heard the man. Let's get moving.'

5

'Right, I've checked,' said Maitland, bouncing back into the room. 'There's a great big rock up against the fire escape on the second floor. Whoever did it would have had a hell of a job getting it up there. The Facilities Manager's going to have a fit when he finds out about it.'

'He hates us anyway. He can just add this to his list of why the HET should be booted out of the building. Have they blocked off the other fire exits as well?' asked Bernard.

'No, just the second floor. Doesn't make sense, does it?'

Bernard thought it did make sense if you were targeting someone who worked on the second floor, and you knew they were alone in the building, more or less. He rubbed his forehead; he could feel the onset of a headache.

'Unless,' said Maitland, thoughtfully, 'it's Bryce trying to put the frighteners on us. Although, to be honest, threatening to shoot us all was probably more frightening.'

This logic made it more likely that it was Scott Kerr's work, which meant he had a worrying level of knowledge about the inside workings of the HET. Bernard tried to put the thought to the back of his mind, and hoped Mona would be back soon to tell him what he needed to do. 'Do you think Marguerite will be OK?'

'Yeah, there was no harm done, was there? She's got a great story for all her Admin pals when they come back to work.' He did an impression of her voice. '"Oh My God, I so nearly died, until Maitland came along and saved me"'.

'Shut up, you did not save her. I bet she'll have a few choice words for her dad when he gets home.'

'Hello? Anybody in?' Marcus's voice floated in from the corridor.

'Oh, crap. Not him as well.' Maitland headed to his computer and pretended he was very busy.

Marcus came in coughing. 'It's kind of dusty out there.'

'Someone put a smoke bomb through the letterbox.'

'Oh dear.' He looked back towards the door. 'Do you think we ought to go home?'

'I think we should stay,' said Bernard, 'but maybe you should go? After all, you did have a very upsetting experience yesterday.'

Marcus closed his eyes, holding up a palm as if he would rather Bernard didn't bring up that particular subject. 'No, no, fellow workers. If you are staying, I'm staying.'

'Great,' muttered Maitland.

'Anyway,' Marcus yawned, 'I stayed up late last night doing some research.'

'What kind of research?'

'I listened to every Arthusian Fall album in turn, and reread my history of progressive rock. I now know everything there is to know about the band. I could go on *Mastermind* tomorrow with them as my specialist subject.'

'Did you find out anything useful?' asked Bernard.

'Not that I could see.' Marcus shook his head, a little

sadly. 'However, I'm not an investigator. So just think of me as an information resource. If there's anything you need to know about Arthusian Fall just go ahead and ask.'

'Maybe you should go home,' said Maitland. 'We'll phone you if we need your help.'

'Actually, I have a question,' said Bernard. 'Dead hummingbird?'

'What's that?' asked Maitland.

'Well, in between entertaining Marguerite, and then nearly succumbing to smoke inhalation, I have actually been doing some work. According to the Land Registry, the piece of land where we found the body is owned by Dead Hummingbird Ltd. I don't recognise the directors' names, but I wondered if they were related to Arthusian Fall in some way.'

'You were not wrong,' said Marcus, happily. He started to sing. Bernard thought he sounded quite flat, but having listened to an Arthusian Fall album he could see it might have been meant to sound like that.

'*And in the darkness of polluted skies, the bees will cease and the hummingbirds die.* It's from their third album, *Apocalypse*. Side two, track three, if memory serves.'

'Does the company own anything else?' asked Maitland.

'Just one other thing. I'm looking it up on Google.' He typed in the postcode, and an aerial picture appeared. 'Does that look like a disused factory to you?'

'It certainly does. Well done, Bernie, I think that you just found where our missing rock star is bunkering down.' Maitland gave him a celebratory thump on the back, which nearly bumped his head off the PC's monitor. 'Time to track down the Guv.'

6

'I'm still struggling to see why anybody would want to shoot that lassie,' said Alfie.

'She overheard something she shouldn't have,' said Paterson, manoeuvring the car through the streets of the Southside of Edinburgh. Despite the public sector curfew, the roads were still busier than they would have liked.

'I assume we still don't know what?'

'Correct. We don't know, and believe me, we'd very much like to. We were hoping she might start crying on your shoulder. Did she say anything?'

'No.' Alfie shook his head. 'I tried to talk to her but she kept banging on about how she's signed the Official Secrets Act and how it was the worst thing she's ever done. Like I said, mostly she just talked about her family.'

'There's going to be a hell of a lot of security here given the circumstances. I don't know how Bryce thinks he's going to pull something off,' said Paterson.

'That's worrying me too,' said Mona. She leaned forward as far as the seatbelt on the back seat would let her. 'Bryce isn't stupid. He's not going to do something that will get him caught. That catering worker he shot in Aberdeen, he didn't shoot her at the official visit Carlotta was making, did he?'

'No, he didn't. That's a very good point.' Paterson looked thoughtful. 'The woman lived in Aberdeen, and he shot her near her home. He must have waited for Carlotta's first ministerial visit up there. She still gets the message that this is related to her, but he wouldn't have to take the same level of risk.'

'So, you're saying that he could be anywhere in Edinburgh?' said Alfie. 'Because I'm not sure how we deal with that.'

'No, I think he'll choose somewhere that's linked to this visit in some way if he can,' said Paterson, 'just to ram home his point.'

'This is a brand-new primary school, isn't it?' asked Mona.

'That's what Stuttle said,' said Alfie. 'Fancy toilets.'

'Where is the old one?' asked Paterson. 'That would send out a message.'

'A good call, Guv.' She looked it up on her phone. 'It's about ten minutes away from the new building. Which one do we go to?'

'All the available security in Scotland will be focused on the new school. On the other hand, if we're right, they're at the wrong place and there won't be anybody else at the old school. If I was a lone gunman wanting to get a clear shot at somebody, an empty playground would seem ideal. Let's at least swing past there.'

'OK, then you need to take the next on the left, Guv.' Mona directed them through the streets under the guidance of the map on her phone. After three or four minutes of driving through tenemented residential streets, she told Paterson to stop. 'It says we're here.'

He looked around. 'I don't see a school.'

'There's a shop over there,' said Mona. 'I'll go and ask.'

'Make it quick,' said Paterson. 'We could just be wasting time here.'

The man behind the counter looked up as she walked in. 'Yes, love?'

'Is there an old primary school around here?'

He laughed. 'That's funny. You're the second person in half an hour to ask me that.'

'Was it a young woman who asked?'

He nodded. 'Yes, a lassie with long dark hair. She was in about twenty minutes ago. Is she all right? She was a bit upset when she was here.' He did a little mime of someone crying.

'She's not OK, and I need to catch up with her. How do I get to the school?'

The shopkeeper seemed to grasp the urgency of the situation. 'Head down to the end of the street. There's a little lane on your right that takes you straight to it. Best of luck.'

She ran back into the street and waved to the others to follow her. She jogged towards the end of the street, and a minute later Paterson caught up with her. 'What's the story?'

'Catriona was also here asking where the school was.'

'Then we're in the right place, thank God. How do we get there?'

'We turn right at the end of the street.'

As the shopkeeper had suggested, there was a narrow lane that ran along the side of the last tenement in the street, bordered on the other side by a six-foot-high wall. At the end of it Mona could see the school building, its windows boarded up.

'Can you get into the school from the other side?' asked Paterson.

'I guess so. This can't be the main way to get to it.'

Mona hurried forward, only to be pulled her to a halt by her boss.

'You need to go back.'

'Don't be ridiculous, Guv. Catriona's out there like a sitting duck.'

'So are we. We've no flak jackets, or helmets or anything.'

'Bryce isn't aiming for us.'

'We don't know that. Also, he doesn't have to be aiming for you and me for us to get hit. I'm not sending my staff into that.'

Alfie caught up with them. 'What's the story?'

'We don't know, but we need to assume that a man with a gun and a grudge is heading towards the school from the other direction. Mona – get on the phone to Stuttle and get firearms officers over here.'

She pulled out her phone, then stopped. 'There she is, Guv.'

'Aw, fuck. Keep hold of her, Alfie.'

Paterson took off in Catriona's direction. Mona tried to follow him only to find Alfie's hand firmly clasped round her arm. 'Sorry, but your boss is talking sense. I'm phoning Stuttle.'

Mona kept half an ear on Alfie's phone call, but most of her brain was focused on watching Paterson and Catriona. She looked deeply unhappy to see him, pushing him away from her while she looked around, her long hair flying out behind her.

'They're on the way.' Alfie put his phone away. His grip on her arm had not relaxed in the slightest. 'She's not too pleased to see your boss, is she?'

'Bryce probably told her to come alone.'

'How long do you think—' began Alfie, then broke off

as they heard the sound of a car approaching at speed. 'I don't think that's the cavalry.'

'Shit.' Mona watched in horror as the car pulled up beside Catriona and Paterson. The muzzle of a gun appeared through the window.

Paterson threw himself on top of Catriona. There was a strange sound, not quite a gunshot, and the car screeched off again.

'Guv!' Mona finally broke free from Alfie, and ran towards her boss.

Catriona was screaming, a guttural cry, over and over again.

'I'm OK, Mona,' said Paterson. 'Get the reg.'

She chased after the car, but it was gone. *Probably false plates anyway*, she thought.

Alfie had his arm around Catriona. She'd stopped screaming, but was now sobbing, making no effort to wipe her tears away.

She realised that Paterson hadn't stood up. He was still lying on the ground, his leg sticking out at an abnormal angle.

'You OK, Guv?'

'Bastard shot me. Did you get the plates?'

She shook her head. 'Sorry, Guv.'

'Ah, well, probably false anyway.'

'There's not much blood, but he might have been shot.' Alfie was on the phone, presumably talking to the ambulance service.

'Of course I've been shot,' yelled Paterson, over his shoulder. 'Just not with a proper gun. I think it was an air rifle or something like that. I'm going to kill Bryce when I catch up with him.'

'We still need to find him,' said Mona.

'Talk to the girl.' Paterson was now speaking through gritted teeth. 'If she's ever going to speak to us it's now.'

'Catriona, what's going on?'

The girl looked up at her, tears streaming down her face.

'My colleague's just got himself shot trying to protect you. The least you can do is speak to us.'

'Come on now, lass.' Alfie squeezed Catriona's shoulder. 'Tell us how Bryce got in touch with you.'

'I knew something bad was going to happen.' Catriona was in danger of hyperventilating again.

'Breathe, Catriona.' Mona forced herself to be patient. 'Deep breath.'

Catriona made an effort to control herself. 'Someone sent me a mobile phone through the post.' She pulled a small phone out of her jeans pocket and handed it to Mona. 'I thought it was a mistake or that it was some kind of promotion or something. Then the messages started, saying things that could only be meant for me.'

'How long ago was this?'

'About a week. The messages were horrible, saying that they would get my mum and my dad and my sister, I should be a good girl and do as I was told.'

'Did you talk to anyone about this?'

'The message said not to, but I was so scared I had to speak to someone.'

'So, who did you call?'

'When the . . . *incident* happened I was given a contact phone number for a man named Ian and told if I ever needed anything, he was the person I should contact. I kept ringing his phone, but I didn't get any answer.'

If the Ian in question was Ian Jacobsen there was a good reason why not, seeing as he was off on an extended period of *rest and recuperation*. Someone should have been monitoring his calls, Bob Ellis or one of other men in suits. She'd so look forward to pointing out this monstrous cock-up to him later.

'I tried Paul Shore's number, but I didn't get any answer there either,' Catriona said. 'Then I saw on the TV that he'd been shot, and I was too scared to speak to anyone else.'

Mona scrolled through the texts. The early ones didn't make any sense. 'What do these messages mean?'

'I can't say.'

Mona sighed, and scrolled on. They became increasingly threatening, until she reached the final message she'd received earlier that day telling her to come to the school.

'What will happen to me now?'

'You come back with me to the flat,' said Alfie, 'and you do as you are told this time.'

'What about my parents and sister?'

'We'll contact the local police, but I think your part in all this is over,' said Mona. 'You've done what he wanted you to.'

She nodded, miserably.

The sound of sirens could be heard.

'Better late than never,' said Mona, as half a dozen police cars turned into the street.

'I'm getting her out of here,' said Alfie. 'I'll commandeer one of the cars to give us a lift. Come on, Catriona.' He helped her to her feet.

As she walked past Paterson she stopped and knelt down. 'I'm so, so, sorry.' Her tears started again. 'Thank you.'

Paterson grunted in return.

7

'Mona still not answering her phone?' asked Maitland.

'No, and neither is Mr Paterson.' This worried Bernard. Given their current circumstances, he'd have thought that his colleagues would respond to his messages PDQ. The only thing he could think of was that they were experiencing difficulties of their own.

'So, we're just going to sit here until they bother to get in touch?'

'What do you suggest?'

'We can have a look at it. I'm not saying we should storm the place, but we could at least scope it out.'

'Even for you, Maitland, that's a ridiculous idea. I don't know what's there, but I'm pretty sure it'll be firearms, and we don't know how Bryce would respond to us just turning up on his doorstep. To say nothing of the fact that it's owned by a rock star who by all accounts is less than stable. I'm not getting myself shot just so you can look macho.'

Maitland tutted. 'I'm not trying to look macho, I'm just fed up sitting around waiting for Bryce to make a move.'

'*Why* do you think Bryce is tormenting us?' asked Marcus.

''Cos he's nuts,' said Maitland, irritably.

'Yes, obviously,' said Marcus. 'But why is he bothering to torment us with this low-level harassment? If he's annoyed with us he could just shoot us.'

It was a good point. There was no way that Bernard's brain could continue to clutch at straws. The evidence was overwhelmingly pointing in the direction that Scott Kerr had worked out what they had done, and now they had to suffer. The only thing worse than their current torment was the fact that when it stopped it would be replaced by something much worse, maybe even fatal. He wondered whether to raise it with the others. Marcus had been complicit in their deception, although with any luck Scott Kerr wouldn't know this. He looked over and caught his friend's eye. Marcus grinned at him. Best not to worry him, at least, not yet.

'Maybe Bryce's trying to make a point through Arthusian Fall lyrics. Is there anything about smoke?' asked Maitland.

Marcus looked excited. '"And smoke shall cover the Earth". It's a line from the title track of *A Message from the Doomsday Police*.'

Maitland sat up straight. 'What about tyre slashing? Do they say anything about that?'

'No, I don't think so.' Marcus thought for a second. 'Unless it's more generally under one of their lyrics about the failures of the modern world.'

'I think that anything that's ever happened to anyone, ever, could be interpreted through the prism of lyrics from Arthusian Fall.' Bernard wished they would all shut up. His phone beeped to indicate a text message, and Lucy's number flashed up.

'Finally Mona gets in touch,' said Maitland. 'What's she saying?'

Bernard read and reread the message. 'It's not from Mona. It's from Bryce.'

There was a second's silence, then they both leapt to their feet so they could look at the phone.

'What does it say?'

'*Hi, Bernard, Bryce here. We have Lucy at the factory. You know where we will be. Bring Maitland and Marcus. Contact the police and I will,*' his voice broke, '*kill her.*' He stood up and headed for the door. 'We need to go.'

Maitland grabbed his jacket and pulled him back. 'Now who is being ridiculous? It's a trap, Bernard. We wander in there, we're not coming out again.'

'But—'

'At least try and track Lucy down. She might not even be there.'

'Bryce was ringing from her phone.'

'Oh.' Maitland thought for a moment. 'He could have stolen her phone, or be hijacking her number. He's a technology guru.'

'I'll phone the museum.' The number rang and rang without being picked up. He slammed the phone down in frustration.

'Does she have a home landline?' asked Marcus.

'No.' His phone beeped again and he snatched it up. '*In case you think I'm joking.*' There was a grainy picture of Lucy, a gun pressed against her head. She looked understandably terrified.

'Right, I'm going. You two can do what you like.'

Maitland did not let go of his arm. 'Bernard, we can't do anything for her. If we go rushing into an isolated factory with nobody knowing where we are, she's going to end up dead, and so are we. Marcus – tell him.'

'Yes.' Marcus nodded. 'Probably. Although Bryce

hasn't actually killed anybody. He's shot people, but he hasn't actually aimed to kill. Maybe my subconscious still has some affectionate feelings for him which are clouding my judgement, but I really don't think he wants to murder anyone. I think he's trying to get a message out, and maybe he needs our help to do that.'

Maitland looked at them each in turn. 'Are you both insane?'

'No. Just considerably braver than you are.' Bernard stared at Maitland.

'I'm not falling for that. You're just trying to psych me into coming with you.' He paused. 'And I am every bit as brave as you. Braver in fact.'

'Right, you can drive.'

Maitland watched his colleagues pull their coats on. 'Well, I'm phoning Mona as soon as we get there.'

'Whatever. Let's just go.'

8

'I'll come to the hospital with you, Guv.'

'You will not!' Paterson was upright, but appeared to be staying so only by gripping tightly to the door of the ambulance.

'But we don't know how badly hurt you're—'

'I'll tell you exactly how badly hurt I am! I've got a flesh wound to the upper thigh, that's all.'

She exchanged a glance with the paramedic, a small wiry man in his late fifties. She would have said the Guv's injury was a bit higher up his body, and suspected that this was the real reason Paterson wanted to travel solo.

'But, Guv ...'

'What about the other pair? They'll not be coping without any management input.'

'I'm sure they're fine.' She pulled her phone out to reinforce her argument and saw several missed calls from both Bernard and Maitland, and one from Cameron Stuttle. She wondered what her HET colleagues' emergency was. Knowing her teammates, it could be anything ranging from their having located the factory, to complaints about Marguerite. Paterson had a point. Without some kind of management directing their every move, they were like a bunch of headless chickens, running around annoying each other.

'Take the car keys.' He dug carefully into his trouser pocket.

She admitted defeat, and took them. 'Maybe I should head back. Do you want me to let your wife know?'

'God, no.' Paterson looked horrified. 'If this one,' he gestured to the paramedic, 'does a half decent job, I can be home by tea time without her having to worry.'

The paramedic grinned. 'Step into my chariot, sir. We'll have you back sitting comfortably on that upper thigh in no time.'

Mona ran up the steps into the building, her nerves still jangling from the day's events.

'Hello?' She shouted up the stairs to her colleagues. 'You won't believe what happened today—'

She broke off as she realised no-one was responding. The building was eerily quiet. She'd been in the building alone before, either when she'd been working very early or very late, but there was a different quality to this silence. It felt more – what was the word? Lonely? Melancholy? She shook herself. She was being silly, probably unnerved by Paterson being shot.

'Marguerite?' She stuck her head around the door of the Admin department, and found it empty. She'd have been surprised if anyone, Marguerite aside, had been working. She wouldn't have turned up for work in their position – why risk getting shot? And, of course, why turn down the chance for a few extra state-sponsored days' holiday?

She hurried up the stairs to the HET office and flung open the door. The room was just as deserted as the rest of the building. Maybe all that her colleagues had been phoning about was to say that they were going home.

Throwing herself onto a chair, she discarded her coat and bag at her feet, and decided to tackle Stuttle first, before tracking down the others. He answered almost immediately.

'Stuttle's phone.'

The unexpected voice took her by surprise.

'Oh, I was looking for Cameron Stuttle.'

'Well, I hope you've got his home number, because as of about an hour ago he was placed on gardening leave. Is there anything that I can help with?'

The voice sounded familiar, but it took her a moment to realise who it was. *Bob Ellis.*

'No, it's fine.' She wanted to get off the phone as quickly as possible. There was no way she was discussing the day's events with him.

'Are you sure I can't help?' He laughed. 'Mona?'

She hung up, trying to get her thoughts straight. Had Carlotta finally finished scapegoating Stuttle and hung him out to dry? She'd thought Carlotta would wait until the Bryce situation had been resolved, which of course, it could have been. She debated phoning Bob back and asking if they'd captured Bryce, but decided against it. He probably wouldn't tell her.

Stuttle sacked. Or on gardening leave, at least, which was probably the first step along the road to getting your jotters. What did his sacking mean for the North Edinburgh HET? It was hard to put a spin on it that was positive for them, although one thing was sure. Her chance of ever gaining Milwood Orders clearance had been buried in the grave next to the remains of Cameron Stuttle's career.

She looked round the room, her sense of unease growing. Where *were* Bernard and Maitland? She dialled Bernard's number, but got no answer. The same happened when she dialled Maitland's. After a moment's thought she also phoned Marcus, and got no response. As a last resort she pressed Carole's number, but it went straight to voicemail. Her colleagues' computers were still on. Maitland rarely switched his off, often forgetting to close it down, even at the end of the day. Bernard, on the other hand, was painstakingly particular about turning his off when he left the office, both to save on energy and to prevent the office burning down through an electrical fire. If his computer was still on, he'd left in a hurry.

With a quick look to check that no-one was about to walk in on her, she slid into Bernard's seat and pressed the spacebar on his computer. The 'Enter Password' box came up and using one finger she typed in *Lucy4321Museum*. In addition to fire safety, Bernard was also meticulous about information security, using a strong and difficult to guess password. However, he'd been less careful about checking that his colleagues weren't watching him type said password, just in case they ever had to find out what he was up to at some point in the future.

The screen cleared to reveal the last thing that Bernard had been looking at. It was a Google satellite image of something. She cautiously zoomed in, worrying in case she accidentally lost the page, and with it, any clue to what her colleagues were up to. It looked like an industrial site. She scrolled slowly around it. Had Bernard struck it lucky in finding the factory recently purchased by the members of Arthusian Fall? That could explain the flurry of missed calls. She looked again around the deserted office. Where were her colleagues now?

They wouldn't have been so stupid as to go looking for the factory. Stupid didn't begin to describe it, lunacy would be better. No, they wouldn't have done that. She wouldn't put it past Maitland to go out for a sneak peek at it, but Bernard's entire life revolved around minimising the risk to his person from his daily HET duties. He'd no more go off in search of their missing rock star's base than he would wander into the lions' enclosure at Edinburgh Zoo.

Her earlier certainty began to crumble, and she scribbled down the postcode. She'd better check this out, although if they had gone looking on their own she was going to kill them.

Unless Bryce and his friends already had.

9

'Bernard, don't be a dick. You can't go in there.'

Bernard ignored his colleague and got out, slamming the car door behind him. 'I'm not leaving Lucy in there on her own.'

'Getting yourself shot isn't going to help her.' Maitland ran round the side of the car, and stood in front of him. 'Let's get some backup.'

'Bryce said he would shoot her if we brought the police. I'm not going to let that happen. I'm going into that building, I'm going to find her, and I'm going to get her out. You stay here if you want.' He stepped round Maitland and crossed the road.

'I'm still calling for backup,' said Maitland.

Bernard kept walking. For all his tough talk, his legs were trembling.

Behind him he heard Marcus say, 'I'm not sure we can get reception here.'

He walked swiftly up the lane to the factory before he could change his mind. He resisted the temptation to look at his surroundings, in case he saw anything that caused his nerve to fail, and send him scampering back down the road. He just hoped nobody took the opportunity to shoot him before he even found Lucy. He reached the door in safety, and slowly turned the handle. To his surprise it opened. Maybe he shouldn't have been surprised. He had, after all, been invited.

He slipped into the building, the metal door clanging shut behind him, wondering if Bryce would be annoyed that Maitland and Marcus weren't with him. He totally understood their unwillingness to wander into the unknown. If it had been anyone other than Lucy, wild horses wouldn't have dragged him in here.

Should he announce himself? He considered shouting out a hello, but decided Bryce was probably well aware of his arrival. He looked round the hallway. It was like standing in a giant tin box, although judging by the puddles on the floor, it was a box that wasn't quite wind and water tight. It was lighter inside the building than he had hoped for. He'd brought a torch, but there was enough light from the cracks in the roof to see by.

He pushed open the first door he came to and found himself in a huge room, which was flooded with light from the windows in the roof. In its previous life it had probably held a whole host of factory equipment. Now, aside from a pool of water the size of a small lake, it was completely empty. Bernard could see a couple of doors on the far side of the room so headed in their direction, in the hope that one of them would open on to a room with Lucy sitting in it, unhurt, unharmed, and very pleased to see him.

The first door he opened led into a space which was only about three feet square, and had probably been a cupboard in its working life, but the next one led to a corridor. Bernard scanned up and down it, but couldn't see any sign of life.

'Hello?'

There was no answer. He almost wished that Bryce would leap out just to break the unbearable silence. He let out a quiet, slightly hysterical laugh at the thought: Scotland's Most Wanted leaping out of a crevice and shouting *boo*. There were two further doors, one of which he assumed had to lead to Lucy. He headed right, and turned the handle. This time the room wasn't empty. A blonde woman in combat fatigues was sitting on an old sofa in the middle of the room, reading a book and listening to music. She must have had some high-quality headphones on, because she didn't look up. He walked into the room, until he was firmly in her line of sight.

She jumped. 'Who the hell are you?'

He half-noted an American accent, but 95 per cent of his attention was taken up looking at the walls of the room. From floor to ceiling there were metal cupboards screwed to the wall. Behind each of their slatted doors, he could see a selection of guns. The room was practically wallpapered with firearms.

The woman pushed her headphones down onto her neck. 'I asked who the hell you are?'

He tried to look non-threatening. Even in his current situation he didn't want to alarm a woman on her own, who might assume that he meant her some physical harm. Although he had to admit she looked more annoyed than alarmed. He lowered his gaze and realised that the gun she was pointing directly at him was probably contributing to her feelings of control over the situation. It was much smaller and less deadly-looking than some of the specimens mounted on the wall, but it was a small space and he was pretty sure she wouldn't miss if she was aiming for him.

'I'm Bernard. I'm here to see Bryce.'

'Bryce?' She looked surprised. 'Bryce has no right to

be inviting people here. Colin!' She yelled loudly over his shoulder.

Rapidly approaching footsteps could be heard in the hall outside. He turned and saw a man who looked almost familiar. He was tall, well built, and sported a neat grey beard. Long silver hair was tied back in a ponytail. In common with the American woman, he was dressed head to toe in camouflage clothing. Also like her, he was carrying a fairly substantial gun.

Colin Karma.

Rock star.

Heavily armed.

Possibly also mad.

'Who the hell is this?'

He looked furious, although Bernard was pleased to see that he wasn't actually pointing his gun at him, unlike his wife. That situation could, of course, change at any moment.

'He says he's here to see Bryce.'

'Bryce? How did you even get in?'

'The door was unlocked.'

Karma looked so furious that Bernard almost took an involuntary step backwards, before he realised that the anger was not directed at him but at Bryce.

'What's he playing at? He can't go inviting random people up here.'

'I'm here to see Lucy.'

They looked at each other. 'Who?'

Bernard fought a rising sense of panic. 'Lucy. She's my girlfriend. Bryce said he had kidnapped her and I was to come here.' He knew that he sounded crazy, but he was also aware that he was probably not the only one in the room who was insane.

There was a long silence, while the two camouflaged

individuals looked at each other. The woman's gun was still pointing directly at him.

Colin spoke to the woman. 'When did you last see Bryce?'

She shrugged. 'Not since yesterday.'

'You come here on your own?' Karma gestured at him with gun.

'Yes,' he said, then panicked slightly as he realised they would find the car and his colleagues with the most cursory of checks of the surrounding area.

'Frisk him,' said Colin.

The woman got to her feet and patted him up and down.

'Please,' he said, his arms raised above his head. 'I just want to find Lucy.'

'We don't know anything about that.' Colin turned to the woman. 'Bryce is out of control. What are we going to do with him?'

'You know what I think about that. Where's his sidekick?'

'Don't know.'

There was a loud crash from somewhere else within the building.

'I don't like this at all,' said the woman.

Colin headed back out through the door. 'You keep an eye on this one. I'm going out to find out what's going on.'

The door clanged shut behind him. The woman, who Bernard had decided was probably the second Mrs Karma, not quite as close to divorce as they'd previously thought, kept her eye and her gun firmly fixed on him.

'So, Lucy isn't here?' This was the only possible bright spot on the horizon.

'Shut up,' she replied.

There was a further crash from outside. The woman looked at him and then at the door, obviously torn between investigating and standing guard. Curiosity won out.

'Don't move,' she said. She dived over to the door in one lithe movement, and stood there, listening. After a second or two she threw open the door, and stepped out into the corridor, gun aloft and poised. There was a squeal from outside, followed by silence.

Bernard fully expected to see Bryce appear. Please God let him be about to say that the Lucy thing was all a ruse to get him here, and that the love of his life was safe and well back at her home.

A figure appeared in the doorway. It was not the person he had been anticipating.

Bernard stared at the new arrival, then slowly closed his eyes. 'This is a really bad time. Is there any chance we could do this later?'

10

The roads were getting narrower, with fewer cars passing her with every turning she took. She'd been travelling along the latest B-road for about ten minutes now, and in that time she hadn't seen a single other vehicle. This whole journey had the feel of a wild goose chase. All she had was a postcode, and in somewhere like this, that could cover a big area. What was she even looking for out here?

Fortunately, just as her GPS was telling her she had reached her destination she saw a *For Sale* sign, with a large red *Sold* pinned across it. It probably wouldn't be a good idea to park right next to it and alert anyone to her arrival, so she drove past and pulled off the road into a lay-by, only to find there was another car already there. Without hesitating she put the car into reverse; there was too much she didn't know about this scenario to assess whether she was in danger. Her foot was on the accelerator to drive off again when the door to the other car opened and the lanky form of Maitland emerged from it. She cut the engine and got out.

'Mona, thank God. Bernard's gone all die-hard. He's headed into the factory.'

The outbreak of lunacy was even worse than she'd feared. 'On his own? Why?'

'He got a message from Bryce saying he'd kidnapped

Lucy and was holding her here. It could be bullshit but the text came from Lucy's phone and we've not managed to track her down.'

'Why didn't you call me?' Her colleagues really could not be left on their own for a minute without some kind of disaster striking.

'Because I was driving, Bernard was pissing about trying to get hold of Lucy on his phone and Marcus was just, well, being a dick as usual.'

'Marcus is here as well? Where is he now?'

'Wandering around the countryside trying to get a mobile phone signal. We're in a black hole here.'

They looked at each other. 'What do we do now?' asked Maitland.

'I can answer that one,' said a voice behind them. 'You put your hands on your head, and stand against the car. Don't turn around.'

Maitland muttered something under his breath, but did as he was told. Mona slowly followed suit. 'Who the hell are you?' she asked, her eyes fixed on the car.

'I'm a man with a gun.'

The voice was youthful, and Mona wondered if it was a bluff.

'Bollocks you are,' said Maitland, turning round. 'Oh, right, you do have a gun.' He snapped back to face the car again.

'Nice one, Maitland.' Mona sneaked a glance behind her, and saw for herself that there was indeed a man pointing a gun at both of them. He had a hoodie up over his head but even so it was obvious to see that . . .

'What happened to your face?' asked Maitland.

'Shut up.'

Mona saw the gun arm wobble a little. This was no

professional killer. This was a university dropout with a bad attitude to women, and a head full of Bryce's nonsense. This was the boy who had led Blair Taylor astray, Blair whose remains were now lying in a mortuary in Edinburgh. She wondered how thoroughly Bryce had trained him.

'Did you have a little accident with your bomb-making perhaps?' asked Maitland. 'Little experiment with your friend Mr Karma go ka-boom in your face?'

'Shut up, I told you!' His voice was agitated. Maitland's taunting was obviously unsettling him, but she just hoped it wasn't going to get them both shot. Maitland caught her eye, and gave a slight nod of his head in her direction, which she took to mean get ready for action. She decided to step up the pressure.

'Anyway, nice to meet you, Aaron. Your mum's been missing you. Remember her? The woman who sacrificed everything to get you an education, which you've pretty much thrown back in her face?'

'Aaron?' The gunman gave a snort. 'I'm not Aaron. He was weak. He—'

Maitland spun round and aimed a flying kick at the gunman's arm. The gun flew out of his hand and bounced down the road, fortunately without going off. Maitland made a grab for the gunman, and Mona made a grab for the weapon. Within seconds, the gun was secured, and Maitland had their captor up against the car with an arm up his back. Bryce might have done an excellent job teaching his protégé to shoot straight, but he hadn't prepared him for the most elementary of police moves.

'So,' she began, walking round the car so that she could get a better look at him, the gun resting lightly in her hand, 'by the process of elimination, am I correct in thinking that you are Blair Taylor?'

He said nothing.

'Your mother and father are at their wits' end,' said Maitland. 'Jesus, Blair, you should see the state your ma is in. She's getting through the day by chucking back pills. And when did your dad's hair go completely white? How could you do this to them?'

'My parents are idiots. They've got no idea what's really happening to the world.'

'They didn't deserve to be put through all this,' said Maitland. 'You could have paid them a visit, let them know you're still alive.'

He made a sound that was half laugh and half hiss. 'Go home looking like this? I'm a fucking freak in case you hadn't noticed.'

'We'll make space for this crybaby stuff later.' Mona jumped in. They were wasting time. Full marks to Bernard for his bravery, but she doubted he had much in the way of a game plan. She needed to get inside, fast. 'First of all, how many people are in there?'

Blair's free hand was inching towards his leg. She grabbed it and frisked him down. 'Second gun in your sock. Very nice.' She shoved it into her bag. 'Now answer the question – who's in there?'

He said nothing and Maitland put a little bit more pressure on his arm. He let out a cry. 'Colin and his wife, and Bryce. Now let me go.'

'What about Lucy?'

'I don't know who you're talking about.'

Maitland put some more pressure on his arm. 'Sure?'

'I don't know her.' His voice was high-pitched. 'I swear to God it's only Colin, Lana, and Bryce in there.'

'Any guns?'

'Guns?' He laughed. 'Guns? There's a shitload of them. You've got no chance once you get in there.'

'We'll see about that,' said Mona, with a confidence she really didn't feel. 'Maitland, get him tied up.'

He stared back at her. 'What with?'

'There must be something in the boot of the car.' She trained the gun on Blair. 'You can let him go. Believe me, I will shoot him if he moves.'

Maitland opened the boot and reached around. 'There's nothing.'

Blair smirked at her, and she cursed the inadequately supplied pool cars. An idea struck her. 'Try the first aid kit.'

'Are you planning to Elastoplast my hands together?'

'Shut up!' Maitland pulled Blair's hands behind him and wrapped a length of bandage around them. 'Sorted.' He looked doubtfully at his handiwork.

'Bryce will kill the pair of you. He will . . .' He struggled for a strong enough word. 'Eviscerate you.'

'Whatever that means,' said Mona. She turned back in the direction of the factory. Where was Bryce? Inside the building, or somewhere close at hand?

'What are we going to do with him?' asked Maitland. 'Put him in the boot?'

'No, he might suffocate. We'll have to lock him in the car. You'll have to stay here and keep an eye on him.'

'What are you going to do?'

She nodded over in the direction of the *For Sale* sign. 'I'm going to have a look around.'

Maitland pulled another bandage out of the first aid kit, and started wrapping it around Blair's hands.

'You're going to cut off my circulation!'

'Shut up.' He turned back to Mona. 'You can't go in there on your own.'

'You let Bernard go in there on his own.'

'Let him go?' He tutted. 'Hardly. I tried everything I could to stop him setting off on this bloody suicide mission.'

'It's still a suicide mission,' said Blair. 'You're both dead.'

'Think we've had enough from you, thanks.' Maitland shoved him head first into the car and locked the doors.

'Take this.' She gave him one of the guns they'd taken off Blair. 'You know what to do with that?'

'I've had firearms training.' He looked worryingly pleased to be holding an actual gun, turning it over on his palm to admire it.

'Don't shoot anyone unless you really have to. Also, don't shoot yourself.'

'No worries. I'm a highly skilled firearms operative when it comes to hitting red circles on paper outlines of people. I'm sure real life's not so very different. What's your game plan?'

'Get in there, get Bernard, and get out.'

'And Lucy?'

She thought for a moment. She really had no idea. 'Her too, if she's actually there. I'll play it by ear.'

11

'Do this later?' Scott Kerr looked incredulous. 'Are you taking the ...' He tailed off as he caught sight of the rest of the room. His look of annoyance was replaced by a grin so wide it reminded Bernard of the Joker in *Batman*. 'What is this place?'

'I'm not entirely sure, but I really think we should get out of here.'

Kerr didn't look as if he was about to move. 'I underestimated you, Bernard, I really did. Man, look at these guns!' He spun round, then abruptly stopped, his face a few inches from Bernard's. He wasn't smiling any more. 'When I heard Alessandra was still alive, I was raging. I don't mind telling you, that my first thought was to track you down and teach you a lesson, you know what I'm saying?'

'Yes, but—'

'Then I thought, why not have a bit of fun with him and his mates first? The fuckers have messed me around plenty, so why not give them a wee taste of their own medicine? Make their life a little bit uncomfortable, you know what I'm saying? So, I've been following you around these past few days, playing a few wee tricks and that on you and Mona, did you notice?' The mile-wide grin was back. 'Did you get that it was me? The smoke bomb in your office, Mona's car tyres, and her front door?'

'I did, and really we need to—'

'And, don't take this the wrong way, pal, but you really are a boring bastard. Work, home, work, home.'

'Yes, I'm very boring but we need to—'

'So, when I was following your car out here, I thought that was you off for a wee picnic in the countryside with your pals. I was going to have a bit of fun making you all beg for your lives over your cucumber sandwiches and ginger beer. But instead,' he took a deep breath, 'instead you've brought me all this. Handed me all these lovelies on a plate.' He did a further 360-degree turn, the better to take in the full wonder of the place.

'Seriously,' Bernard looked nervously at the door, 'the people in this place are nuts and dripping in guns. You need to get out of here.'

'Sounds like my kind of people, to be honest. I'm amongst my ain folk here.' He still didn't move. 'But if you're talking about the bitch in the camouflage outfit, I just knocked her unconscious.'

Bernard's heart skipped a beat. 'Her husband's going to be really, really, pissed off.'

'Yeah, probably, especially if he's that big dude also in camouflage gear, because I used one of the bitch's keys to lock the door he went through, so he can't get back in.' He stared at the weapons on the wall. 'Now help me get this gear shifted out of here and into my car, and I promise I'll only break one of your legs instead of both of them.'

Bernard's as yet unbroken legs went from under him, and he collapsed to the floor.

'Come on now, Bernard, you must have known this day was coming. You couldn't really have believed that I would fall for the stunt that you and that old dyke

Annemarie pulled. Now you help me with this gear, tell me where my missing tart is, and I might just settle for slapping you about a bit.'

'I don't know where she is.' This wasn't entirely true. Bernard hoped to God that he could stick to this lie, whatever Kerr had planned for him.

'What about Annemarie, does she know? If I give her a kicking would *she* talk to me?'

'Leave Annemarie alone.'

'Too late.' He grinned. 'Your flat's also in a bit of a state, I have to say. Remind me, what is it that gets out blood stains? Is it salt or white wine?'

Bernard closed his eyes and weighed up who he was more worried about. Scott Kerr was easily the scariest person he had ever met, and would have no qualms whatsoever about beating him to a pulp until he gave up whatever knowledge he had of Alessandra's whereabouts. However, Kerr was a rational individual and after he was done with him, he might well let him live. The Karmas, on the other hand, were preppers awaiting the apocalypse. Who knew how trigger-happy they were? Added to which, if Bryce found them all here, how he would react? He couldn't risk him hurting Lucy. 'Mr Kerr, I can't impress on you too highly that you need to get out of here.'

Kerr grinned at him again, and rattled the cage of the nearest gun cupboard. 'Pity these are locked or we could be out of here a lot sooner. And whatever it is that you are worrying about, Bernard, don't fret on my behalf, I'll be just fine.' He opened his coat and Bernard could see a gun tucked into the waistband of his jeans. He admired his optimism but one handgun was not going to be a match for the arsenal that the survivalists could lay their hands on. 'Now where do you think they keep the keys?'

Something strange was happening over his head. Bernard looked up, and could see the roof moving slowly up and down. He had a horrible feeling that merely locking a door behind him wouldn't be enough to keep Karma out.

'It doesn't matter where the keys are, because we're not about to touch the guns, are we?' he said loudly in the direction of the ceiling.

'Speak for yourself.'

The ceiling vibrations were increasing. With an almighty ripping sound, one of the panels gave way in a cloud of dust. Bernard closed his eyes and tried not to think about asbestos. The missing panel released fourteen stone of angry survivalist, who landed in a direct hit on top of Scott Kerr. With a knee in Kerr's back he whipped out a revolver. 'What's your fucking game?'

'I'm sure we can sort all this out amicably,' said Bernard, in a doomed attempt at diplomacy.

Scott Kerr seemed less than keen on this idea and stabbed Karma in the ankle. Karma let go of him, and he leapt to his feet. The rock star was quick, though, and despite his injury, grabbed Kerr and pointed his gun straight at his head. 'I'm going to kill you.'

The fleeting thought went through Bernard's mind that at least one of his problems might be about to be solved.

'They'll never even find your body out here.' Karma cocked the trigger.

Bernard gave a swift undercut to Karma's arm. The gun went up in the air and shot through the ceiling. The sound was deafening in the small space, and he clasped his hands to his ears.

'Oh God, please tell me there wasn't anyone else up

269

there?' He stared at the ceiling half expecting a red stain to appear.

There was another gun shot. Bernard's hands went to his ears again; the ringing sound was unbearable. He turned round slowly and looked down to see Karma lying on the ground. Half of his face was missing. Bernard closed his eyes, desperately fighting the urge to throw up. 'What did you just do?'

Kerr was already on his phone, looking for backup.

'We need an ambulance,' said Bernard.

'Bit late for that, don't you think? I just blew his fucking head off. The reception here sucks.' Kerr shoved his phone back in his pocket. 'Right, it looks like it's just you and me then.' Kerr started playing with the keys on Karma's belt. 'Which one do you think unlocks these little beauties?' He waved a hand in the direction of the gun cupboards.

'I'm not helping you.' Bernard took a step towards the door.

'Oh, but you are.' Kerr lifted his gun a fraction of an inch in his direction. 'You're not going anywhere.'

12

Mona surveyed her options. The tarmacked road to the factory stretched in front of her, long and straight. If she went that way she'd be there in five minutes, maximum. She'd also be an easy target if anyone was keeping watch and looking to defend their territory. Bernard might have had a formal invitation to visit, but there was nothing to say that the same welcome would be extended to her. The other option was cutting through the woods that surrounded the factory, though from what she'd come to know about Bryce she wouldn't be surprised if he had booby-trapped any approach to his base. The trees could be full of unpleasant surprises.

She tossed a coin in her head which came down on the side of the woodland, and she picked her way very gingerly through the vegetation. She stopped when she was level with the building. From what she could see from her hiding place, the front door was open, and she guessed Bernard had gone in that way, without stopping to firmly close it behind him. That wasn't like him, but obviously a sign of the stress he was under in trying to get to Lucy. She could attempt to follow him in, but it was a bit too obvious for her liking.

The trees continued beyond the factory, so she carried on picking her way through, in an attempt to get a look at the back of the building. There might be a more discreet way to get in. There were no windows in the building which was a blessing, as no-one could look out and see her, but, of course, it did limit the number of ways to get in. The only possibility seems to be some kind of fire exit, though tampering around with that would definitely attract somebody's attention. Or she could try ...

'Hello, Mona.'

The accent was Northern Irish.

'Hello, Bryce.'

'Probably best if you don't turn around, because I would have to shoot you.'

Twice in ten minutes. This was turning into a theme. She suspected that Bryce couldn't be disarmed with a swift kick to his gun hand.

'How do I know you're actually armed?'

'You don't, but take it from me even if I wasn't, I could have you dead within seconds. Assuming I wanted you dead. I could also provide a range of injuries from broken limbs to full-on paralysis.'

'I get the picture.' She believed him, and had no desire to find out exactly which level of injury he would choose to inflict on her. 'Who are you, Bryce?'

'I'm an IT officer. Sci-fi fan. Friend to Marcus.'

'Threat to the state? Special operative gone rogue?'

He just laughed.

'OK, answer me a more straightforward question,' she said. 'Why are you out here instead of in there?'

'Well, having extended the invite to Bernard and his chums, I decided to come out and check whether they came alone, as instructed. I did send my, let's call him an assistant, out to look for them, but he didn't come back. You know anything about that?'

She was pretty sure Bryce already knew the answer to that. 'Maybe.'

'Maybe, she says. If I have to find myself another gopher, I'm going to be well pissed off. There's a whole load of training went into that one. I'll probably swing by later and get him back. After all, judging by the motley crew that seem to be dealing with him, I don't think you've brought anyone that can seriously hurt me.'

She began to feel an unwise irritation, which was probably fuelled by adrenaline. 'Why did you want us here anyway?'

'I don't remember inviting you to join us, Mona. I'm not sure what I've got to say to the lads is any of your business.'

'So it's boy talk, is it? If you've got a message for Bernard I'll see that he gets it.'

'Oh, will you now?' He laughed. 'I underestimated you lot, you know. This was supposed to be our bunker. We were settling down for the long haul, but the intrepid investigators from the North Edinburgh HET found us even before we'd had time to unpack the china. We'll have to move on now.'

'You're breaking my heart.'

'It was the last place, wasn't it? Once you'd found that it was easy to track us down. How did you find out about it?'

'I don't know – it was Bernard's doing. Pretty stupid, leaving a body lying there for anyone to stumble across. You're lucky some kids or a dog walker didn't find it.'

'This is what happens when you work with amateurs, Mona.' He gave an exaggerated mock sigh. 'First I knew about the little burial display was when I heard you guys had been talking about it in the office.'

'Our office is still bugged?'

'Yeah, you really ought to have had the office professionally swept, but resources are tight, I know. Added to which, I'm very good at what I do.'

'You can't possibly be doing all this and listening to our conversations with just the four of you.'

'I don't remember saying we were just a lone band of stragglers, Mona. There's plenty more people who share my views. Are you armed, by the way?'

'No.' She cursed herself for having stuck the gun in her bag instead of her pocket. She'd have to work out a way to hold on to it. Being armed felt like the best chance of her and Bernard getting out of here alive.

'Just in case you are lying to me, I'm going to give you a quick frisk down.' He started patting her sides. 'And if I do find out you are ...' He broke off as the sound of a shot rang out.

'Was that ...?' Mona let the word hang, as the sound of a second shot rang out.

Bryce sighed. 'See, as I said, this is what happens if you work with amateurs.'

'If Bernard has been shot I will kill you!'

'Save the hysterics. We'd better go in.'

13

Bernard said 'everybody keep calm' for the third time. This was mainly for his own benefit as Scott Kerr looked as completely and utterly calm as a Zen Buddhist master. Bernard sank back onto the sofa and took several deep breaths.

'Does this look like the kind of key that would open those cupboards to you?' he asked.

Bernard wasn't entirely sure what happened next. There was a bit of a blur in the doorway, and suddenly Scott Kerr's arm was being held halfway up his back, his nose down on the concrete floor.

'Hey, Bernard.'

'Hello, Bryce. And Mona.' He'd never been more pleased to see her. He'd never been more pleased to see anyone. 'Mona. You're here.'

'Are you OK?' she asked.

He nodded. He had no idea if he was OK or not, but he wasn't dead and neither was she, so relative to at least one of the other occupants of the building they were doing well. To his surprise Mona put her arms around him and gave him a lingering hug.

'Break it up, you two. Mona – empty the contents of your handbag on the floor.'

She did as she was told, and Bryce looked at the debris over the top of Scott Kerr's head.

'No gun. Glad to see you weren't lying to me, Mona, and I don't now have to kill you. OK, so, is this the gobshite who's responsible for the two dead people?' asked Bryce.

'Two?' asked Bernard.

'There's a dead woman lying in the corridor,' said Mona. 'I think it's Lana Murray.'

'I never killed her,' said Kerr. 'I just give her a bit of a slap.'

'Yeah, one that caved her head in on the concrete floor,' said Mona.

'Right.' Bryce placed his gun against Scott Kerr's head and cocked the trigger.

'No! Don't shoot him!' Bernard was horrified.

'Why not?'

'Because ...' He didn't actually have an answer to that. Scott Kerr was a despicable human being, who caused misery to anyone unfortunate enough to get mixed up in his world. He'd also just beaten up Annemarie, and had had plans to do the same to him, plans which may only have been temporarily shelved. It was hard to find a compelling argument that he deserved to be spared. 'Just don't shoot him. And take a step back because he still has a knife. He stabbed the last guy in the ankle.'

'Who is he anyway?' asked Bryce, heeding Bernard's advice.

'Scott Kerr.'

'Again, who?' said Bryce.

'Drug dealer.'

'Oh, one of them.' He pulled Kerr up by his hair so he could look at him. 'Bet you thought all your Christmases had come at once, getting a sight of all these guns?' He laughed. 'OK, Mona, can you frisk him for knives and anything else that you might find?'

'Sure.' She patted Kerr down, and removed a knife and a knuckleduster from his trousers.

'Be seeing you about this later, bitch,' he muttered.

Bryce hit him on top of the head with the gun. 'I wouldn't bet on that.' Kerr fell forward, and hit the stone floor with a sickening thump.

'Right, you grab one arm each,' instructed Bryce.

Neither of them moved.

'What are you going to do with him?' asked Mona.

'Stick him in a cupboard for now.' He walked into the corridor, and opened a large metal door. 'Shove him in there.'

'Will he be able to breathe?'

Bryce shrugged. 'Probably.'

'I will absolutely not be party to a man being killed,' said Bernard.

'Do you want me to throw you in there with him?'

'OK, let's calm down,' said Mona.

In response, Bryce pointed a gun at her head. For the first time, it occurred to Bernard that they might not be able to talk their way out of this one, that Bryce might just be too far beyond the bounds of reason to negotiate with.

'Move him.'

They reluctantly dropped Kerr on the floor of the cupboard.

Bryce threw a set of keys at Mona. 'Lock him in.'

She fumbled through a number of different keys until she found one that worked. Bryce gave the handle a try, to make sure she had actually locked it.

'Right, now he's out of the way, we can have that conversation, Bernard.' He pointed to them to return to the gun room.

'I'm not saying anything to you until I've seen that Lucy is safe and well.'

Bryce laughed. 'Seriously? She's not actually here, you eejit. The worst thing that happened to your girlfriend today is that someone mugged her for her phone.' He paused. 'And used the phone to take a picture of her with a gun placed against her head, which I'm willing to allow might have been a little bit traumatic.'

Bernard stared at him. 'Is that true?'

He nodded.

'Oh, thank God.' He sat down heavily on the chair recently vacated by Lana. Mona sat down next to him.

'So, Bernard, Lucy is safe for the moment and will remain so provided that you do exactly what I say.'

'Me? What do you need me for? I can't think of a single skill that I have that you don't already.'

'Yes, but you've got one thing that I've definitely not got, Bernard. You've got credibility.'

Bernard and Mona exchanged a glance. She didn't look any clearer than he was about what Bryce was getting at.

'You see, I'm a dead man walking. Sooner or later, no matter how careful I am, my former colleagues are going to catch up with me. When they do, it's not going to be a public trial and justice seen to be done. No, I'm going to get a bullet to the back of the head. I'm resigned to that, but my work is not done yet, so I need someone to buy me a bit more time. That's where you come in, Bernard.'

'Really?'

'Yes. You see, I can get all kinds of messages to Carlotta Carmichael, or Bob Ellis, or whoever I need to. What I can't do, is credibly pass on *misinformation* to them. They already take everything I say with a pinch of salt. So, listen carefully, because this is what I need you to do.'

'I'm not going to do anything illegal.'

'Lucy is a sweet girl. You've really done well for yourself...'

'Leave her alone!'

'Then do as I say!' Bryce's composure slipped. 'Or I'll shoot her, I'll shoot Mona, I'll shoot your fucking mother. Shut up and listen.'

Bernard looked at Mona who nodded vigorously. 'OK.'

'I want you to tell Marcus to hack into Carlotta Carmichael, Paul Shore, Catriona McBride and Emily Keith's medical records, download their vaccination logs, and e-mail them to *The Guardian*. Tell him I can't do it myself because my former IT colleagues have finally woken up to some of my methods. Tell Marcus he has certain IT privileges that I've recently had revoked.'

'Marcus won't agree to do that.'

'I know, and I don't need him to. I've already downloaded the files. That's just your cover story for why I've called you out here. What I *actually* want you to do is phone Bob Ellis, and say that you were summonsed here by me, for the reasons we've already discussed, and while you were here I left you locked in a room while I stood outside giving instructions to Blair. You overheard me discussing mobilising our troops to undermine Operation Trigon.'

'What's that?'

'You don't need to know.' He smiled. 'But believe me, when you drop that little gem in his ear, he's going to freak the fuck out, and start diverting his resources into all the wrong places. It'll buy me enough time to do what I have to.'

'Which is what?' asked Mona.

'Which is none of your business.'

Bernard rubbed his head. 'What do I say about Colin Karma's death, and his wife? And,' he took a deep breath, 'Scott Kerr's?'

'You say nothing. The only people in the building were you, me, Blair, and I suppose we'd better mention Mona.'

'But . . .'

'Bernard, don't sweat it. Believe me, there won't be a trace left in the building that anything unpleasant happened here. Trust me, I can clean up a crime scene.'

'When am I supposed to do all this?'

'Well, not right away, obviously. Give me some time to get out of here. Go and see Bob tomorrow, tell him Marcus needed to sleep on it. You'll know when the time is right.' He grinned. 'So, Bernard, go and release Blair from wherever your colleagues are holding him.'

Bryce shifted the gun so it was pointing at Mona. 'Then you and Maitland get in the car and drive away. Any attempt to come back here, or any police appearing on the scene, and I'll shoot her.'

He didn't move. 'There's no way I'm going to be able to persuade them just to drive off and leave Mona here.'

'Fair point, Bernard, so I'm going to give you some good reasons. Lucy. Kate. Marcus's mum. Oh, and your pregnant ex-wife. I know where they all live, so you'd better get your friends persuaded.'

Bernard looked at Mona.

'Go,' she said. 'Do exactly what he said.'

14

Mona's frustration had given way to something resembling boredom. Bryce had locked her into what appeared to be living accommodation, with a polite entreaty to make herself at home. She'd have been happy to oblige, if there had been anything remotely homely about the room. Her choice of entertainment was either to lie down on the not very clean-looking mattress for a quick kip, or sit and stare at the four walls. She'd have helped herself to a cup of coffee, but the sole catering facility seemed to be a primus stove, for which she didn't have any matches.

The only sensible use of her time had been to go over the room inch by inch, looking for any possible weakness that would allow her to escape. She'd no idea what Bryce's plan was for her, beyond her immediate use as a hostage. He didn't seem to have any compelling reason to kill her; after all he'd let her colleagues go, and Bernard had seen just as much of the situation as she had. It would be better not to have to put that particular theory to the test, though, so she had hammered and prodded her way round the door, the slit of glass that passed for a window, and several acres of flat, metal wall. Nothing gave.

She checked her phone. Bryce had secured her in here over an hour ago. She'd heard some banging and crashing when he'd first locked her in, and some shouted conversations, but for the past forty minutes or so there'd been total silence, aside from the creaking of the building itself as the metal expanded and contracted in the sun. She was just contemplating whether she should actually brave the dirty mattress and lie down, when she heard footsteps, and the door swung open.

'Apologies, Mona. I hope you weren't too bored.' Bryce grinned at her.

She glared. 'When can I go?'

'Soon, soon. Just waiting for young Blair to come back with the van. We've got so much stuff that it'll take a couple of trips.'

'What stuff? Guns and dead bodies?'

He shrugged. 'That pretty much sums it up.'

'Is Scott Kerr still alive?' she asked.

'What do you care? One less deadbeat drug dealer on the streets. Everyone wins.'

'It's still murder, Bryce, whatever he is. Jesus, there's a lot of dead people around you.' She got to her feet. 'People are going to be looking for Karma and his wife, you know.'

'Are they?' He raised an eyebrow. 'They've no family to speak of, and I'm not sure Colin did what you'd call friendship. Do you really think anyone will miss the bullying, thieving, doesn't-pay-his-bills bastard? Even I'm not going to miss him.'

'Why were you working with him then?' She returned to the starting point of their investigation. 'Did you come round to his way of thinking? Did you decide to join his gang?'

'His way of thinking?' He threw his head back and laughed. 'The guy is nuts! Did Stuttle think my pretty little head had been turned by him? Get real, Mona, I sought these people out.'

'Sought them out?'

'Yup. I needed assistance with some of my, ehm, projects, and Aaron had come on to my radar, so I suggested to my superiors that his activities required some surveillance. Gave me the time and the expenses account I needed to win his trust.'

'Aaron Mitchell was a misogynist fantasist, who never did anything more daring than hand out a few leaflets, from what I can make out.'

'True.' He grinned. 'I did have to exaggerate his importance more than a little to get the go-ahead. He was also utterly fearless, totally lacking in compassion, and very willing to take orders from me.'

'Obviously, that worked out well for him.'

'I salute my fallen comrade, although he didn't die in battle. It was the good old-fashioned Virus that did for him. I am pissed off with him, though, for dying and landing me with his dopey mate.'

She felt almost sorry for Blair. 'And Karma had the money.'

'Money, and a few useful contacts. You can't start a revolution without guns. Of course, there were his wife's special skills, too.'

She remembered her earlier conversation with Sharon Murray, which seemed a lifetime ago. 'Prosthetics?'

'Yup. It amused me to have Bob Ellis and his mates chasing all over the country because they'd seen "Bryce" using a cashpoint. Except, of course, it wasn't me, it was Blair in about three grand's worth of Bryce-suit. I'm almost going to miss Lana. Well, I'll certainly miss her more than her loser so-called rock star of a husband. Jesus, have you listened to the man's music?'

Mona stared at Bryce. He *looked* like the guy she

remembered coming to fix her computer, the one who never said boo to a goose. Yet here he was, casually discussing guns, murder and insurrection. 'So, you want a revolution?'

'A revolution of truth.'

'What does that even mean?'

He stared at her for a moment, a smile playing around his lips. His gun was lightly balanced on his knee, still pointing directly at her. 'You know, Mona, I've never liked you. You, Paterson, Maitland, and Stuttle, all cut from the same cloth. All desperate to obey orders so that you can curry favour with the man above, get yourself on to the next rung of the ladder.'

'There's nothing wrong with being ambitious.'

'Yeah, the only problem is, the system promotes stupid people, doesn't it?'

In spite of her situation, she could feel her anger growing. 'I'm not stupid.'

'Aren't you? All the time I was spying on the HET, not one of you noticed. The only one who came even close to suspecting I was up to anything was Bernard, and I don't see anyone rushing to promote him.' He grinned. 'I like Bernard. He took the time to get to know a lowly IT support officer. When you heard about me, did you even recognise my name? Did you remember what I looked like?'

He'd got her there. She'd had no idea who Bernard had been talking about when he'd first raised his suspicions about Bryce. She decided to come out fighting. 'It's a bit much to complain about other people being careerist. You've been on the government payroll for years. What makes you suddenly so virtuous?'

'I had what you might call a light-bulb moment.' He

thought for a moment. 'Actually that's not quite right. It was more a slow burning realisation that the people I was working for were evil.'

'Evil?'

'The embodiment thereof.' He nodded. 'You know the Carmichaels. It would be difficult to spend a lot of time in their company and remain convinced of the integrity of our elected leaders. And, you know, Mona, they're not the worst, not by a long shot.'

'The African drugs trial.'

'Yeah, that tested my loyalty to its limits. Nobody likes to see innocent kiddies sacrificed like that. The trouble is, there's a lot more where that came from. And, as I said, I don't like you, so I'm going to share something with you.'

She was tired of Bryce's nonsense. 'Why would you share something with me if you don't like me?'

'Because I want you to suffer like I'm suffering. I want your brain to hurt as much as mine does.'

She could probably beat him on that one. Even now, underneath the adrenaline, she could feel a painful throbbing.

'Have you seen Alexander Bircham-Fowler recently?' Bryce asked. 'The good old Prof, Scotland's leading virologist, as the TV news is always fond of telling me, and, I believe, a close personal friend of yours?'

'He's not a friend of mine.'

'I know, you just shared some adventures together, didn't you? Both nearly got yourself killed in pursuit of him getting a Health Check. Anyway, my former employers really hate him. I mean, loathe with a vengeance. Personally, I think he's a smart guy and well worth picking his brains. So, next time you catch up with him, assuming there is a next time, ask the Prof how pandemics develop. Ask him about the tiny mutations you'd expect to occur naturally as a virus progresses. Ask him when you would anticipate that the pandemic would die out, *naturally*.'

'It *is* dying out. That's all over the news. The incidence of new cases is way down on last year.'

'Well, keep watching the news. I predict that in a couple of months there will be a fresh outbreak of the Virus in Haiti. In that particular outbreak we'll see a Virus that has considerably mutated. Mutations that virologists like Bircham-Fowler wouldn't expect.'

She stared at him, uncertain what he was trying to say. He laughed at her expression. 'Wake up, Mona! The Virus wasn't just a random natural occurrence. It wasn't caused by some careless chicken husbandry, or some human interaction with chimpanzees. The Virus was man-made.'

She rested her head carefully on her hands while she thought about whether this was actually possible.

'Man-made, Mona, man-made. And they made it once, so they can make it again, only slightly different. Just tweaked enough for us to lose our immunity to it. Think of that, Mona. You've had a year now of thinking you're safe from all this nonsense, you and Bernard and Paterson and Maitland, and the one that used to be a nurse. But when the Haiti stuff kicks off, nobody's going to be safe.'

'You're making this up.'

'Quite a thought, isn't it? Of course, the Health Enforcement Team will have been a complete waste of time.'

'If this is true,' Mona said, 'who's responsible for it? It's not the *government*?'

'A lot of people think Bircham-Fowler's past it, you know.'

'What?' Mona was irritated by the sudden change of direction.

'Some of his research projects have gone nowhere. People were muttering that he was too old to be leading on Virus research, saying that secretary of his had been propping him up for years.'

'That's bullshit, and what does it have to do with anything?'

'Why would someone try to shoot a has-been, out-of-touch Professor, whose research doesn't make sense?'

She stared at him.

'We, as in my former employers, don't know who created the Virus. But Bircham-Fowler's research had begun to throw up anomalies. Lovely, self-deprecating man that he is, he assumed that his research was flawed, not that he was researching something that has never been seen before. It suited the likes of Carlotta to have him sitting on his research puzzling over it, while the government try to work out what the hell is going on.'

'He doesn't know—'

'He knows something significant enough to get him shot, he just doesn't know he knows it.'

'So, it wasn't you guys who shot at us?'

He shook his head. 'No. We don't know who it was, but if we did, we'd be a lot closer to finding out who created this nightmare. So, now you know, Mona, and I hope it hurts your head every bit as much as it's hurting mine.'

Her head *was* hurting, a low dull ache. She paced up and down as she tried to make sense of what Bryce was saying. 'I still don't understand why you're shooting people?'

He grinned again, a smug, self-satisfied baring of his teeth that was beginning to infuriate her. 'Well, I think you've already worked out I'm not shooting at random, am I? The people I've shot overheard a frank exchange of views between me and Carlotta Carmichael on the matters we've just been discussing.'

'So, you just went ahead and shot them? The poor bastards overhear something and that makes them fair game?'

He shrugged. 'I wanted Carlotta to get the message.'

'That's a bit harsh on the people you shot.'

'I agree it *would* be, if they were just innocent bystanders. But these folk, well, they're a little more involved in it than that. None of my shots was meant to kill; even Paul Shore's injury is basically a shoulder wound.' He laughed, throwing his head back. 'Hitting Paterson's fat arse was just the icing on the cake.'

The pain in Mona's head was deepening. She struggled to keep following the conversation. 'What message are you trying to send Carlotta?'

'Carlotta and a few select others are well aware that this Virus is man-made.'

'Why isn't she telling people that?'

'The official line is that she doesn't want to cause panic in the street.'

'Well, there would be,' said Mona. She couldn't imagine that people would react in any other way.

'Better panic then complacency. People have stopped taking even the simplest of Virus precautions. When was the last time you even saw somebody wash their hands before going in a shop?'

At the height of the Virus there had been an alcohol wash dispenser at the front of every public space. Bryce was right on that one at least. She couldn't remember the last time she'd seen somebody taking the time to do that. As the Virus was dying down people were getting sloppy.

'When the next wave of influenza hits, people going to be totally unprepared for it.' Bryce said. 'It's going to spread every bit as quickly as the original Virus.'

'There must be something that the government can do.'

He shrugged. 'They could try vaccinating against the other likely forms of influenza.'

'That didn't work very well this time.'

'Rumour has it they are on the cusp of a breakthrough on that. Just in time to be of no use at all. Carlotta, though, obviously thinks it's worth a shot having vaccines for a range of related, but not identical strains, because she's spent the last six months getting jags.'

The penny dropped. 'The people you shot were vaccinated as well. That's why you want their medical records released.'

'Yep. I bet when you spoke to them they were all, woe is me, I've had to sign the Official Secrets Act so I can't even talk about what happened to me. I'd wager, though, they skipped over the huge bribe they accepted in the form of access for both themselves and their immediate family to state-of-the-art immunisation.'

'I can't take this in.' She stopped pacing. Every step was hurting her head. She sat down next to Bryce. 'If it's all true—'

'It *is* true. The past six months have been a slow revelation. The scales have fallen from my eyes.'

'OK, OK, let's suppose for a minute this is true. Why aren't you shouting it from the rooftops? Why didn't you stick that information on the HET website?'

He laughed. 'Maybe I've got a bit of a self-esteem

issue, Mona, but I'm not sure that anyone would believe me. There are a million nutters out there already putting forward theories that the Virus has been created deliberately by the Russians, or the North Koreans, or whoever it is we're currently afraid of. The Virus has behaved more or less as it should have done up until this point, so people like Bircham-Fowler would be rushing to say I'm talking nonsense. Carlotta, of course, would back him up; it might be the only time they've ever agreed on anything. I'll just be some rogue HET officer who's gone completely and utterly loopy. I worked in IT, for God's sake! I'll just sound like any other conspiracy nut.'

'You think that when you release the vaccination records to the press they'll do your work for you?'

'You have to admit the press is going to be curious about why the Chair of the Virus Committee, and three apparently random civil servants, have all had the widest possible range of vaccinations currently available. I can drip-feed them the rest. Then if my theory about Haiti is correct...not that we want things to wait that long. We want action now. We want people looking after themselves. Anyway—' he stood up '—enough chatter. We've both got things to do. Try not to have nightmares about what I told you.'

Mona didn't move. 'I'm finding it a bit difficult to see you as a force for good, Bryce. You've worked for the government for years – you must have done lots of shit things.'

'I've been in the pay of the government since I was a seventeen-year-old squaddie. I've done things in war zones that have kept me lying awake night after night. But I was a soldier, not a mercenary, and this isn't a war, it's a public health crisis. Some of our politicians see it as an opportunity to undermine all the freedoms I thought I was fighting for. You know the worst thing that Paul and those girls overheard?'

'Struggling to think of something worse than a mutated Virus.'

'I phrased that wrong. You want to know the worst thing they heard from Carlotta's point of view?'

She nodded.

'They heard her yelling at me that there wasn't going to be a word of this in the public domain for at least four months.'

'Why four months? Oh ...' She got the point. 'There are elections in three months' time.'

'Yup, Carlotta and her party are so desperate to cling on to power that they'll squander our chances of preparing properly for what might be about to happen – just so it doesn't mess up their electoral chances. Anyway, time for you to go.'

Mona tried to stand up, but a red sea of lava swam through her head and she gave up.

'You OK? You look kind of pale.'

'I'm fine. So I'm free to go now?'

'Assuming you can find your way back to your car, yeah.'

She hesitated. 'What about Scott Kerr?'

He grinned. 'I wouldn't lose any sleep over him.'

'But—'

His grin vanished. 'I'm losing patience here, Mona. Get out and keep your mouth shut.'

This time she managed to stand without giddiness. She retraced her steps to the former gunroom where she'd left her bag. The cages which had previously held the firearms were all now open, their doors swaying a little as if blown by a gentle wind. Mona blinked and the swaying stopped. What she desperately wanted to do was lie down and close her eyes, get her focus back, rest her aching brain, but she knew she had to get out. She compromised by sitting for a moment on the sofa. When she put her hands behind her to push herself up again, one hand touched metal. The gun she had put there under the guise of giving Bernard a hug was still there. She debated her options, as she tucked it into her bag. She could go back and threaten Bryce with it, but she was pretty sure he could outdraw her, even when she could see straight. The only viable option was just to leave, but she wasn't sure she could actually walk, never mind drive.

Her thoughts were interrupted by the sound of a single gunshot, which reverberated deafeningly around the metal walls. She slipped her bag across her body and moved cautiously towards the door. Peering out she could see Bryce standing at the end of the corridor, with what appeared to be a body at his feet. She blinked, hoping her eyes were playing tricks again. No, the body was still there, but there was something wrong with Bryce. Like the gun cabinets earlier, the skin on his head seemed to be flapping. She blinked repeatedly and the scene came into sharper focus. The skin on Bryce's head *was* moving, slipping and sliding as he walked around the body. She realised what she was looking at. It wasn't Bryce. Bryce was dead, and someone wearing a badly fitting prosthetic mask was standing over him.

She quietly lifted her gun. 'Drop your weapon!'

The gunman turned toward her and raised his arm.

Mona fired.

15

'Leave her? Are you insane? We can't just leave her here.' Maitland looked horrified. 'And there's no way I'm letting shit for brains in there go free.'

Blair was obviously listening, as he chose this moment to kick against the car door with both feet. Marcus, recently returned from a failed attempt to find reception, had been leaning against the car and found himself jolted by the movement. He removed himself to a safe distance, shaking his head as he went.

'We don't have any choice.' Bernard felt weary. 'That's what Bryce instructed us to do.'

'I'm not taking any orders from that bastard.'

Bernard reached for the handle, and released Blair. He climbed out, a grin on his face. 'Untie my hands then.'

'Just go.' Bernard gave him a gentle push in the direction of the factory. He stumbled then hurried off, cursing over his shoulder as he went.

Maitland returned the compliment, before focusing his attention back on Bernard. 'We're not leaving without Mona, and that's final.'

'We have to. He said he will shoot Mona if we don't do what he says. He also said that he would shoot Lucy, Kate, and Marcus's mum.'

Maitland folded his arms. 'Well, he's not actually going to do that, is he?'

'Not going to do it?' Bernard couldn't believe what he was hearing. 'If there is one thing that we know Bryce is perfectly capable of doing, it is shooting people! Take a minute to think this through: he knew Kate's name. He didn't say "Maitland's girlfriend", he said "Kate". He probably knows where she lives, what she's studying, and exactly where he can find her. Do you want to take that risk?'

This led to a long silence, which Marcus opted to fill. 'I for one am furious about his threat. Bryce has met my mother. We all went to see *Les Misérables* together.'

'We shouldn't just run off,' Maitland said. 'We should . . .' He tailed off as he realised his limited options in dealing with a psychotic armed man and his sidekick, with only the massed ranks of Bernard and Marcus as backup.

'Let's just go home.' Bernard was weary to his bones. He didn't know what the right thing was to do. He thought, hoped, Bryce wouldn't shoot Mona, but he also knew there was nothing the three of them could do about it if that was Bryce's plan. Then for the rest of his life he'd have to live with the knowledge that Mona had been coming in to rescue him.

Maitland gave in to the inevitable and slid into the driver's seat. 'So, what were those gunshots anyway?'

'Nothing. Just warning shots,' he lied. He wasn't entirely sure why he was lying, he just couldn't work out the right thing to say. He needed to go home, lie in a darkened room and think about things, except he realised, he couldn't even do that. If Scott Kerr had been telling the truth about Annemarie, there was going to be a situation to deal with when he got home as well. 'Just Bryce trying to show he was serious.'

'Why did he drag you out here anyway?' asked Marcus, as the car pulled away.

Bernard swallowed hard, and began the process of lying. 'Actually, it wasn't really me that he wanted to speak to, it was you.'

'Me?' He looked both surprised, and slightly scared at this news. 'What did he want with me?'

'He wants you to hack into the medical records of Carlotta Carmichael and the three people that he shot, and release their vaccination records.'

There was a silence from the back seat. 'That's a criminal offence, Bernard,' said Marcus. 'I could go to prison.'

'But he's threatening Kate and Lucy if Marcus doesn't do it?' asked Maitland.

'Yes, and Marcus's mother, and God knows who else he sees as fair game.' He turned round towards Marcus, who looked utterly miserable. He couldn't look him in the eye. 'I'm sorry.'

'I can't do it, Bernard. It's just wrong.'

'But ...' began Maitland.

'Don't try and bully me! I'm not doing it.'

'OK, OK,' said Bernard. 'I was pretty sure that was what you would say. Will you at least think it over and give me your final answer in the morning?'

'OK, but it will be the same.'

Bernard closed his eyes. He felt ill. He felt nauseous, weary, and sick to the death of the Health Enforcement Team and the chaos that surrounded it.

'Bernard,' began Marcus.

'Can we not talk, Marcus? I really need to think.'

'I just wanted to let you know that we've got reception again. Are you really sure that we shouldn't be phoning for police backup?'

'If the police turn up mob-handed there's a very real chance Mona will be killed. I'm not phoning them.'

'But—' began Maitland.

'No buts! For all we know he'll opt to go down in a blaze of glory rather than be captured. He could blow the whole place up.'

Maitland sighed, but thankfully stopped talking. The welcome silence was interrupted again by Marcus.

'If you wanted, Bernard, you could try and phone Lucy again now we're connected to the outside world.'

At this precise moment there was nobody that Bernard wanted to speak to less. What on earth was he going to say to her? He took out his phone and saw there was a voicemail message from an unfamiliar number. He pressed to hear the call and heard Lucy's voice. She sounded tired.

Hi, Bernard. It's me. I've really had the most terrible day. I'm going to stay at my mum and dad's tonight. Please ring me on this number when you get this.

She was safe, thank God. He took a moment just to revel in that thought, before he moved on to a number of less positive thoughts. Although Lucy might be safe, she was probably traumatised. She might be horrified if she found out that her bad day was down to her connection to the North Edinburgh HET. And right at this minute she would, no doubt, be in need of some kind words and reassurance from her boyfriend. *Deserving* of some kind words and reassurance. He still hesitated.

'Come on, hurry up,' said Maitland. 'After you're done with your bird, I want to give Kate a ring and tell her to go to her parents', just in case Bryce is actually planning to try something.'

Bernard stared at the phone, realising that he did not

have the emotional wherewithal to speak to Lucy right at this moment. He'd just lied to Marcus, one of his best friends, heaping guilt and emotional turmoil on a man he knew to be a pillar of integrity. He'd lied to Maitland, who for all his other faults, did truly love the woman that he was worrying about. Bernard needed some recovery time from that before he could bear to start lying to Lucy as well.

'Here – take my phone. You phone first.'

Maitland didn't have to be asked twice. Bernard listened to one side of a very forceful conversation, by the end of which Kate did seem to have agreed to make an unscheduled visit to her parents. There would have to be a lot of flowers and apologies changing hands at some point in the future, but for now his aim of getting his girlfriend to safety had been achieved.

'Right, here you go.' Maitland flung the phone into his lap.

'I'll phone her later.'

'Later?' Maitland was surprised. 'Aren't you worried about her?'

'Yes, of course I am, but she's at her parents' already. That's all I would have said to her anyway – go to your mum and dad's.'

'*That's* all you would have said to her?' Maitland sounded disbelieving. 'She had an encounter with Bryce, he held a gun to her head, she probably thought she was about to die, and you don't want to speak to her directly to check she's OK?'

'I DON'T WANT TO SPEAK TO HER.' All the anger that had been building inside him burst out. 'I don't know what to say to her. My ex-wife is pregnant, possibly with my baby, and I think I'm going to have to get back together with her.'

The car swerved, and they drove along the grass verge for a few nerve-wracking seconds before Maitland righted the car. 'She's *what*?' he asked.

'Pregnant. Expecting. With child. You get the picture?'

Marcus leaned forward from the backseat. 'I don't see how it could be your baby though. Unless I'm missing something, you've been separated for quite some time?'

'I don't know.' Bernard frowned. 'I think she might have stolen some of my sperm or something like that. She was desperate to have another child. It was pretty much the only reason we split up.'

'*Another* child?'

He stared out the window. 'We lost our son in the first wave of the Virus. He was still a baby.'

The car felt very, very quiet.

'Did you want another child?' asked Marcus.

'Yes, very much, but how could anyone bring a child in the world as it is? Just for it to have to take its chances with the Virus?'

There was another silence. Maitland and Marcus were exchanging glances in the rear-view mirror. He couldn't say he blamed them; he sounded crazy, he knew, but then today had been all about crazy people.

'It's probably not yours, mate,' said Maitland.

'It doesn't matter if it's my child or not. Carrie is still my wife, and she's too fragile to bring up a child alone. We seem to have slowed down?' The car appeared to be driving around at 20 miles per hour at the moment.

'Of course we've slowed down,' said Maitland. 'That's a hell of a lot to think about.'

'You don't need to think about it. It's my problem, not yours.'

'Absolutely.' Maitland paused, thinking about this.

'Well, actually no, not absolutely at all. It's your ex-wife's problem. It was her decision to have a baby, not yours, and she's the one who needs to stand by that. I can't believe I'm going to give you some advice here, Bernard, mate, but stick with your girlfriend. You deserve to be happy.'

'I'm in total agreement here with Maitland,' said Marcus. 'And that's such a rare occurrence you really should pay attention.'

Bernard stared out the window, with something like tears stinging the back of his eyes. The last thing he'd expected from his colleagues was compassion.

'Stick with Lucy, mate. You've found the only woman in the world as dull as you are, and I really don't think you're going to get a shag out of anyone else.'

'Shut up, Maitland.' He picked up his phone, and pressed the number to return Lucy's call.

'Bernard, thank God. I've had a terrible, terrible day. Didn't you get my messages?'

'Yes, but I've been really, really busy . . .'

'Too busy to call?' There was a slight frostiness to her voice. 'Anyway, if you are at all interested, I was just phoning to let you know that I was mugged today.'

'Actually, no, you weren't.'

'What do you mean I wasn't mugged?' Frostiness had developed into full-blown anger. 'How dare you tell me what did or didn't happen to me today! I was there, I saw the gun! I was mugged.'

'No, I meant that it wasn't an actual mugging. It was . . .'

'You don't care at all, do you? You've been avoiding me all week. I get it, I can take a hint. You obviously want to break up with me. Well, I'll save you the trouble.' The phone went dead.

He placed it gently on his lap. 'Did you hear any of that?'

'The volume she was yelling at, Bernie, I think there are people in outer space that could hear you being dumped,' said Maitland.

'What do I do now?'

'You can tell her the truth? Why you've been so distracted?' suggested Marcus. 'Then plead with her to take you back. I don't agree with the way that Maitland phrased things, but you and Lucy are remarkably well suited, and she is willing to, ehm, you know, with you.'

'Yeah, I'm not usually in favour of telling birds the truth about stuff,' said Maitland, 'but in this case I think it's your only hope.'

'God, let's just get home.' Bernard sighed. Lucy was just the last in a long list of things that he had to worry about. 'I'll think about it all tomorrow.'

FRIDAY

GREATEST HITS

I

'Are you sure you're OK?' Bernard watched Annemarie gingerly raise a cup to her lips. A light purple bruise had spread over her chin. By the time he'd finally got home it had been after midnight. Showing an admirable ability to self-manage, Annemarie had taken herself off to be bandaged up, and when he'd walked in had been hobbling around the flat attempting to tidy up.

'Aye, son. I've had worse on my backside and sat on it.' She started to laugh, then winced, holding her side. 'I shouldn't laugh.'

Bernard wasn't laughing. 'I'm surprised the hospital let you out.'

'Well, it wasn't *actually* a hospital, son. I try to avoid them if at all possible. I've got a couple of pals who can help me out every time I need it.'

'Every time? How often do you get beaten up?'

She laughed, and winced again. 'Don't make me laugh, son. I wasn't meaning me. When I was working with the girls they were always getting into bother, and I didn't always want to involve the authorities, if you get my drift.'

'OK,' said Bernard, not entirely sure if he did. 'Can I get you another cup of tea?'

Annemarie was on the Earl Grey, although his tipple was a little bit stronger. He'd cracked open the expensive rioja he'd bought in anticipation of the day he finally brought Lucy back to his flat. It wasn't going to be required anytime soon, he was sure of that.

'No, no, son, I'm fine.'

A thought occurred to him. 'Where's the dog? Kerr didn't do anything to her, did he?'

'No. He booted her a couple of times then shut her in your room. She got a bit upset. I'm afraid there might be a bit of a mess in there, but I never made it that far with my tidying.'

Bernard resolved to stop thinking his day couldn't get any worse. He attempted a smile. 'Don't worry about it. So, where is Sheba?'

'She's back at the flat.' She paused. 'As is my good-for-nothing brother, talking a load of nonsense and with no idea where he's been and how he got back. I'm not sure whether he's borrowed any money or not. I'm sorry, son, for getting you involved in my problems.'

He sincerely wished he'd never met Annemarie, but he took a deep breath. 'You've nothing to apologise for. We all agreed to get involved to save Alessandra. We all knew what would happen if Scott Kerr found out what we'd done.'

'Where is the wee bastard now?'

'I don't know. He might not still be—'

His phone rang, and Mona's name flashed up. He grabbed it. 'Are you OK?'

'It's not Mona, Bernard, it's Carole. I've got some bad news.'

2

Her first impression was that everything was very white, blinding almost. It hurt to try to focus on so much brightness, so she closed her eyes again. A series of images flooded into her brain. Bryce, dead at the factory. An assassin taking aim at her, and her bullet finding his gun arm. Running from the factory, with the marksman in full pursuit. A frantic drive, her head pounding and her eyesight clouding over. Stopping in the first populated area she came to, the kids outside the chip shop crowding round her car.

Where was she now? Was she in danger? She forced her eyes open again, staring out again into the snow. Fortunately, this time things fell more into place. *Bed. Chest of drawers. Monitor.* She was in a hospital room.

OK, so someone was trying to keep her alive, rather than kill her. The question now was, was this some top-secret medical facility, or the good old NHS? Mona tried to sit up, which prompted a loud beep from the machine next to her. Within seconds, the door opened and the familiar figures of Paterson and Carole burst in. They were promptly elbowed out of the way by a nurse.

'Out until I've sorted this, please.'

'Is everyone OK?' asked Mona, over the top of the nurse's head.

Paterson nodded. 'Everyone's fine. All accounted for.'

'I need you to relax,' said the nurse, looking not at Mona but at her HET colleagues. They took the hint and retreated to the corridor. 'You've had a nasty bump.'

'Which hospital am I in? Who brought me in here?'

The nurse gently patted Mona back into place on the pillows. 'Time for all these questions once you've had a proper rest.' She took a final look at the machine and, apparently satisfied, headed to the door. 'Sleep,' she commanded.

Mona watched the door, in the hope that her colleagues would reappear and tell her what was going on. The minutes passed, and she was just beginning to think the nurse had demanded they leave, when the door was cautiously pushed open. Paterson sneaked in, a finger pressed to his lips. Carole closed the door gently behind them.

'Keep your voice down, Mona. We've been given our marching orders by that nurse.'

'Is everyone really OK, Guv?'

'Yes.' He scowled at her. 'No thanks to you and your idiot friends disappearing into an ambush, with no thought of telling your line manager.'

'Don't blame me, Guv, I didn't know what they were up to. We were overtaken by events.'

'Yes, I had a very long conversation in the early hours with Bernard. What happened to you, though? He said you were alive and well when he deserted you.'

'He didn't desert me, Guv, he didn't have a lot of choice. As for me, I'm not entirely sure what happened.' She wondered what to tell her boss; she felt a desperate need to process the evening's events before she got any of her colleagues dragged into it. She opted for a lie. 'The last thing I remember is arguing with Bryce, then I felt a really sharp pain in my head. How did you find me?'

'You were found slumped over the wheel of your car in West Collie,' said Carole. 'I was the last number you'd called so the police phoned me, and I phoned Mr Paterson...'

'Who managed to persuade them that you had a head trauma, and weren't some random stoner,' said Paterson. 'So, what's going on?'

She didn't know what to say, so bought herself some time. 'Oh God, has anybody told my mother?'

'We've told her something. Said you wouldn't be allowed any visitors before morning, which actually is true. Are you OK?'

She tried to nod, but little sharp pains ran up the back of her head. 'Maybe I came back to work a little bit too soon. I'm not about to pop my clogs, so go home and get some sleep. I'm pretty sure you have a lot to do in the morning.' A thought occurred to her. 'I need to speak to Bernard. Where's my phone?' She tried to sit up.

'You're not phoning anyone, and I'm not going anywhere until you tell me what the hell is going on.' Paterson pulled a chair up to the side of the bed.

'The thing is...' She sat forward, a lot less cautiously than before. As she'd hoped, the machine started bleeping again.

'You two are still here?' The nurse stood in the doorway. 'Can you please leave now, before I have to call for security?'

Paterson glared at the nurse, then admitted defeat. 'OK, OK, we're going.'

'Goodnight, Mona.' Carole gave her shoulder a squeeze, her eyes anxious.

'Later,' said Paterson.

She reached over to her locker to get her bag. The drawer was locked. Frustrated, she slumped back on the pillow and closed her eyes. Darkness overcame her.

3

Despite Paterson's instructions to take it easy, the next day Bernard found himself walking up the stairs of the Cathcart Building at ten past eight in the morning. It had been after 1am when he'd finished speaking to Paterson, and had crawled into bed. He'd thought he'd be unable to sleep, particularly as his room had a strange, unpleasant smell which he was attributing to a frightened Sheba being incarcerated in there. However, he'd surprised himself by falling asleep as soon as his head hit the pillow, although he'd woken up at half past five, the events of the day playing over and over in his head.

As he reached the first landing, his phone alerted him to an incoming text message.

Have been up all night thinking. I can't do want Bryce wants. I'm sorry. What now?

Thank God. This would have been a terrible time for Marcus to decide he would sacrifice his career and reputation to keep Bryce happy.

He put down his bag, and meticulously typed an answer. *Don't worry. I will deal with it.*

A noise from upstairs attracted his attention. Someone was already in the office. It was probably Maitland, as he was the only member of the team who had had any chance of a full night's sleep. Carole potentially could have— The sound of furniture being knocked over, followed by a loud burst of colourful language narrowed the possibilities down. He ran up the remaining stairs, and stuck his head round the door. He might as well get the yelling over with.

'Bernard, you clown! You're supposed to be at home taking it easy.'

'Shouldn't you be doing that as well, Mr Paterson?'

Paterson grunted in response, and returned to the cubbyhole that passed for his private office. Bernard followed him, hovering by the doorway. 'Any more word on Mona?'

'I spoke to the hospital about ten minutes ago. She had a good night.'

'Can we go in and visit?'

'The nurse I spoke to wasn't very keen on the idea, but I say we go down there and see what happens.' He yawned.

'How much sleep did you get last night?'

'About four hours. I was woken by a phone call at 6am.'

'From Mr Stuttle?'

Paterson shook his head. 'From Paul Shore. He's decided he wants to make a "clean breast of things", his words not mine. He's asked me to get him a solicitor and meet him there.'

'A clean breast of things? What do you think he means by that?'

'I honestly don't know.' Paterson sat back and folded his arms. Bernard felt himself growing hot under his gaze.

'It did occur to me, however, that you and your pal Mona might have more of an idea. Seems to me that you two know a lot more about what's going on than I do.'

The rising sense of panic that Bernard had been feeling

all week was threatening to overwhelm him. 'I really need to talk to Mona.'

'Why? To get your story straight about what you are going to tell me and the rest of the world about what happened last night? Well, I've got some bad news for you. Whatever has been happening in Mona's brain over the past few weeks, it's not good. She says she can't remember a thing about last night after getting to the factory.'

'Oh dear.' Bernard grabbed the orange plastic visitor's chair and sat down heavily.

Paterson stood up, walked past him and closed the door. 'So,' his voice was low, 'how about, while it's just the two of us, for once in your life actually telling me the truth. What happened last night?'

Bernard mulled this suggestion over. He desperately wanted to talk to someone about yesterday's events. He would love to be told exactly what he needed to do next. Paterson would certainly have plenty of ideas about the correct course of action. On the downside, however, there was the very real risk that his boss might feel compelled to report their activities to the authorities.

Paterson gave up waiting for him to speak. 'Well, you better have some kind of story prepared for when Bob Ellis and his pals catch up with you.'

Panic bubbled up again. 'I'm not sure they know anything about what happened last night.'

'Maybe not. But you found that factory, so why can't they? They're not stupid, and this might just have piqued their interest.' He motioned to Bernard to come round to his side of the desk to look at something on the computer. Bernard saw that the BBC News website was open.

'*Firefighters tackling an inferno at a disused factory.*'

Paterson read aloud. 'Not a small blaze, Bernard. Not some accident. No, an *inferno*. Care to tell me what exactly might have gone up in that blaze?'

Bernard stared at the screen, taking care not to actually catch his boss's eye. There was a danger he might cave and tell him everything that had happened this week if he did.

'Nothing to say?' Paterson sighed. 'Oh, well, on your head be it.' He turned off his computer. 'I've got to go and brief a solicitor. You take some time to think about things. I'll give you a ring and tell you what time I'm going to be at the hospital. Meet me there.'

Bernard nodded. Bryce had said he would know when the time was right. The blazing factory indicated that the time was now.

'What do you want?' Bob barely looked up from his desk. Aside from his laptop, every inch of it seemed to be covered in files or sheets of A4. 'We're kind of busy here, Bernard.'

'Yeah, but, ehm.' He stared at the back of Bob's head. 'We tracked down Bryce.'

The words came out in a rush. Bob's head snapped up, a small grin on his face.

'*You* found Bryce?' he said. 'You, the North Edinburgh HET, just stumbled across a major terrorist, who the entire Scottish police force is looking for?'

Bernard felt his sap rising. 'We didn't just stumble across him, Bob. We used detective work and found him.'

Bob stared at him. It took all of Bernard's self-control to stare back. Eventually Bob's expression softened from disbelief to a tentative curiosity. 'So, where is he?'

'I don't know. We had to let him go.'

'You let him get away?' The little grin returned. 'You found him, then you just let him go? Aye, right.' He swivelled back to his laptop.

'I didn't have any choice.' He ran through the approved story, right up to the point where Marcus had said he would have nothing to do with it. He could hear his voice getting faster and squeakier as he talked.

'Is this for real, Bernard?' He turned round, slowly. 'Because if you are shitting me . . .'

'I'm not,' he said, hastily.

Bob stared at him in silence for a further moment, then leapt into action. He pulled out his chair, and pointed to it. 'Sit there and do not move.'

Bernard sat and watched as Bob instructed, delegated, and shouted at what felt like every other person in Fettes. He closed his eyes and rested his head on his hand, taking care not to mess up any of the paperwork on the desk. He was on the point of dropping off when Bob punched him on the arm.

'Right, we need you in an interview room so we can get this all on tape.'

He opened his eyes to see Bob and an equally large man in a dark suit standing staring at him. 'Come on, move it.'

He was hustled down so many corridors and turnings that he had no idea where in Fettes he now was. The thought crossed his mind that nobody else knew he was here.

'OK, Bernard, once more for the tape.'

He repeated the story, hoping he'd kept the details the same.

Bob's colleague, who hadn't introduced himself, spoke. 'OK, we need you to think really carefully about anything else you might have seen or heard while you were there.'

'I didn't see much, to be honest. He was there with Blair, and I tried to listen to what they were saying when they were outside the room, but it was quite difficult, you know, the place is a factory, it's got big metal doors and things ...'

'I know it's difficult.' Bob broke in, a trifle impatiently, he thought. 'Just try, Bernard, anything you can remember.'

'Oh, oh, oh, OK.' He nodded. 'Well, when they went out of the room they were having, I suppose, a discussion you'd call it, maybe a bit of an argument, about something.'

'Did you hear what they were talking about?'

'Only little bits. They were talking about trying to undermine something, some operation or other.'

The room was very, very silent. 'Which operation?' asked Bob.

He shook his head. 'I couldn't hear very well, but it sounded something like try-on?'

'Trigon?' The man in the dark suit was staring at him.

'Yes,' he said, feigning delight. 'It could have been that.'

The two suits looked at each other for a second, then without another word both of them got up and hurried out of the room.

He rested his head back in his hands. They'd bought it, thank God, and hadn't asked any questions he didn't have answers for. Most importantly, they had left the door open behind them. He gave them a few minutes' head start then wound his way back through the corridors. After a few dead ends he finally made his way back to reception area, and out into the daylight.

4

'I thought I looked shit until I saw you, Bernard.' Mona sat up on one elbow to get a better look at him.

'We're in so much trouble, Mona. I've just been to see Bob Ellis...'

'Shit.' She lowered her voice. 'Bryce is dead.'

'How do you know? I thought you couldn't remem—'

'I remember everything. I just need some time to process it, and decide what we need to do.' She gave Bernard a rapid update on everything she had seen the previous night.

'So who shot him?'

'I don't know. I shot at the fake Bryce, but I think I didn't do much more damage than a flesh wound.'

Bernard's face contorted. 'Oh my God, please tell me Scott Kerr's not still alive? He could have come to in that cupboard and come out fighting.'

'I don't think so – he was in a pretty bad way after Bryce hit him.'

'But you don't know for sure?'

'I didn't have time to check on him. After I'd shot the fake Bryce I was pretty busy running for my life.'

'Could Blair have shot him?' he asked.

'But why? Aren't they on the same side?'

'True. Oh...' A thought occurred to Bernard. 'Kerr

was texting his mates. There wasn't any reception, but if they moved his body . . .'

'The messages could have been sent, and his friends could have come looking. *Jesus.* Whoever shot him, there are a lot of guns out there in the hands of people who really shouldn't have access to firearms.'

Bernard put his head in his hands. 'And I've just lied to Bob Ellis and all his mates for nothing.' He looked up. 'Couldn't you have contacted me?'

'I was unconscious! Anyway, I don't know that it was for nothing.'

'You think Bryce's accomplices could target us?'

She gently shook her head. 'No, well, maybe, I suppose. It was more that I was thinking Bryce might not actually be the bad guy here.'

'What did Bryce say to you?'

'Knock, knock.' Maitland, Carole, and a very large bunch of flowers were in the doorway to her room.

'Later,' she whispered to Bernard.

'How are you feeling?' asked Carole.

'A bit sore, and a bit stupid, to be honest. I can't remember what happened last night.'

'I would sum it up,' said Maitland, 'as Bernard did something incredibly stupid, and you went and bailed him out as usual.'

Bernard stood up suddenly, sending the hospital chair flying. Without a glance at anyone, he walked quickly out of the room. She had a pang of guilt that she hadn't been able to reassure him.

'Nice work, Maitland. He's had a terrible time worrying about Lucy.'

'Well, she's no longer his problem as she dumped him last night.' He picked up the toppled chair and sat in it.

316

'Really? He was trying to save her, wasn't he? Doesn't she get that he's a hero?'

'I don't think he managed to get his point across very well. Plus he's only heroic occasionally. The rest of the time she'd have to put up with him just being Bernard.'

'Poor Bernard,' said Carol. 'Anyway, Paterson's on his way over. He's meeting with Paul Shore and a lawyer apparently.'

'Yeah.' Maitland plonked himself down on the side of her bed. 'Paul Shore wants to make a clean breast of what's been going on. What do you think he's done?'

'I don't know.' Mona pretended to think this over. 'Whatever it is, I'm pretty sure it's going to involve Carlotta and maybe a lot of other important people too. I'm assuming he's not planning to go back to work after this. Maybe he could retrain as—'

The door to her room flew open so fast it nearly came right off its hinges. 'Can you walk?' said Paterson.

'Can I walk?' asked Mona, surprised.

'Yes, can you get your arse off that bed and walk, do you think?'

Paterson was looking slightly crazed.

'I don't know, Guv, I haven't been upright yet.'

'Well, I need you to try. Maitland, help her.' He began pulling back the covers on the bed. She made a grab for them before he uncovered her completely.

'Mr Paterson,' Carole protested. 'Mona shouldn't be moved without a doctor OK-ing it.'

Paterson had given up on the bed sheets and was busy putting her possessions into a bag. 'Paul Shore is dead.'

'What?'

'Paul Shore died an hour ago. The wound to his neck had been healing well, but he apparently developed some

317

kind of infection that put a strain on his heart blah blah blah. I turn up to his hospital room with a lawyer to help him get something down on paper about what's been going on, and he's dead.' He slammed the locker door shut. 'Forgive me if I don't think this is a safe environment for one of my staff.'

Mona gave this scenario a moment's consideration, then swung her legs round to the side of the bed. 'Carole, I'm attached to a catheter.'

Carole looked round at her colleagues, obviously unhappy at what was going on. With her nurse's head on she would never have sanctioned someone in Mona's state leaving the hospital. Yet she'd learned a lot in her time at the HET. 'You pair, avert your eyes.' She turned back to Mona. 'When I take it out, every health professional in the corridor is going to come bursting into this room, and they're not going to be happy about this.'

'Mona, I assume you are willing to take responsibility for your own health, and discharge yourself?'

'Damn right, Guv.' The fighting talk was undermined a little bit by nearly falling over as she tried to stand upright.

'Then you two get Mona down to the front door. I'm going to get my car.'

The machine started beeping as predicted, and a man in hospital scrubs appeared. 'You shouldn't be out of bed.'

'Sorry, I need to go,' said Mona, wobbling at the side of her bed.

'But . . .'

'I'll get the car.' Paterson pushed past the doctor. Carole took a firm hold of one of her arms and Maitland held on to the other, and they staggered down the corridor, the protests of the doctor ringing in their ears.

Paterson was waiting at the front entrance, the car on a set of double yellow lines, its engine turning over. At the sight of them he flung open the passenger door. 'Get her in.'

'Gently!' added Carole, as Maitland dumped her on the front seat.

Paterson leaned over, and gestured to her colleagues. 'If anyone asks where we've gone, say you don't know.'

'We don't actually know, Guv. You haven't told us.'

'Well, then you won't need to lie.' He sped out of the car park, nearly crashing into the barriers in his haste to be gone.

'Are you expecting someone to stop us leaving, Guv?'

'Not sure what I'm expecting, Mona. I'm more focused on what I wasn't expecting, like I wasn't expecting Paul to die.'

They drove in silence. Mona closed her eyes. The light was once again hurting her head, and there was a low-level feeling of nausea. She wasn't sure if it was a physical reaction, or a manifestation of stress. Paul was dead. Was she safe? Was Bernard?

'Thanks, Guv, for getting me out of there.'

'You're welcome, but please don't die, otherwise I will be in such trouble for springing you from hospital.'

'I'll do my best.' She opened her eyes again. 'Where are we going anyway? Are you going to drop me back at my mother's?'

'Your mother's? Do you really think you'd be safe there?'

'I don't know.' She really had no idea. 'What do you think?'

'I don't know what to think, Mona! You and your idiot partner never tell me what is going on! I know this much, though. If an amiable civil servant like Paul Shore can get himself killed, then anyone can. Anyone, that is, that's stupid enough to cross swords with Carlotta bloody Carmichael.'

'You think she's behind Paul's death?'

'She seems to be a common link.'

She closed her eyes again, the nausea in her belly growing stronger. She also had an inconvenient feeling of hunger. She hadn't eaten for almost twenty-four hours, but it seemed somehow inappropriate to suggest they stop for a cheeseburger. 'So, where are we going?'

'You're going on a couple of weeks' enforced holiday. I'm going to get you some medical attention at a hospital that isn't under the jurisdiction of one of Carlotta's mates. Let's see if we can't work on that *amnesia* of yours.'

The Guv obviously didn't believe her memory loss was real. She kept her eyes firmly shut. Paterson could be perceptive.

Of course she remembered everything.

She remembered that Bryce was dead. She also recalled that he had hinted he wasn't working alone, that he had resources at his disposal. Whoever he had been working with, they were still out there, presenting either a threat, or possibly their only hope.

She remembered that the Professor was in possession of information, important information, that he didn't realise he possessed.

She remembered that Bryce had claimed the Virus was man-made, with all the implications that meant for the future health and happiness of the world. She remembered Haiti. She remembered that Bryce had been playing for time to get his message out, time that they hadn't been able to give him.

'Are you sure you don't remember anything, Mona?'

She remembered that Bryce had said he hated her, that he was sharing this information to hurt her. She was hurting. Christ, was she hurting! There was no way she was putting this on Paterson, or Bernard, or any of her colleagues. Not, at least, until she'd worked out what they could do.

'I'm kind of hungry, Guv. Any chance of stopping for some food?'

'Ignoring the question?' He sighed. 'Have it your way. Let's get the hell out of Dodge, then we'll stop.'

'Thanks, Guv.'

The car sped on. She closed her eyes again, and started to plan.

ACKNOWLEDGEMENTS

Thanks to everyone at Sandstone Press for their continuing support for the series, with especial thanks to my editor, Moira Forsyth.

Love and thanks to Gordon, as always. And I'm not going to mention my children at all because the only bit of my books they ever read is the acknowledgements, just to see if they are there.

Mum 1 - Kids 0.

Also in The Health of Strangers series

ISBN: 9781912240524   ISBN: 9781912240821   ISBN: 9781912240814

The Virus is spreading. Monthly health checks are mandatory. Enter the Health Enforcement Team, an uneasy mix of police and health service staff. Stuck with colleagues they don't like, politicians they don't trust and civil servants undermining them, Mona and Bernard are fighting more than one losing battle.

www.sandstonepress.com

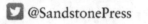 facebook.com/SandstonePress/

@SandstonePress